F
WILLIAMS, M
Ravenscarne

1 7 MAY 1992

1992

1992

1992

1993

Ravenscarne and Other Ghost Stories

Ravenscarne and Other Ghost Stories

Mary Williams

PIATKUS

To all my friends in Cornwall,
my home for so long

Copyright © 1990 by Mary Williams

First published in Great Britain in 1991 by
Judy Piatkus (Publishers) Ltd of
5 Windmill Street, London W1

British Library Cataloguing in Publication Data

Williams, Mary
  Ravenscarne and other ghost stories
  I. Title
  823.914 [F]

  ISBN 0 – 7499 – 0057 – 1

Phototypeset in 11/12pt Compugraphic Times by
Action Typesetting Limited, Gloucester
Printed and bound in Great Britain by
Billing & Sons Ltd, Worcester

Ravenscarne

A harsh wind blew down the hill as I climbed the steep slope above the sea. The lane was no more than a track winding between clumps of furze and bracken from which the barren land stretched desolately on either side. There was no sign of human habitation except for a cottage huddled in a hollow to my right, and the gaunt shape of a building half-silhouetted against the lowering clouds. It was hard to imagine anyone living in such a benighted place, and I wondered if I had been directed wrongly. The sense of loneliness was pronounced, filled with desolation and foreboding.

This was not the scene I'd expected – a mellowed landscape of sunlit hills above the great Atlantic – but one overhung, it seemed, by a vast shadow, suggesting: 'Go back. There's no place for you here. Better you'd never come.'

I paused by a boulder, pushed the windblown hair from my eyes and automatically took my cousin Anne's letter from the pocket of my windcheater, absently studying the old address – 'Ravenscarne', Tregale, Nr. Mirronporth. The house which once had been my grandfather's home.

I'd been there occasionally as a child. But that was long ago, and the wild landscape before me now touched no chord of remembrance, provided no guiding landmark to say, 'This is it. You are back.' Everything seemed alien, hostile, as though I was a stranger treading forbidden ground.

I read the note through again: So short, but somehow urgent:

1

It's a long time since we met, and now Grandfather's dead I feel very cut off here. Please come and see me if you can, Belinda. I'm not well, and Lucien thinks your company would cheer me up.

With love,
Anne

It hadn't been easy for me; I'd had to get special leave from the fasion house where I worked as a designer. I wondered once more why my presence was necessary to Anne. She had her husband, and friends surely, because since our grandfather died she must have been quite well off, and able to lead the kind of life she wanted without having to consider ways and means. Her mother had been my father's sister, and because she'd been widowed when Anne was a little girl, my grandfather had provided for them both, and shared his home with them. Later, when Aunt Lucy died, my cousin had gone on living with the old man. She must have been about twelve then, and nineteen at the time of his death. Everything, except a small legacy to me, went to Anne. There was no one else. If anything happened to my cousin, I was to come into the estate.

I didn't mind. I liked my job, which was interesting and quite remunerative, and I'd never anticipated inheriting much. My grandfather for some abstruse reason of his own hadn't approved of my mother's marriage, so family relationships had gradually faded into the limbo of 'what-once-had-been'.

From time to time I'd thought vaguely of Anne. We'd exchanged cards at Christmas, and when she'd married last year she'd sent me a piece of cake. However, as I'd gone to Canada with my parents when I was seven, my memories of her were necessarily hazy.

The letter had been quite a shock. I could easily have refused. I could have told her how busy I was, but because she was my only living relation I'd accepted the invitation.

Now I wished I'd insisted that the man who'd driven me by taxi from Penzance should take me on through Tregale to Ravenscarne. But he'd said the district was not suitable for cars. So carrying my light suitcase, I'd walked. Less than a

2

mile, he'd told me. It seemed much more.

I'd called at the inn in Tregale to ask the way to the house, and when I'd mentioned Ravenscarne the barman had paused before replying, looking sidelong at a girl standing nearby, polishing glasses. 'Round the curve of the hill,' he said curtly, 'then left.'

I'd thanked him, had a shandy, and presently left.

As I climbed higher, the wind shrieked with a high-pitched reed-like quality through the heather and gorse. At last, when I saw the house ahead, it was quite obvious that Ravenscarne was quickly falling into complete decay. Light penetrated the empty eyes of windows, giving a semblance of phantom movement through the shadowing wind. Gaps yawned from what once had been the garden wall; the doorway was a jagged scar overhung by weeds straggling from the broken bricks. The wrought-iron gates were tumbled from their hinges, the desolate drive overgrown by bramble, nettles and furze.

I stood staring, sensing that something must be dreadfully wrong. Why had I been lured here from half across the world, to be confronted by such chaos and desecration? Yes, 'desecration' was the only word to describe the scene. This place was the one I'd come to find, yet only the shell remained. And Anne? What of her? Had some trick been played on me? Some monstrous lie to get me to the vicinity? If so, why?

I was still trying to get things into some sort of perspective when I was startled by the crackling of twigs and the sudden appearance of a figure clawing upwards along a narrow path between high clumps of bracken and foxgloves.

A man.

'Good morning,' he said. My heart steadied. He was smallish, with bright eyes and a clipped goatee beard. He wore a sports jacket and flannels.

'Can I help you?' he asked.

'I was looking for my cousin's house, Ravenscarne,' I replied, relieved to find someone so obviously normal in what seemed to me such abnormal surroundings.

He smiled and held out his hand. 'I thought so. You must be Miss Carn.'

3

'Yes,' I said quickly.

'I heard about you from the Wildings — Anne and Lucien.'

'You know them?'

'I have a cottage close by,' he told me. 'I'm a friend of Lucien's — and Anne's too, I hope, though doctors aren't always popular.' A slight accent suggested he might be French.

'I see. You're — ?' I broke off hesitantly.

'I keep an eye on her,' he replied lightly, too lightly I thought. But before I could question him, he continued: 'My name is Dendas, Louis Dendas. I expect we shall be seeing quite a bit of each other whilst you are here. But come along. You've gone out of your way, you know. The house is further down. It's years since the old place was lived in: didn't you know?'

'No,' I said.

'Oh, yes. The old man found it inconvenient as he grew older; there was the water problem among other things. So he had the manor farm modernised — if you can call it that; quite comfortable really. It must have puzzled you, seeing this place in such a condition.'

'It did,' I admitted. 'But in Anne's letter the address was the same. Why didn't she tell me?'

'Oh, the *farm's* known as Ravenscarne now — it used to be just "The Manor".' He paused then added, 'You must be tired.' He took my case. 'Follow me.'

He turned and went to the right, taking a narrow track downwards, pushing through tall curling fronds of fern and undergrowth. When we reached a bend the descent became more rocky and less overgrown, revealing some distance below the mellowed walls of a house silhouetted against the rim of sea and sky.

A few minutes later we were there, walking down a flagged pathway to the front doors which were obviously of early Georgian architecture, as were the tall windows overlooking the garden, though I guessed the original structure was considerably older, probably Elizabethan.

Inside, the hall was wide, cool, with a broad staircase spiralling off to the right. I didn't remember the dark antique furniture or carvings, the Persian rugs on the flags, or the ebony figure on a pedestal at the foot of the stairs. There was nothing here to remind me of my grandfather – no tang of tobacco, or heady hot geranium smell from the conservatory – nostalgic reminders of my childhood. But of course this was a different place. I had never set foot in it before; any sleeping far-away memories I had were those of the deserted shell I had just left, lonely and bereft now in its shroud of weeds and cobwebs. It was as though a cold hand touched me, and I shivered. Doctor Dendas must have noticed. I felt his hand on my shouder, heard him saying, 'Wait here. They must be at the back.'

But I didn't have to wait. A door opened down the hall, and a man appeared. My first impression was that he was slender, tall and dark, and that he had a nice voice. Voices are important. They can instil confidence or destroy it; put one at ease, or on edge. Lucien's warmed me, and made me feel secure for the first time since I had left the station at Penzance.

'Belinda?' he queried quickly.

'Yes,' I answered as his hand closed over mine. His grip was firm. I could feel his palm pulsing.

'I'm Lucien. I see you've met Louis.' He paused, then added, 'I'm so glad you've come. It was a great deal to ask; but when you see Anne – '

'How is she?' I interrupted.

'Not too bad today. But you must be prepared for change.'

'Of course. She's grown up now. We both are.'

'I didn't mean that. It's – '

'Your cousin has a blood condition,' Doctor Dendas interposed before Lucien could finish. 'A form of anaemia. It makes her tired, and she's naturally weak.'

'Do you mean she's seriously ill?' I asked.

'She could be,' the doctor answered. 'Unless she makes an effort. At the moment she doesn't try to help herself.'

'That's why we sent for you,' Lucien explained. 'Someone she knows, someone young – it could make all the difference.'

I was at a loss. 'When we were children, Anne was so full of vitality. Perhaps a specialist?'

'Do you think she hasn't seen the best doctors and neurologists in the country?' Lucien said.

Something in his voice implied a rebuke. I turned my head so that he wouldn't notice the flush staining my cheeks. Then I asked, 'When can I see her?'

'She resting now,' he replied. 'After tea we'll see how she is. Would you like to wash first?'

'Yes, please. I do feel rather grubby.'

Just then a girl came through a door at the bottom end of the passage, a tray in her hands. As she drew nearer I saw she was very dark, dressed simply but smartly in a cream dress with an orange scarf knotted at her neck. Young, too. Obviously no ordinary servant. An au pair perhaps? In that case why had Lucien referred to Anne's need for youthful company? Perhaps the two girls didn't get on. Perhaps ... My musings were interrupted by Lucien saying, 'Katherine, this is Miss Carn — Belinda. My wife's cousin. Could you show her to her room? I'll take the tray. Katherine helps us in the house temporarily,' he explained. 'She's just left university and wants to write. Cornwall's a good place for ideas.'

'Yes, it does have something,' I agreed ineffectually.

I followed Katherine upstairs to a room overlooking the moors. It was a nice room, surprisingly modern, furnished in light oak with peach-coloured draperies. From the window I could see the roof of the ancient family home, lit to silver by the dying spring light.

'Fancy!' I couldn't help saying. 'My grandfather once lived there with Anne.'

'It wouldn't be my choice of a home,' the girl said. 'Picturesque and all that, but it can't ever have been practical.'

'I suppose not. I don't remember much about it. I was only a child when we went to Canada.'

There was a pause. I couldn't think of anything else to say. Something about her unsettled me; or perhaps it was just tiredness after my journey. I smiled. 'Well, thanks.' I went over to the mirror. 'What a sight!'

'I wouldn't say that. Your hair's gorgeous.'

I turned. 'Do you think so?'

'Copper-beech,' she remarked. 'Now don't tell me you've

6

never heard *that* before.'

I had, of course, so I said nothing. She went to the door. 'There's a bathroom and the rest opposite, across the landing – there. Just for your use. Why there aren't wash-basins in the bedrooms, I don't know.' She shrugged. 'Still, there's something about these old places ... very atmospheric, aren't they?'

'Yes,' I agreed.

Lucien and the doctor were waiting for me when I went downstairs. The lounge, with wide French windows overlooking a lawn sloping down towards the sea, was a gracious room. The silver tea service was, I guessed, genuine early Georgian. Lucien must be rich, I decided, although the silver could have been my grandfather's.

Katherine came in carrying two plates of sandwiches.

'Hope they're cucumber,' Lucien remarked. 'Katherine is an expert with sandwiches. Just that little extra, you know – they taste better than anyone else's.'

I guessed he was talking just for the sake of it, to make me feel at ease. I glanced at Katherine; her face was expressionless. She didn't appear to have heard. But Lucien! For the first time I noticed how handsome he was. Well, 'handsome' was hardly the word. He was more than that – beautiful, in a male way. Not effeminate, quite the reverse, but startling because of his long slatey-blue eyes shaded by thick black lashes, above a mouth and nose reminiscent somehow of Greek sculpture. A half-smile played round his lips, tender and kind when he looked at me. 'Surely he's a poet,' I thought. 'He must be. Or an artist. No one could look like that and not be something unique.'

In contrast to Lucien, Doctor Dendas appeared commonplace. Even Katherine looked the sort of girl one could meet anywhere, in any street or any town. I suppose from that first brief meal together, I was encompassed by the magic of Lucien, just as Anne must have been when she fell in love with him. How tragic to be ill when she had much that would be envied by other women.

After tea Lucien took me up to see her. She was lying in a bedroom which had the same outlook as the lounge. Everything about it was exquisite – reminiscent of some elegant stage-set in ivory and pink, providing the ideal setting for my cousin's fairness. She was a natural blonde, and as a child had always been considered the best looking of the family. Now she was more than that, with a delicate magnolia bloom that gave her an ethereal quality.

Her face lit up when she saw me. 'Belinda, how good to have you here. You haven't changed. At least – ' She broke off, still smiling.

I kissed her lightly. 'It's a long time, Anne, but I'd have recognised you anywhere. I'm sorry about your illness. Are you feeling better?'

'At the moment,' she answered. 'Sometimes I feel all right, then at others simply awful. I can't explain. It's not the sort of thing you can easily convey.' She broke off, turning her face away.

'Nerves? Anaemia?' I said uncomfortably. 'It'll pass.'

'Anaemia! I wish I could believe that.'

'That's what the doctor said. He should know.'

'Oh, him.'

I couldn't help noticing the dislike in her voice.

'Lucien has faith in him,' I reminded her.

'Yes, that's the trouble. He doesn't understand. "Louis says this" and "Louis says that" – anything Louis says goes.' For a moment bitterness flooded her voice.

'And you don't believe him? Lucien, I mean.'

Her eyes widened. 'It isn't a matter of believing. I know he's doing what he thinks right, for my good. You mustn't think, ever, we're unhappy. From the very beginning he's been quite wonderful. Kind, understanding ... But –'

'Yes?'

'Sometimes I wish we could have had a more ordinary start. I know I should be used to living in the wilds. In a way I am, of course. At least, I was – when Grandfather was alive. But here at the manor – it's different. Sometimes I feel I don't belong, Belinda.'

'Why?' I asked, noting the bewildered crinkling of her brows.

She waited a moment before answering. When the words came they held a lifeless quality that brought back all my former apprehension. 'It's theirs, really.'

8

'Whose?'

She shrugged. 'Louis, Katherine – all of them.'

To say I was puzzled would have been putting it mildly. 'What do you mean, Anne? The house belongs to Lucien and you. He's your husband. Katherine has nothing to do with it.'

'Oh, but she has. Far more than you'd think.'

I took her hand in mine. It was very cold. 'What is it?' I insisted stubbornly. 'I think you ought to tell me. Surely you're not suggesting that there's something between Lucien and her?'

Her eyes widened. She shook her head almost wildly. 'Oh, no, no. I told you – Lucien's been marvellous. He loves me. We're everything to each other. Until I met him I didn't know what living was.'

I could well understand that.

'And so patient,' she went on. 'He never scolds or gets irritable, and it must be a strain having me like this for such a time.'

'How long have you been ill?' I asked.

'Five months – no, six. Perhaps more.'

'Well,' I forced myself to sound cheerful, 'that's not an age.'

'It seems so sometimes,' she said. 'Sometimes it seems an eternity. At nights, when I dream, it's hundreds of years ago – hundreds and hundreds. And I'm still lying here, only there's no house – only the hillside, and it's always cold. There are stones, too.'

'Stones?'

'Big ones. And there's someone above me – someone tall and terrible with flaming hair. His body's like white fire –'

I heard the rising hysteria in her voice, saw the terror cloud her eyes.

'A dream,' I said firmly. 'As you said. One of those nightmare things people have when they're ill. It was the same with me when I had pneumonia – all I saw were little green men dancing on the blankets.'

She managed a smile. 'You did? Really?'

'Honestly.'

9

She relaxed and lay back against the pillows. They were pale pink silk with frilled edges.

I sat with Anne until Lucien came in. He went straight to her and kissed her. 'How are you feeling?'

'Not too bad,' she answered. The love in her eyes was all too apparent. In his too. They stared at each other as though entranced. I just didn't exist for them. I left them together, wondering again why they had sent for me. I doubted very much whether there was anything I could do for my cousin. It was quite clear that all she wanted was Lucien.

I could understand that, and should have been fore-warned. From the beginning I did my best not to fall in love with him. He was Anne's husband, and I happened to be old-fashioned about that sort of thing – a fact that excluded the possibility of having an affair with him, even if I'd wanted it, which I didn't – then. His attraction for me in those first days was either mental or emotional – perhaps both. I didn't want his arms round me, or in the proximity of his body. I just wanted to look at him, and hear him talking in his warm voice, succumbing to the magic of his presence so that I lived on a kind of dream-plane. That's the way it was, as though the real world had moved to another sphere where physical things were non-existent.

Looking back now I can see that I was very naive and thinking like an infatuated schoolgirl. I'm sure Katherine was aware of it. At times I felt her watching me and when I looked at her, her eyes were cold, holding a hint of scorn. I sensed that she could be a cruel person as brilliant people sometimes are. I knew she was clever, she had taken a First in English and had already started writing a book.

'What kind of book will it be?' I asked one day. 'A novel? Love story?'

'Love?' She laughed jarringly. 'Don't be ridiculous! One look at me should tell you different.'

'Sorry I asked,' I said lightly, but already on edge.

'You needn't apologise. I'm a realist. And I know that beneath your shy little-girl-lost look, dear Belinda, you're eaten away with curiosity. You don't understand us. Even your cousin's got you guessing.'

10

'About what?' I said sharply.

'Everything. And there's something else too.' She paused before adding, 'You don't like me much, do you?'

I could feel my lips tightening. When I made no comment she moved nearer, and in an uncomfortable moment I saw her as she would be when she was forty: high-coloured, buxom and bold-looking, with the suspicion of bags under her eyes. Involuntarily, I drew back.

'Oh, don't worry. I'm not going to touch you. The feeling's mutual,' she said casually. 'As a matter of fact, you rather bore me. When we first met — when you were standing in the hall with the light shining on your copper hair — I thought, "Here's someone exciting. Someone I could mind about very much." But after all, I was mistaken. You're just ordinary.'

She walked away from me, then turned and added maliciously, 'You've fallen for Lucien.'

I was shocked, because in a way it was true.

I never asked her about her book again. It became, for me, the key to things I didn't want to know. That small incident marked for me the beginning of my unrest at Ravenscarne.

After the first week the dream-like days became sultry and oppressive, burdened with rain that did not fall, leaving the tired smell of dry earth and parched undergrowth heavy in the air. The foxgloves in the hedges wilted. It was as though Nature waited for some climax to shatter the tension — for a clean wild storm to sweep the lanes and moors, leaving us purged and free of emotional conflict. How much of this Anne sensed I do not know. After her first enthusiasm at seeing me she relapsed into increasing indifference. I mentioned this one day to the doctor when he'd taken me to point out his cottage, a quarter of a mile along the field path from Ravenscarne.

'I really don't think she needs me at all,' I stated. 'There's no reason for me to stay on.'

'Oh, but there *is*,' he exclaimed, and his voice sounded quite startled. 'Believe me, it would be a great mistake for you to leave just now.'

'Why?'

11

'Anne's lethargy is just a symptom,' he explained. 'A good sign, in fact. It shows she's relaxing.'

'Well,' I said doubtfully, 'it can't be for too long. I have my work to think of – responsibilities.'

'Isn't Anne one of them?'

'As a relation, I suppose so,' I conceded. 'But she has Lucien. I don't count really, except as a mild diversion when she feels like it.'

'Please stay,' he said.

I didn't reply at first. When I looked up he was regarding me with an intensity I found disturbing. I noticed for the first time the curious, almost colourless, quality of his eyes; the tiny black pupils and the cold set of his lips above his clipped pointed beard.

'Well?' he persisted.

'I'll think about it,' I answered. The muscles of his face relaxed into his usual friendly smile.

'Good girl. Now, I won't ask you in to see the cottage today – it needs tidying. But what about the garden? Would that interest you?'

I replied politely that it would, very much. We walked on. It did not take long to get there.

He led me past a patch of rough field bordering one side of the cottage to the back, where the ground sloped down abruptly between rocks and ferns, threaded by narrow paths leading to secret pools and small green clearings. The vegetation there was surprisingly lush compared with the wild surroundings. Far below I could hear the breaking of the waves against the rocks. 'One day I'll take you down to the cove,' he said. 'The rock formation is rather unique. But tell me – what do you think of this?'

Pushing aside a branch of some exotic bush I saw a piece of sculpture which at first glance might have been merely a macabre natural rock formation. But it wasn't. It had been crudely carved from stone into a primitive representation of a male figure with grotesque features, leering uncannily above the thick growth of creepers and entangled plants.

'What is it?' I asked. 'Modern? African, perhaps?'

'Oh, no, not African,' Louis answered. 'It was done by a friend of mine; quite brilliant in his own sphere. A rising

12

reputation.' His eyes lingered almost lovingly upon it, then turned to me questioningly. 'You don't appreciate it, no? Not many people do. It is not beautiful in the ordinary sense, of course. But beauty –' He broke off, shrugged, and added, 'What is beauty? It depends what one is looking for. Comparative only. There can be no final assessment.'

I was suddenly overcome by the sultry air and smothering growth around me. I had the momentary trapped feeling of being in a nightmare, struggling for freedom and unable to move.

'Yes, well, you're quite right, I suppose,' I managed to say. 'I'm not very knowledgeable about modern sculpture.'

I turned to go up the path.

'It is not modern,' I heard the doctor say very quietly behind me, 'it is timeless – expressing the creative urge from earliest days. Didn't you feel *that* even? The reaching out for life from the darkest consciousness?'

Feeling his breath close against my neck, my spine tautened, went rigid.

'No, I didn't,' I said sharply, hurrying on, clutching at the grass and ferns as I went. 'I don't delve into such things.'

When we reached the top, I stopped to get my breath.

'Quite a climb,' the doctor said. 'You went too quickly.'

I glanced at him and saw then only a perfectly ordinary-looking little man in tweeds facing me, with apparent concern on his face. The abruptness of the change was in itself unnerving, but later I decided I'd merely been over-imaginative.

Anne came down after tea, and I was surprised to see her looking so well. The boy who worked in the garden and helped Katherine about the house, brought some roses in which my cousin arranged in bowls. She seemed happy for the first time since I'd arrived, and looked quite beautiful in a blue dress which brought out the violet shade of her eyes.

'Something's done you good,' Lucien said. 'It must be Belinda.'

'Of course,' Anne agreed. 'Come on, Belinda, I feel quite capable of taking a short walk.'

13

Lucien glanced at her sharply. 'A walk?' he said anxiously. 'But you've not been outside for a month. Are you sure?'

'Yes, quite sure,' she interrupted quickly.

I took her arm, steadying her as we went out to the front of the house. The sky was lifting a little, spraying a glitter of silver above the horizon, where the ruin stood blind-eyed to the evening.

'I expect it will rain,' my cousin remarked. 'When everything's clear like that it generally does. I wonder – ' She broke off, hesitating.

'Wonder what?'

'I wonder what it's like in there now,' she said, glancing up at the old house.

'I'm sure it's all very neglected and dismal and dank,' I answered promptly. 'Just an empty horrid shell.'

'Oh, no, it isn't,' Anne stated definitely.

'What do you mean?'

'It's never empty,' she said.

'But, Anne – '

'There are some things you can't kill,' she told me. 'However much you try, they go on and on.' I felt her hand gripping mine, and fancied that she shivered.

'You're cold,' I said. 'There's a wind getting up. Don't you think we'd better go in?'

'Yes, all right,' she replied, in normal tones.

I didn't ask her to explain her strange allusions to the ruin. I was not even sure that she would be able to. But it was obvious to me that Anne was still far from well.

That night I couldn't sleep. My mind was unable to dispel the forebodings that, like some sinister malign force, seemed to fill the atmosphere, hovering in every shadow, every corner of my bedroom – moving soundlessly down the corridor outside, and in the rising wind which tapped the branches of the sycamore against the window.

I thought of Anne, wondering if she was sleeping or lying awake like me. Obviously Ravenscarne was not really the right place for her at the moment, and to steer my thoughts into more practical channels I played with the idea of taking her back with me to Canada for a holiday. If it was for her

14

good, surely Lucien would agree? He might even come himself. Lucien! With a stab of pain, the magic of Lucien — his face and movements, the memory of his rich warm voice — obscured my morbid fancies, leaving me inexplicably restless, longing for his presence. This was ridiculous, I thought. I had known him only a few days. Besides, he was Anne's.

Presently I got up, slipped on my light dressing-gown, took a torch, and went towards my cousin's room. Before I got there she appeared round a corner of the landing, looking like some ghostly child in her short flimsy white nightdress. When she saw me she stood for a few seconds, glanced back over her shoulder, then hurried to meet me. Her eyes were brilliant in her pale face, haunted with terror, and I wondered if she'd had a nightmare.

'Anne,' I whispered, 'I was just coming to see — '

'Shhh!' She put a finger to her lips and continued urgently in a soft voice, 'You must get away from here, Belinda, as quickly as possible. For your own sake. Leave tomorrow as soon as you can. It's terribly important.'

'But — '

'I can't wait now. But, whatever else I say, *this* is the truth. Get away from this place!'

'You must come and talk to me,' I begged.

'No.' She wrenched her shoulder from my hand, turned and went back. I waited, and a few moments later heard the closing of a door.

I returned to my room and sat on the bed, trying to think. But my mind was awhirl, circling from the loathsome sculpture in the doctor's garden to Anne's contradictory statements and fears. Then, as always, back to Lucien.

Should I say anything to him? I wondered. Confide in him about Anne's nocturnal visit? There seemed no satisfactory answer. At last I put the problem aside until the morning. Before getting into bed again I went to my window and opened the curtains. The outline of the moor was visible in a shaft of watery moonlight, the great boulders crouching like primeval beasts in the sparse furze. To my disordered fancy they seemed to move, in the play of the shadows from the sullen clouds, and I remembered Anne's reference to the cold hillside and the stones.

15

'Hundreds of years ago,' she'd said. 'No house – only the cold hillside and the stones.'

But this happened to be the twentieth century and there *was* a house, a house I had visited as a child; the genuine castle-like Ravenscarne where my grandfather had lived, empty now with all life gone. But was it empty? Anne had said it wasn't, and as I stared at its crumbled silhouette I thought a light flickered just once, then died. It could have been the moonlight, of course. I told myself it must have been, and closed the curtains with hands that trembled.

After deciding to walk up to the old place some time soon and explore the interior for myself, I fell into a fitful sleep towards dawn.

The next day, to my surprise, Anne's mood had changed. When I went in to see her she was having breakfast on a tray, looking relaxed and welcoming.

'Hello, Belinda,' she said. 'Spoilt, aren't I? Bacon and eggs for a change. I usually only have cereal. But I was hungry this morning.'

'Anne,' I said, 'about last night – '

She stared at me and wrinkled her forehead. 'Last night?'

'Yes, surely you remember? I met you in the corridor, and you said – you said I ought to leave.'

She put down her knife and fork abruptly. 'I said what? And what do you mean, I met you?'

'Don't you remember?'

She laughed. 'No. And neither do you. You must have been dreaming.'

I shook my head. 'No. I couldn't sleep. So I thought – '.

I broke off, seeing the disbelief on her face, realising she really did not recall a thing about our nocturnal interview.

'You *thought* you weren't sleeping,' she said. 'But you were. I suppose you were having a sort of nightmare like me. The last thing I'd want is for you to leave me, Belinda. I like having you. That's why I'm so much better. You *must* stay for a time. You can, can't you?'

I didn't know how to answer or what to think. It seemed to me that I was caught in a welter of uncertainty and morbid conjecture like a fly in some sinister cobweb that every moment grew stronger and more constricting, smothering my capacity for independent thought.

That afternoon I went for a walk along the cliffs. The air had freshened, and a glimmer of sun and blue sky spattered the clouds in a variegated pattern of light and shade. With the light wind fanning my face, my spirits lifted. I almost laughed at myself for having what must have been, after all, no more than a bad attack of nerves, though I had never in my life suffered that way before.

I walked sharply for about two miles, enjoying the scenery and sweet tangy scent of heather and short turf. When I reached the Gap − the name given to a creek cutting down steeply to a rocky cove − I saw a man coming towards me with an alsation dog. He had sketching materials under his arm, obviously an artist, though he didn't look like one of the modern variety. His hair was comparatively short; he wore respectable flannels with a scarlet shirt, and when we were face to face I saw that he had a friendly expression, rugged kindly features, with those grey far-seeing eyes many sailors and naval men have, and brown unruly hair which gave him a boyish look though he must have been in the late thirties.

'Lovely day,' he said, smiling.

'Yes.' I was about to go on when he added, 'Forgive me, but are you a stranger round here?'

I knew this was no ordinary "Haven't we met before?" approach. He was too nice for that.

'Very much so,' I told him. 'I've come from Canada to stay with my cousin. She's ill.'

'Oh?'

'At Ravenscarne, the manor house,' I said. 'Do you know it?'

He nodded. 'I've seen it; I know Mr Wilding by sight. But I've only been in the district a month. Taken a cottage near Tregale − the other side − to paint.'

'It's painting country, isn't it?' I remarked. 'For wild landscapes, I mean − the tin mines and everything.'

'Yes,' he agreed. 'The trouble is the winds that blow up suddenly from the sea. Not that it matters. I'm a very raw amateur.'

'Have you anything with you?' I asked.

17

'No. I gave up in despair. To be quite honest, I didn't start today. Instead I found a warm spot and read the paper. By the way – ' His eyes scrutinised me kindly but shrewdly.

'Yes?'

'Have I met your cousin, I wonder? I did see a youngish woman in the little shop the other day. We got chatting about photography.'

'Oh, no,' I told him. 'I'm sure it wasn't Anne. She's in bed most of the time.'

'I'm sorry. Well, any time you like to look in you can see some of my unsuccessful efforts,' he added. 'Valley Cottage. The name's Grey. Martin Grey. Be glad to have you any time, won't we, Rex?'

Hearing his name the dog jumped up, barking playfully. He was young, I could see; not more than a year old.

'I'll remember,' I said. 'I'll look forward to it.'

'In the meantime, if I can be of any help, count on me.'

'Help?'

'Yes. Well, in lonely places like these you never know, do you? Accidents, fire, punctures – I happen to have a jeep. Handy sometimes.'

A moment later he had gone on his way. I sat on a rock for a few minutes before turning back in the same direction I'd come. I was glad to have met him. His company had cheered me; more than that, it had helped. Why? Because he had been so perfectly normal, I suppose. I knew I was not quite alone. But did I?

As I walked across the moor Martin Grey's offer to be of help and his reference to lonely places niggled at my mind. Perhaps it was because the blue sky lowered suddenly to yellowing grey, bringing a chill prediction of rain, that doubt rose in me, dimming the spurt of newfound optimism. What exactly had his casual remarks implied? Was he suspicious of Ravenscarne? Of Louis Dendas, perhaps? Did he know more of Anne than he'd professed? The apparent nonchalant surprise when I told him of my cousin's illness could have been assumed, in which case he was not quite the genuine character I'd believed.

I tried to dispel the idea and mostly succeeded, but as

troubling thoughts succeeded one another in my brain I unthinkingly took the wrong path – a sheep track, probably – and abruptly found myself staring over the cliff edge to the sea. The rocky face was not sheer there. The granite sloped at a gradual angle with occasional wide layers of green turf enabling a comparatively easy climb down to the beach. I was further away from Ravenscarne than I'd thought, and the surprising view disclosed something else – a shack built a quarter of the way down, with a rough pig-shed adjoining, and a white goat tethered to a stake. A few straggly greens waved untidily behind a roughly made fence, and a lean gypsyish youth was leaning on a fork, staring up at me, open-mouthed. He had shoulder-length black hair under a wollen cap, and a long, pale face.

He said nothing, but his expression was uninviting. I was turning to go when an old woman appeared round a corner of the shack. She was short and stout, with an aggressive set to her square jaw.

'Who be 'ee?' she shouted. 'Watcher want?'

I didn't reply, just started back the way I'd come, hoping to join the proper track to Ravenscarne as quickly as possible. All the way I had the feeling someone might be following me, and whenever possible broke into a run, although the dense undergrowth mostly made this impracticable.

I was scratched and breathless when the wider coast path suddenly appeared ahead. I stood for a moment, trying to be calm, annoyed with myself for having been so unnerved. A nasty woman and a simple-minded youth – what cause had they to follow me or wish me ill?

And Martin Grey?

How wrong I'd been to doubt him for a moment. Obviously the Cornish atmosphere had got on top of me, and if I was to be the slightest use to Anne I'd have to keep a strong hold on my imagination in future.

When Ravenscarne came into view the sun was shining again, and the clarity of the air was intense, giving everything a rather stark, too-clear appearance, like a contrived set for a play.

Little did I realise then that drama indeed would soon follow, and of a kind far different than ever I had contemplated.

That evening there was a heavy shower of rain, but in the morning the sky had cleared and the wind dropped. The garden and moors looked fresh and glistening in the sunlight; the parched hedges and undergrowth had revived as if by magic, filling the air with a heady summer sweetness that had a tang of salt in it from the sea.

I went up early to see Anne, but she was worse again and didn't want my company. Katherine was in the hall when I went downstairs. She was wearing red; it suited her full bright lips and abundant dark hair.

'What are your plans today?' she asked.

'I haven't decided,' I answered. 'I might walk up to the old place — the house.'

'Why?'

'Why not?'

She shrugged. 'It isn't exactly welcoming just now, except for rats.'

I stared at her. 'You're trying to put me off?'

'Put you off?' She laughed contemptuously. 'You sound as neurotic as — '

'Anne?'

'That's right.'

'I don't think she's nearly as neurotic as you try to make out,' I said bluntly. 'I think — '

'Well? Go on.'

'I think you and the doctor are — ' I broke off, because I couldn't find the right word.

'Are evil influences, is that it?' she asked mockingly.

'I didn't say that.'

'No, but I'm sure you meant it,' she retorted. Adding after a brief pause, 'perhaps you're right. Even that's better than just vegetating. Most people do, you know. They haven't the first inkling of what real life is. They don't know how to taste and touch and feel to the full. *You* don't, because you're afraid.'

I forced myself not to look at her, although I could feel

20

the magnetic force of her eyes on me. Just then I was grateful to hear Lucien's voice.

'What are you two gossiping about?'

'Nothing important,' I said.

Lucien was just going to speak again when Katherine remarked, 'Belinda's going up to the old place.'

'A nice walk in the proper weather,' Lucien said. He smiled at me. 'Wait till tomorrow. I'll go with you. It'll be a bit boggy today after the rain.'

'All right. I'll do that.'

I spent the day rather aimlessly, reading, walking, and writing a few letters to my friends in Canada. I was just going to have a wash before tea when the sound of raised voices echoed from the front. I went to the door. As I'd thought, the woman was Katherine, and to my surprise I saw that she was arguing with a middle-aged man wearing a dog-collar. The vicar I supposed, though I hadn't met him. The church was at Merrinporth, a distance which so far had deterred me from braving the Sunday morning trek. I wondered what the trouble was, and was about to amble casually down the drive when Katherine turned abruptly and hurried towards the house, leaving the clergyman at the gate. The next second he, too, had walked sharply away. Katherine's face was angrily flushed when she reached the door. She gave me a brief glance, then hurried past and up the stairs without a word.

I put the incident behind me, and thought nothing more about it until the next day. As it was a fine morning and there were a few things I wanted, including stamps and envelopes, I decided to walk to Tregale where the tiny general shop sold most things from a tangle of ribbons and cottons to toothpaste and tintacks.

As soon as I went in I sensed an 'atmosphere'.

An elderly woman in black carrying a shopping basket was talking in undertones to Mrs Pender, the owner, who was listening intently from her side of the counter. They both stopped when they heard me, and the shopper said brightly with an obvious change of subject, 'Well, that's all today, thank you, Alice. See you later.' She glanced at me rather disagreeably as she passed, slamming the door behind her so that the bell tinkled harshly.

I made my purchases, and was about to leave when a man who looked like a farm worker came in. 'Got the baccy in yet?' he asked, and in different tones, 'Awful about vicar, edn't et?'

'Real sad,' Mrs Pender agreed. 'And in the best of health yesterday.'

'Heart they do say,' the man remarked.

'Heart? Hmm! They can *call* it that if they like,' Mrs Pender said ominously, 'but I'd give it a different name.'

I went back to the counter. 'Excuse me,' I began, 'but has anything happened to the vicar?'

The woman eyed me warily. 'Do you know him?'

'I think it must have been him I saw at the gate yesterday,' I answered. 'Ravenscarne.'

The suspicion in Mrs Pender's eyes deepened to active hostility. 'If you did,' she remarked tartly, 'I'm not surprised at what's happened, poor man. Them up there should be driven off, proper smart, and the guilty ones should get what they deserve.'

'That's right,' the man agreed darkly.

'Look,' I said, 'I don't know what you're talking about. Mrs Wilding happens to be my cousin. She's ill. That's why I'm here. If there's anything I should know – anything discreditable – I think you should tell me to my face, or not gossip at all.'

I waited. After an exchange of glances, Mrs Pender said, 'There's plenty you should know, but I'm not saying yet, except for the vicar. Found dead on his bedroom floor this morning, early.'

'Dead?' I echoed, shocked.

'That's what I said.'

'Oh. But how? What happened? His heart, I suppose.'

Mrs Pender gave a dry simulation of a laugh.

'According to the doctor from Merrinporth – a new man he is, Lawson's his name. Yes, that's what he said – the housekeeper told me when she called in a bit ago, and a terrible state she was in too, poor dear. But if you ask me –' Her voice dropped a tone.

'Yes?'

She fixed me with her dark pebble eyes under their thick grey brows. 'If you ask me,' she reiterated, 'it was murder.'

I stared at her, hardly believing my ears. 'Murder?'

'That's what I said,' Mrs Pender stated, fetching the tobacco from a shelf. 'And he's not the first, not by a long chalk. There was Miss Sibley, who fell down a mineshaft, back over past the ruin. "Accidental", they brought in. But Miss Sibley wasn't the one to be caught like that. She knew every inch of those moors, bog and all, because of her bird-watching. A silly arty sort of woman she was – pleasant though, in her way, and rich too. Still, I never did have much use for her. All the same, right is right. Oh, she was murdered, make no mistake about it. Pushed. And who got her money? That foreign man. Dendas, they call him.'

'But how can you know?' I said. 'That she was pushed? I mean –'

'Pushed or not,' came the quick rejoinder, 'it was murder.' And the narrow lips tightened into an obstinate button shape.

'Then perhaps you should have told the police,' I suggested rashly.

'Ha! Them's no use,' came the short reply. 'But I'm telling *you*, young lady, there's things going on up there that would shame the devil hisself. So if you take my advice, you'll get out before it's too late.'

I left the shop feeling more bewildered than ever, telling myself – and trying to believe – that the unpleasant conversation had been merely country antagonism to strangers, 'foreigners' as they called them in Cornwall, who were resented by the natives. But I couldn't stifle my growing doubts of the whole set-up at Ravenscarne. There was the arrogant Katherine, for instance. Why was she really there? Although she did a few things about the house, a great deal was shouldered by the boy, a sullen youth who though a bit simple-minded was strong and good with his hands, and by a daily who came four mornings a week to clean and cook. The latter was a silent woman, the wife of a farm labourer, whose first consideration was probably the good money paid by Lucien.

I couldn't somehow accept his explanation that Katherine was there merely to write a novel although *he* evidently believed it. But she wasn't the kind of girl to be satisfied by mere mental pursuits. She was far too full of vitality. There was a lust for life about her that I found mildly unpleasant, and a certain slyness that was discomfiting. She seemed always to be watching me, although of course with my imagination all fired up, I might have been imagining that. I wondered frequently if she wanted Lucien for herself. I couldn't picture her loving him – I doubted that she had the capacity for love at all. Passion, yes. But what had Ravenscarne, so remote and cut off from civilisation, to offer? The doctor wasn't exactly attractive, and I knew she hadn't a chance with Lucien who was obviously devoted to Anne. Though even he sometimes, I thought, must feel a bit benighted. He had apparently no job of work although, like Katherine, he dabbled with writing. His chief concern, indeed, appeared to be his wife, which was natural I supposed. She was so beautiful.

But there was another side to him I didn't understand.

I would watch him sometimes, standing quite motionless, looking through the window towards the moors, and his eyes would be remote from me, faraway. If I spoke he would not hear. When he came to himself again there would be a look of pain about his face until he pulled himself together and smiled. Then he was once more a real person, apparently concerned for my comfort as his guest.

At lunch time that day he said, 'You'd like to walk up to the old place, you said. What about this evening, after tea? It's fine and the ground will have dried out a bit.'

'Yes,' I said. 'I'd like to. Thanks.'

We set off about four-thirty, taking the narrow path up the hill which I had walked down with the doctor. A thin wind shivered through the bracken and scrub, but under the clear sky the gorse flamed gold, interspersed with the deep pink of bell heather and tossed tall foxgloves. When we reached the castle only a tangle of sparse bushes and humped wind-blown trees dotted the skyline. There were

24

no flowers here, no birdsong save the high screeching of a seagull. Through the ruined doorway of the house sinister shadows played upon the damp flagged floor, lit to pale patches from the vacant holes of windows. I went in, followed by Lucien, staring at the weeds and cobwebs on the crumbling stone walls which once had housed a well-loved home. I shivered, imagining ghosts.

'Not very pleasant, is it?' Lucien said.

'No. But why did they let it get like this?' I said. 'I should have thought my grandfather would have used it for something.'

'For what?' he said. 'It has very little historical value. A "folly" originally – mistakenly known as castle in these parts. It was built considerably later than the manor, and it doesn't even mark the highest spot of the moors. The Quoit can top it by sixty feet or more. And the stones – '

'Yes?' I interrupted quickly, remembering Anne's dream with its cold hillside and the stones.

'Well, there are the remains of a circle and relics of an ancient village half a mile away,' Lucien explained. 'Pre-Druid, according to the authorities. Probably 3,000 B.C. That is something. But this – ' He broke off, adding after a pause, 'Come along, Belinda, it's damp. I·don't want you to catch cold.'

His voice was gentle. I looked up at him. In the half-light, with his wonderful head bent towards me, he seemed to possess the beauty of some legendary young god. Just for a moment I forgot my surroundings, even my identity, swept by the magic of Lucien's presence, into a golden nimbus of eternity out of time. Written down it does appear fantastic – the romantic idealisation of a girl in love. But it wasn't simply that I was attracted to Lucien physically; it was that he seemed to give meaning and beauty to ordinary existence.

The moment was fleeting. A second or two later I heard myself saying in ordinary practical tones, 'Yes, it is getting a bit chilly.'

I turned for a last look round, and then I saw it – a curious-looking carved emblem of stone – or it could have been tarnished dark metal – lying near a rock a few yards from my feet. 'What's that?' I said.

'What?'

I pointed to the object and went forward to pick it up.

'Leave it alone,' Lucien commanded, with unreasonable sharpness.

'Why?'

'It's covered with dirt. Those things can — they can carry germs.'

I laughed. 'Anything can. I was just curious how it came to be here. What is it? A symbol or something? A relic of the past?'

'Perhaps.'

'Well, isn't it valuable then? For a museum or collection?'

'Museums have no right to anything found on Ravenscarne property.' Lucien told me, and his voice was cold. 'Please, Belinda, I know what I'm talking about. Leave it alone. I don't want anyone — even you — foraging around here.' I thought he was being quite unreasonable about the matter, but shrugged lightly, saying, 'Oh, all right, if you say so. But I should've thought —' I broke off as he touched my hand.

'Don't think, just enjoy the present.'

I glanced up at him. His face was once more friendly and smiling, and for the moment doubt died. It was not, after all, difficult to enjoy things in Lucien's company. I knew then that I might really be falling in love with him.

A verdict of death from natural causes was recorded at the inquest on the vicar, and I hoped fervently the whole matter would end there, and that I should hear no more sinister allusions concerning the dead man's association with Ravenscarne. I tried to put it from my mind, but on the night following the funeral, when I'd gone to bed, I heard the shattering sound of breaking glass from below; not once, but several times. I lay rigid for minutes, then slipped on my housecoat and went downstairs. Lucien and Katherine were already in the lounge. One of the lovely French windows was shattered, and Lucien was picking up the bricks and stones scattering the floor. A piece of Ming china had been smashed.

26

When Lucien saw it he said nothing, just replaced the broken pieces on the table. There was complete silence between them both. The quietness, following the violence, was somehow terrifying. I couldn't even force myself to ask, 'What is it? What happened?'

Menace seemed to flood the room. Then I heard Katherine say, 'They won't get away with it, of course.'

'No,' Lucien agreed, in a dead kind of voice.

'People who do this sort of thing always suffer for it. It's inevitable.'

Her tones were emotionless, quite cold and remote, but faintly vengeful.

'But why? *Why* is there such hatred for you all here?' I asked.

Lucien turned sharply, his strange, slatey-blue eyes searching my face.

'What do you mean, Belinda?'

I hadn't meant to tell him about the gossip in the shop, but now I had no choice and related what had happened.

For a moment or two Lucien and Katherine just went on looking at me, then he said gently, 'You shouldn't have worried about that kind of thing; it always happens in villages. Didn't you know that?'

'That's what I thought,' I said. 'That's what I told myself. But when I asked the way at the inn — that first day when Doctor Dendas met me on the hill — there was a sort of silence then. An atmosphere. And now — this. This isn't just idle gossip, is it?'

'No, it isn't,' I heard a woman's voice cry shrilly. I turned quickly, and saw Anne standing in the doorway, with her fair hair tumbled loose about her shoulders.

Lucien went towards her. 'It *isn't*,' she echoed desperately, almost wildly. 'I told you before — get away, Belinda. Go away from here, quick, quickly! It's all there, just as I said, like it was then. The cold hillside — and —' Her voice wavered; her figure seemed to crumple as Lucien caught her, gathering her into his arms. Her eyes were closed. She lay limp and unconscious, her head supported against his shoulder.

'Just one of her turns,' Katherine said contemptuously.

27

'What do you mean?' I demanded. 'She's ill. Haven't you any sympathy? Can't you do something?'

'I'll take her back to bed,' Lucien said, after he'd eased Anne into a chair. 'She's had a nightmare. Katherine, get some hot milk, will you? When she comes round I'll give her one of the tablets.'

As Katherine went out I asked on impulse, 'Who prescribed the tablets?'

Lucien looked surprised. 'Who? Louis, of course. He's her doctor.'

'Don't you think perhaps – ' My voice wavered.

'Yes?'

'Well, perhaps a second opinion would be a good idea?'

He was obviously taken aback. In the short pause that followed, I sensed he was not only annoyed but hurt.

'Do you imagine I haven't had more than one? My dear girl, we've had specialists here. I told you when you arrived, if you remember; but no one's done as much for her as Louis.'

'I see.'

'I hope you do.' He eyed me reflectively before continuing, 'You mustn't be offended, Belinda, but the fact is – in the beginning we were doubtful about having you here, just at this point in her illness. Apart from the blood condition, you'll have gathered she has mental lapses.'

'It seems so.'

'However – ' I could still feel his eyes searching my face intently, ' – in the end I agreed to her contacting you. She seemed so anxious to see you. And now, believe me, I'm glad.'

'Thank you for putting me into the picture,' I said.

'I can understand your anxiety,' he told me with a smile. 'Everything here must seem very strange to you. If I were in your shoes I'd probably feel the same. But I'm afraid our private affairs have to remain our own. Try and remember that. It's not meant to be a snub. Just – advice.' He touched my shoulder lightly, then gathered Anne's limp form into his arms again and went upstairs, leaving me standing there, aware that I'd been subtly yet effectively put in my place, and that even from Lucien I was unlikely to get any practical co-operation where my cousin was concerned.

When Katherine returned I said ineffectually, 'Can I do anything? If you have a sweeper − '

'Oh, no. It's all right,' she said. 'I can cope.'

Before she left for the kitchen, I asked, 'Are you just going to leave things as they are?'

'What do you mean?'

'This vandalism − the window and glass. Surely someone should 'phone the police.'

Katherine regarded me thoughtfully before replying: 'In some ways you're very naive. Don't you realise that the police are hand-in-glove with the locals? Do you think we'd have a chance in hell of getting recompense?'

'But whyever not?'

Katherine shrugged. 'Because, as you said, they don't like us. It's quite true. We're in very bad odour at Ravenscarne.'

'But there must be some reason,' I persisted.

'Oh, yes, there's a reason,' she answered. 'We *live*; we appreciate things they don't understand. Why − they haven't the first inkling about the history of their own countryside. If you mentioned primitive culture, they wouldn't know what you were talking about. That's why they detest Louis and Lucien.'

'Lucien?'

She smiled; and then she looked very handsome indeed, bold, beautifully arrogant, with her well-modelled chin held upwards in the regal manner of some modern Boadecia. 'Oh, yes,' she said softly, almost in a whisper. 'Lucien most of all.'

'But − '

She shook her head, still smiling. 'You don't understand − no. Maybe you will some time − and when you do, you won't dislike me so much.'

I didn't contradict her; there was no need. From that moment we had no illusions about each other. At least she was honest. Perhaps she really did believe that one day I might grow to like her. But her reference to Lucien disturbed me. I couldn't imagine anyone having a grudge against him, despite the proof of it which lay before my eyes in the shattered Ming and splintered glass on the floor.

I didn't see Anne until the afternoon of the following day.

29

When I went in she was smiling and looking refreshed.

'I slept late,' she said. 'Awful of me, isn't it?'

'I don't think so, not after last night.'

Her blue eyes widened. 'Last night? What about last night?'

'Don't you remember?' I broke off, angry with myself for referring to the unpleasant incident over which she'd obviously had a black-out.

'There was a storm,' I lied on impulse. 'Well – almost. It thundered.'

A little frown puckered her forehead. 'Did it? I didn't hear. How funny, I usually do.'

'A good thing you didn't,' I said. 'I hate thunderstorms.'

'Yes, so do I.' Her voice had changed, become very quiet; it was as though a veil had crossed her face, leaving only a dead blankness and despair.

'Oh, Anne,' I said suddenly, taking her hand, 'what's the matter with you? What is it? Can't you tell me?'

She shook her head. 'I don't know, Belinda. I really don't.'

'But –'

'That's the awful part of it,' she went on. 'I'd tell you if I could.' She clung to me, and I held her hand against my shoulder, feeling completely useless as the tears slowly welled from her eyes, coursing down her cheeks like a child's.

'Yes,' I said, getting up and easing her gently back against the pillows, 'I know you would. I know, too, that you should not be like this, happy one moment then confused and miserable the next. There's something wrong, and it isn't you. It isn't Lucien either. It couldn't be. But you're not so sick as the doctor and Katherine want you to believe. At first I thought there was nothing I could do, that my journey had been useless. But that's not true. I *am* going to do something about it, and you *will* be well again. You must believe it.'

After a long look, she nodded. 'I'll try.'

And with that the subject was dropped.

After tea, I decided, I'd make a visit to Martin Grey's and put a few questions to him.

The afternoon sky had a queer greenish tinge when I set off across the moor, giving the lonely landscape a desolate look.

Bushes and twisted trees were starkly accentuated, rising from clumps of heather and gorse. I recalled fairytale books of my mother's, containing weird illustrations by Arthur Rackham that had always entranced me. So I was not really surprised when I saw a bent black-clad figure coming towards me along a narrow track leading from the high lane. I wondered at first if it was the woman from the shack on the cliff. But this one was different. As she drew nearer I saw that she was very old; hawk-nosed, with beady black eyes under thick grey brows, and thin lips above a jutting chin. Probably of Spanish ancestry, I thought, knowing that in the past many sailors from Spain had settled in Cornwall. She was swathed in a large black shawl with a battered felt hat perched on her head. She was carrying a basket and was obviously out to gather something. I'd have passed her by if she hadn't stopped directly in front of me and said, 'Come from up theer, do 'ee?' She made a vague motion with one arm towards Ravenscarne, and having learned the attitude of the locals, I tensed myself to be on my guard.

I nodded. 'Yes, I'm staying there.'

She shook her head. 'You shouldn' be then. You do look a nice sort of maid to me. I seed you the other day leavin' the shop, an' when I went in I was told you be from Ravenscarne.'

'I'm Mrs Wilding's cousin,' I told her, rather ineffectually, 'I expect you heard that too?'

She nodded. 'There b'ain't many things I *doan'* know round here. Lived a long time, I have. Judith's my name – Judith Paynter – an' ninety summers I've already seen come an' go. Many things, too, some good an' some of the devil's making.'

'Yes, I'm sure. Ninety – that's a wonderful age.'

Her thin lips widened and took an upward tilt. The effect completely changed her from a gnome-like character to a whimsical-looking old lady with a twinkle in her eye.

'Wonderful?' she said. 'Well, maybe. Eatin' right an' thinkin' right does a deal to livin' long. Spinach now –' she glanced into her basket, adding quickly ' – in half an hour this 'eer'll be full of spinach, the wild kind that grows in a dip near the cliff. Real life-givin' 'tis. Natural stuff. When

31

you do live so near to nature you do learn to know the good things from the false. Up theer at Ravenscarne 'tis mostly the false an' the wicked they preach, so I've heard.'

She stopped speaking, staring at me contemplatively, obviously waiting for my reaction.

I thought quickly and said in what I hoped were placatory tones, 'Just stories, I think — small things exaggerated.'

The smile died. 'Oh, no, m'dear. I'm sure the truth up theer is worse than what is said. Whether the poor Reverend gentleman's death can be laid at their door I can't be sayin', not for certain. But things go on at Ravenscarne an' the old house, too, that's sinful an' dark; things that the Law should know about.'

'Why are you telling me this?' I asked.

'To warn 'ee. Just to warn 'ee, m'dear.'

'But —'

'Ais?'

'If people know something's wrong, why don't they get the police there themselves? Surely it's up to them?'

'Oh, no 'tedn'. They be thinkin' of themselves,' the old woman asserted, with a hint of fear in her voice. 'Frit they are, an' no wonder. There's things beyond the law of man. Things that can curse an' kill or turn a body into a toad if the thought's strong enough.'

'A toad?' I couldn't help smiling.

'Ais. *Ais*!' She thrust her chin at me. 'An' doan' 'ee laugh, chile. You jus' tek care. That's what I say — tek care.'

She turned away, and before I could reply passed sturdily on, an old bent figure, prodding the bracken and undergrowth with her stick, basket swinging on the other arm.

When her figure had disappeared round a clump of gorse and heather, I continued in the opposite direction. Though trivial in itself, the casual meeting with Judith Paynter had been a revelation. The inhabitants of the district were not necessarily ill-disposed to *all* visitors. The suspicion and dislike they felt — well, hatred was a better word — were mostly for Ravenscarne and those living there. Their fear was genuine and based on some dark knowledge I too sensed but had no evidence of. How was it that Lucien could be so enmeshed in such matters? Over and over again the tormenting question rose to bewilder and frustrate me, with a frail niggle of doubt I was unwilling to accept. Anyway, I told myself stubbornly, his loyalty and friendship for Louis Dendas were sufficient excuse for any professed ignorance of malpractice at Ravenscarne. Lucien, like myself, could be, and probably was, a mere innocent bystander in any curious practices going on.

I shivered slightly as a chill little wind quivered through the undergrowth. Through sheer tension I felt suddenly lonely and alien in a strange world where only Anne and Martin were real. Martin I hardly knew. And Anne? It seemed as I thought of her that a whole life-time lay between us. The years between our last meeting as children were hidden and filled with mystery. She had told me nothing that really mattered of that long period. All we had in common was the blood-tie and a beloved grandfather.

Yes, I had loved him, despite separation and the fact that I'd obviously been second best with him.

But had Anne?

How did I know?

I didn't, of course. There was no way of knowing such things. One could only trust and believe in the good.

I'd have to cling to that, I told myself stubbornly. Whatever happened I must not begin to have doubts about those I cared for.

It had gone five when I reached Martin's cottage, which stood a stone's throw from the village in a small neglected field spotted with a few loose boulders and patches of furze, between the road and the cliffs. The door was open, and the dog came to meet me, barking in a friendly way. A moment later Martin appeared.

'Hullo,' he said, taking the pipe from his mouth. 'Nice to see you. Come on in — down, Rex.'

I went inside. Although the cottage had been renovated, with a number of modern alterations, it was obviously very old. There was no hall. The door led immediately into a sitting room, with stairs branching from it to the right. I guessed the kitchen was at the back. The genuine ancient oak beams curved slightly in the middle, as though tired from the weight of years. But the effect of the cream-washed walls mellowed by the late afternoon sunlight was warm and welcoming. Though it was early summer, a fire glowed in the grate.

'I like my creature comforts,' Martin told me as I sat down in a luxuriously relaxing easy chair. 'The evenings get chilly sometimes.'

'Yes.'

There was a short pause before I said casually, 'I've had tea, and felt like a walk. That's why I – well – I just came to see you, because you said if I needed advice any time, or help, I could call.'

'Of course. I meant it.' He paused. 'I'm glad you remembered. And I'm glad to see you. Now what is it? Come on, unburden yourself, Miss Carn.'

I was surprised. 'You know my name?'

He laughed. 'In a village, it isn't difficult to be a nosey-parker.'

'I didn't suggest you were.'

'Well, that's what I am, of course. Cigarette?'

I shook my head. 'No thanks.'

He took one himself, and after he'd lit it, continued, '*Miss* Carn, isn't it?'

'Yes. Belinda actually,' I replied.

'And I'm Martin. But you wanted to tell me something. You're worried. What's up?'

'I don't know exactly. That's the trouble,' I confessed. 'My cousin's ill, of course, but there's something else. Something about the place.'

'You mean Ravenscarne?'

'Yes.'

'I'm not surprised.'

'Why? How did you know there was anything –'

'Strange going on?' he interrupted, adding almost immediately, 'I have a confession to make. It's my business to know things. My name *is* Martin Grey, and I do a few daubs now and then. But my real job's quite different – detecting.'

I stared. 'You mean you're a –'

'Police Detective Sergeant Grey,' he said. 'But for Pete's sake, don't be scared. I hope it'll help, knowing there's someone like me around.'

34

'That depends,' I said cautiously, 'on why you're here.'

'I'm afraid it's a secret for the time being. At the moment it's for *you* to tell *me* as much as you can. Every detail you can remember about what's been worrying you.'

'It's not easy.'

'Take your time,' he urged, and added, 'You *do* trust me, don't you?'

'Yes,' I said, and felt I could. There was something direct and dependable about him that left me in no doubt of his integrity. Naive of me perhaps, since villains were known to be extremely plausible sometimes. I could have asked for his card, of course, but it didn't occur to me. I *had* to trust someone, and clutched at Martin Grey like the proverbial straw.

And so I recounted as best I could the accumulation of small, sinister events, including Katherine's confrontation with the dead vicar, the conversation at the inn, my cousin's fears and nightmares, which she later denied – everything I could think of, culminating in the stone-throwing of the previous night. I didn't mention my visit to the old Ravenscarne with Lucien or finding the emblem because I wanted at all costs to avoid implicating him in anything unpleasant, and the incident didn't seem important to me then.

'I see,' he said thoughtfully when I'd finished. 'And that's all?'

I nodded. 'Yes. It doesn't amount to much, does it? I mean, most of it's just hearsay, or as though I was imagining things. But I'm not. I'm frightened. Most of all for Anne. And Lucien, too. He doesn't seem to realise anything's wrong.' I paused then continued, 'Perhaps there isn't.'

'I'm sure there is,' Martin said very definitely.

'But what? If you won't tell me anything, how can I be expected to co-operate? It's difficult working in the dark.'

'I realise that,' he answered, 'and believe me, there's nothing I'd like better than to have you in on things all the way. But the police have their own methods of working – and I'm just one of them, Belinda, a cop with a job to do. So leave it to me, will you?'

'I haven't really any alternative, I suppose.'

'No.'

'All right.'

'In the meantime take care of yourself. And if you feel in any kind of danger – any at all – 'phone me.' He wrote a number on a small piece of paper and handed it to me. 'Put that safely away,' he said. 'It's not in the book.'

'I didn't expect you to be on the 'phone,' I remarked, putting the paper into an inner compartment of the purse I always carried.

'You wouldn't make a very good policewoman then,' he replied, smiling. 'I saw that a line was connected before I took the place.'

The knowledge cheered me, made me feel more secure.

'Of course, if anything prevented you 'phoning, you'd have to get me as quickly as you could – make a dash for the cottage,' he said. 'In fact, it might be better for you to try and see me most days, just in case. You usually come this way for a walk in the afternoon, don't you?'

'After tea, yes.'

'Make it morning tomorrow, about elevenish, if you can,' he told me. 'That is, if the weather's okay, and you're not tied up with the rest of the household. Then the next day about this time – alternately. We don't want to arouse suspicion.'

'You *do* know something, don't you?' I queried. 'It's not just suspicion.'

'I'm afraid not.'

'Oh.'

'Don't be frightened. If you keep your head, and I think you can – you look to me that kind of girl – you can be of tremendous help. On the other hand, it might be better for you to leave.'

'No,' I said definitely. 'I wouldn't dream of it; not with Anne as she is. But I do wish – oh, well, like you said – I'll leave it to you.'

'That's right. Just keep your eyes and ears open, and report anything suspicious. Promise?'

I nodded. 'I promise.'

I left a little later. When I looked back he was standing at the gate watching. He waved, then turned and went back into the cottage.

As I left the village I walked quickly, because the sky quite suddenly clouded and a chilly wind sprang up, bringing mist from the sea. At one point, where the path verged closer to the precipitous coast, I dimly saw a boat approaching an inlet of the steep cliff face. It looked like one of the Breton fishing boats, which surprised me because I knew they weren't allowed so near to land unless it was for supply purposes or to shelter in harbour. Still, it could be a local boat, I supposed; its shape was indeterminate in the mist, which was thickening every moment. I walked on, forgetting about it, realising how easy it would be to get lost in the bewildering tangle of undergrowth which at intervals encroached upon the narrow path. I was not used to the sea-fogs and ever-changing skies which could be clear one moment, the next no more than a swirling density of wreathing shapes. I shivered as the cold air brushed against me, touching my face with icy fingers. It would be dangerously simple, I knew, to wander in the wrong direction and slip over the cliffs, or step unwittingly on a mat of bramble which covered the yawning gap of an ancient tinmine shaft.

I had been reading a book on Cornwall recently which had described such hazards. There was Miss Sibley, too. No death could be more terrible, surely, than to lie injured at the bottom of one of those dank places, crying for help with no one to hear. I tried not to think of such things, but it was as though the landscape itself was possessed by elemental evil, forcing sinister suggestions into my mind.

I knew I couldn't be far from the house, and looking down located the grey thread of path cutting to the left. I took it thankfully, knowing that I had not much further to go.

Then I heard what I'd noticed before but refused to acknowledge: the soft pad of footsteps behind me. I turned sharply with my heart pounding. There was no one there, or if there was I couldn't see because of the mist.

I went on, quickening my pace, with the bracken and wind-blown bushes creaking and sighing as I passed. That was it, I told myself, it was only the wind or the snapping back of the undergrowth where I'd disturbed it. There had been no footsteps except in my troubled imagination.

I was wrong. Suddenly there was a temporary clearing of the mist, and a voice saying in my ear: 'Miss Carn, you should take care in weather like this. It can be very dangerous.'

I turned my head. At my side, staring down at me in the grey light, was the pale faintly smiling face of Louis Dendas. 'I hope I didn't frighten you,' he added.

'You made me jump.'

'I'm sorry. It's so hard to know what is what in this infernal fog,' the doctor said softly. 'I wasn't even sure you were real. I had been down to the cove and had quite a business finding the track. Then I saw something move — like a ghost. I'm so glad you're not one.'

'So am I!' I remarked.

'These sea-fogs can be very dangerous. If you take my advice, you'll avoid the moors when possible. Roads are best for walking on.'

'Is the weather often like this?' I asked. 'The mist, I mean, coming up so quickly?'

'Oh, yes, often,' he answered. 'And it's not only the mist. There are shafts — bogs — adders.'

'Adders?'

'Didn't you know? Of course, they're about more when it's hot. You can see them in the sunshine sometimes, curled up on the stones.'

I shivered.

'Rather beautiful really,' he went on, 'in an evil kind of way. But then beauty *can* be evil.' His voice trailed off. I sensed that he was looking at me, that he wanted in some way to make me more aware of him. I didn't answer; I had no intention of letting him know that he had succeeded.

Yet when we reached Ravenscarne later he appeared genial and perfectly ordinary. Ordinary? Well, not quite, perhaps. I tried to determine what it was about him that was so disturbing, but couldn't — unless it was that faintly lascivious look in his shrewd eyes, the same quality that had been so obvious in his strange assembly of garden sculpture.

He left me at the door, saying that he would be back later to have a look at Anne. 'I expect you know she's had another bad turn today?' he said.

38

'Yes, unfortunately.'

He shook his head. 'Very sad. And distressing for you, too. Lucien is very grateful to you; and so he should be.'

Such normal words. Spoken with such apparent sincerity. He gave me a brief wave and was gone, leaving me with the worrying thought that I might, after all, be badly misjudging him.

When I went into the lounge I was surprised to find Lucien with two strangers, a girl and a man. They were having drinks, and appeared to be very friendly. The girl was slim, small, pale, with very large eyes and a quantity of honey-coloured hair piled on top. The man was dark and bearded. He looked like an artist.

'Thank goodness you're here, Belinda,' Lucien said. 'We'd have been out looking for you if you'd been much longer. Moors aren't the place to go wandering in the fog.'

'So Louis told me,' I said.

'You saw him?'

'Hardly *saw*. We almost banged into each other. He thought I was a ghost, and I thought – ' I laughed, knowing how silly it sounded, 'he was one.'

'An astral collision,' Lucien said with a smile. 'Rather intriguing. But highly improbable.' He put his hand on my shoulder and urged me forward. 'These are two good friends of mine, Helen Welsh and Marcus Raine. Helen – this is Belinda Carn. Anne's cousin.'

Both came to meet me. We shook hands, exchanging the polite formalities, and as we talked I learned that the couple had something to do with a film unit and were in Cornwall looking over possible spots for location work.

'Lucien's asked us to stay for a few days,' Helen said, 'which is perfectly sweet of him. It will be a marvellous rest. Filming can be such a rat race, especially in this bloody climate of ours.'

'Glad you made it,' I heard Lucien saying. 'It hasn't been much fun for Belinda so far with Anne as she is.'

'How is she now?' I asked.

'Sleeping at the moment. When she wakes up she'll probably forget she's had a bad turn. She generally does.' I glanced at him and saw a shadow momentarily cloud his eyes. Then he forced a laugh and suggested, 'Let's forget illness for a bit, shall we?'

He was trying to be nonchalant, but I could sense his unhappiness and felt great pity for him because the light-hearted chatter was obviously a facade, a brave act to mask his concern for Anne. I noticed with a stab of compassion the sensitive curve of his lips, the gentleness of his smile when he looked at me.

'Oh, Lucien,' I thought, 'it's wrong that *you* should have to suffer as well as Anne. You and I — we're both caught up in this; both victims, somehow, of this evil — this dark thing that seems everywhere. And it's not only because of Anne, it's . . .'

But what was it? And did it really exist? In that short pause, as I stared at him and he at me, I didn't really care. All I minded about was Lucien. All my past and future became unified somehow in the presence of Lucien, his beauty and remoteness. It was as though for some dark recess of time he had returned to recognise and know me. For a brief interim I *was* Lucien, and he was me. I loved him; not with my body, perhaps, but with my whole spirit.

And then the moment was over.

I heard him saying, 'Sherry, Belinda?'

I took it gratefully. Its warmth brought me back to the present. I saw Marcus Raine glancing at me curiously, heard Helen saying, 'Well, one thing's for certain — there'll be no point in looking round tonight. The fog's hellish.'

It was. I went to the window where she was standing staring out into a wall of grey. It pressed against the glass, furry, thick, with an obscene menace that reminded me of the stone beasts crouched in Louis Dendas' garden. 'Hell' described it exactly, I thought. I felt suffocated, as though imprisoned by forces beyond my control, understanding for the first time something of Anne's terror.

The tension was broken by my cousin's voice. 'Hullo.'

I turned. She was standing in the doorway in a loose flimsy blue dress, with her pale hair falling to the shoulders. Lovely Anne! Her face was radiant. She stared at Lucien reproachfully. 'Why didn't you tell me Marcus and Helen were here?'

He put his arm protectively around her. 'You were resting,' he said. 'As you'd had a headache, I thought it better to leave you.'

'Headache? I'd forgotten. Well, I haven't now.'

Her manner was emphatically lighthearted, almost febrile. Observing her closely I noticed the bright flush in her cheeks, the feverish sparkle of her lovely eyes. She went forward and kissed Helen on the cheek, then Marcus spoke.

'You look fabulous, Anne darling.'

'So do you,' she said. 'That beard suits you. You look like − now what is it you look like, Marcus dear? I know,' she giggled, 'a high priest. Yes, you look just like a high priest.' The giggle developed into a laugh as Marcus stared at her, his face, I imagined, a shade paler. The laughter went on, increasing in volume. I felt a sudden twinge of alarm as Lucien caught her up in his arms, saying quietly, 'Shhh. Stop it, Anne. Stop it, darling.' Then I saw her head fall back across his arm. She had fainted.

Dinner, following Anne's relapse, was a rather strained and morose affair. Lucien's thoughts were obviously with his wife, and I had no appetite, despite the admirable meal which Katherine had prepared. She alone seemed unaffected by what had happened, appearing if anything more vibrant than usual, flooding the room with a vivacity that subdued even Helen to silence.

Once or twice I caught Marcus looking at her. His eyes were watchful, uneasy and, I fancied, desirous at the same time. I had an instinctive feeling that they were no strangers to each other. Yet Lucien had introduced them as though they were. But then, I told myself, if for some reason or other they did not wish it to be known they were friends, it would be easy to deceive Lucien who frequently seemed to live in a half-dream world of his own.

After dinner Lucien went up to see Anne. When he came down again he said she wasn't too bad, and if I wanted to go up I could as Louis was coming round shortly to have a look at her.

I noticed Helen and Marcus glance at each other, and guessed they wanted to have Lucien to themselves. I was glad to get away. Making friends was never easy for me; I

41

had to get to know people for a while before I made up my mind about them, and so far I was mystified by the couple – by their unnatural air of restraint and watchfulness, which I found strange.

Anne was sitting up in bed when I went into the room.

'Are you feeling better?' I said.

'I'm all right,' she answered lifelessly. 'I know I fainted; Lucien told me. It was seeing that man Marcus. I don't like him. That's why I laughed. I was nervous.'

I sat on the side of the bed. 'I don't like him much either,' I agreed.

'Don't you?' Her eyes widened. 'It's not just me, then?' she queried, with the helplessness of a child wanting reassurance.

I did my best to speak convincingly. 'Nothing's "just you", Anne. Maybe this place gets on people's nerves – I don't know. Just because you fainted doesn't prove you're very ill. You're not. You'll get well and strong again once you're away from here. And when they've gone – Helen and Marcus, I mean – I'm going to see that we go away somewhere together, you and I.'

'You may mean it, and I wish we could. But it won't happen.'

'Why not?'

'There's Lucien.'

'He can come along, too. Probably he needs a bit of a change as well.'

She lay back and relaxed, the faint colour deepening in her pale cheeks.

'You're a comfort, Belinda. So normal. But I don't think – ' Her voice wavered.

'Well?'

'I don't think he'll let me,' she concluded. 'Louis.'

'What has he got to do with it?' I asked. 'He's only a friend. It's Lucien who counts.'

She shook her head. 'No, he's my doctor. Lucien believes in him.'

'Well, then, we'll just have to persuade Lucien to think differently,' I said, with an effort.

'If you can. But it won't work. They're great friends.

42

Lucien says Louis is much cleverer than any other doctor he knows; for nerves, you know. Not that he's done *me* any good. The last one was better. The one in London. But – '

'Who was he?' I asked. 'Can you remember his name? His address?'

She shook her head. 'No. I forget an awful lot of things nowadays. It worries me.'

'Don't let it. It's just a symptom of being run down. I was a bit like that myself once when I'd been overworking.'

This seemed to comfort her. She closed her eyes, and presently fell into a doze.

I was just going to leave when there was a knock on the door and Louis Dendas came in. Anne abruptly woke up. The doctor moved forward, smiling. I got up as Anne said quickly, 'Go away, I'm not ill; I don't want you here.'

'Now, now, Anne,' the suave voice said softly, 'you know I'm your friend. You don't mean that.'

'I do mean it, and you're *not* my friend.' She turned to me imploringly. 'Make him leave me alone, Belinda. Make him go.'

I saw Louis' expression harden, until the eyes were colder than ice in his face.

'Don't you think – ?' I began as he went forward. But he took no notice.

'She's been overdoing it,' he said. 'At the moment she needs as much rest as she can get. Now, Anne, I'm going to see you have a good night's sleep.'

She stared at him silently for a moment or two, and when, after a brief pause, she spoke again, the resigned hopelessness in her voice hurt me.

'He's trying to kill me, you know, Belinda,' she said dully. 'Don't let him.'

The doctor flung me a wry glance as though to emphasise her instability.

I shook my head helplessly. 'Don't talk like that, please.' Then I faced Louis. 'Is it really necessary to give her anything?She was asleep when you came in.'

'If you had ever been a nurse, Miss Carn,' he said with a hint of annoyance, 'you would know better than to question a doctor's judgement.'

If felt the warm blood staining my cheeks. Obviously there was nothing I could do.

I watched him roll up the sleeve of her bedjacket and busy himself with a needle and syringe. In a few seconds she was apparently asleep.

'You shouldn't get so upset,' Louis said, trying, I supposed, to put me at ease. 'I didn't mean to speak sharply, but it isn't easy dealing with your cousin. Do you think I enjoy seeing her so worked up?'

'I suppose not.'

He glanced at me sharply. 'Suppose?' When I didn't answer he resumed calmly, 'She'll be better in the morning. These delusions happen quite frequently with her type of − ailment. The thing is not to take them too seriously. They pass, and the best hope of a cure is to take as little notice as possible.'

Everything passes, I thought. In the meantime how long would the nightmare continue? And who was I to believe?

I lay awake for hours that night, listening to the sound of the summer rain falling, searching for an answer to the problem that troubled me. I could not find any. Only one person now could give any sense of security, and that was Martin Grey. He alone seemed free of the sinister pattern which had enmeshed me, like a monstrous spider's web, in the dark world of Ravenscarne.

The thought of him comforted me. His image was with me still when I fell at last into a troubled sleep.

Once in the night I woke sharply, thinking I heard my name called. I lay alert and tense for a few moments, listening. Imagination, of course, can play strange things with the mind, and it could have been just my overwrought nerves that gave a whispered impression of the wind outside, still sighing, 'Belinda − Belinda −' on a note so incredibly mournful I shuddered before getting out of bed.

At the window I paused. Then, hearing the insidious call again, I pulled the curtains aside.

The heavy rain had thinned and was no more than a drifting vaporous curtain filming a thin watery moon. Bushes and trees were distorted and blurred, almost clear one moment then taken again into curdling uniformity. I was conscious of a sense of extreme loneliness and desolation, and was about to go back to bed when a grey figure took shape against the luminous light filtering through the trees and undergrowth of the empty garden. A pale face was lifted to my window, featureless but with eyes so compelling I felt powerless to move away. At the same time my name rose with a whining reed-like quality above the soughings and sighings of nature. 'Lucien,' I thought, 'it must be Lucien.'

Why, though? What did he want?

I made no answering gesture, and as I stood there the rain unpredictably thickened, spattering the glass and covering the moon once more with cloud. When it had thinned again the figure had gone, leaving only the twisted shapes of trees and undergrowth against the watery night sky. Long shadows streaked across the grass. Somewhere a lone gull screamed. I closed the curtains and went back to bed.

But there was no comfort there — only a confusion of doubts and conjectures that made no sense, even when I fell into a fitful doze.

Was it Lucien I'd seen? Or had the whole thing been an illusion? If the latter, I had to pull myself together or I'd be no earthly use to Anne. It didn't occur to me then that the whole incident could have been a trick, something conjured up by Louis Dendas to frighten me. When the possibility *did* penetrate my brain, anger slowly dispelled fear.

Prematurely, as later events were to prove.

By the morning the rain had faded to a thin drizzle, lapping the landscape into grey uniformity.

Everyone was down for breakfast except Anne. Helen, refreshed by sleep, appeared brighter and was, I realised, better looking than she had seemed the previous night, with a fey quality accentuated by the Pan-like slant of her eyes. Marcus, too, seemed in more robust mood. 'When the rain clears,' he said, 'we'll have a look round. Tregale might be just the spot for village location. The name could be changed, and the locals used as extras.'

'*You'll* be lucky,' Katherine stated emphatically, with a

short laugh. 'We're not exactly popular round here. Our daily's already taken herself off.'

'Vanity is a characteristic of the human genus,' Marcus retorted. 'The chance of being seen on the screen is an infallible remedy for local antagonism. Mark my words, they'll leap into the loving arms of the publicity man.'

I was not so sure. Marcus had not heard the women in the village shop. He had not listened to stories about the dead vicar, or the sinister allusions to Miss Sibley's death in the mine-shaft. He certainly underrated the staunch independence of the Cornish people — their loyalty to each other and suspicion of strangers.

After breakfast I went up to see Anne. She had recovered but looked rather tired, so I did not stay long with her.

When I went downstairs again, I was surprised to see Katherine in the passage with a young girl I hadn't met before. She was round-faced, dark-haired, with a high colour, and small eyes set rather close together. She was wearing a short red dress revealing a good deal of plump thigh, and was in no way prepossessing. When she moved I saw that one leg was slightly shorter than the other, giving her a limp.

'This is Mary,' Katherine said. 'Mary-Ellen. She's come to help us in the house; for a few days anyhow. Perhaps longer.' She looked haughtily at the girl, adding, 'Miss Carn is Mrs Wilding's cousin. If she wants anything, see that she has it. I'm not always about the kitchen.'

'Good morning, Mary,' I said. 'I hope you like it here.'

The girl mumbled something, staring at the two of us in a rather scared way. Katherine, meanwhile, flung me a derisive glance as though to say, 'Whether she likes it or not is of no consequence. She's *here*, and here to work.'

Irritation filled me. In some moods Katherine had the power to anger me more than anyone I knew. Mary, after a half-hearted attempt at a smile, reverted to what was, I guessed, her natural sullen expression. As I went into the lounge I heard Katherine telling her imperiously what and what not to do. I didn't envy the new house-help.

I found Lucien still chatting to Marcus and Helen. He turned when he saw me and smiled. 'Helen and Marcus are

46

going to Tregale,' he said, 'in the car. Want a lift there for anything?'

'No, thanks,' I answered, suddenly remembering my promise to meet Martin Grey. In any case, I had decided to keep away from the shop as much as possible.

About a quarter to eleven I went to my room, put on a light waterproof and headscarf, and ran downstairs as quietly as possible, because I didn't want anyone to notice me going out. But Katherine did. As I opened the front door I heard her voice behind me.

'Going out, Belinda, in this weather?'

'I want a breath of air,' I told her. 'I shan't be long.'

To my dismay she said, 'I'll come too.'

I searched wildly for an excuse, and nearly said, 'I'd rather be alone,' but stopped the words in time. She would only have been suspicious, and that was the last thing I wanted.

'All right,' I managed to say, 'good.' I knew that Martin would understand as we'd arranged I'd not be there if the weather was bad or household matters made it difficult.

'Which way do you want to go?' Katherine asked when we got outside.

'I hadn't thought,' I lied, then added quickly, 'not the cliff way.'

'I agree. It'll be very wet underfoot. All right, we'll skirt round below the castle.'

As we climbed the slope in the direction of the ruined house, the thin rain blew at our backs, driving Katherine's dark sweep of hair before her. She wore no hat or scarf; her bold profile against the grey sky was arrogant and proud. Beautiful in a compelling way. I had never felt her magnetism so strongly before. She seemed to belong to that pagan landscape, to be as one with the bracken, the windblown trees and great humps of rocks. We did not climb to the top of the hill but went to the right, immediately round the curve, beyond the point where I had met Louis Dendas that first day.

'There!' she said suddenly, stopping and looking towards the coast. 'What do you think of that?'

Before my eyes the landscape swept, barren and desolate, to the great cliffs which rose dark against the indeterminate

47

line of sea and grey sky. On my far right I could distinguish the chimneys and towers of Ravenscarne, standing like pygmy things in the cluster of sparse trees and bushes, and beyond that the yawning Gap, guarded by two black tongues of rock thrusting into the sullen water. Further on, the stark shape of a derelict mine-works stood skeleton-like, wreathed in drizzle and cloud.

'Primitive, isn't it?' Katherine said.

'Yes.'

'Marvellous, though, don't you think?'

'It has a weird atmosphere,' I replied.

I felt her hand gripping my arm. 'You haven't seen anything yet,' she remarked.

She must have felt me wince, for she added quickly, 'What's the matter? Afraid?'

I turned sharply, staring at her face, at the dark eyes gleaming from the tangle of windblown hair. 'Why should I be afraid?'

She laughed. 'I think *I* should be, in your place.'

'Why?'

'Because you're a foreigner here — a stranger,' she replied. 'So am I, in a way. But *I* know a bit, I've made it my business to find out about this place, and believe me, pretty nasty things can happen.'

I wrenched myself free. 'I'm sure they can. But they can anywhere.'

'This is different. This is unique.'

'In what way?'

'You'll find out,' she said. 'In time; if you're sensible. You see, I have protection.'

'Protection?' I echoed.

'That's right. There are some things that will master *you* if you don't master *them*. Everything's conflict. But the power is ours if we want it — to overcome.'

'Do stop talking in riddles,' I said impatiently, though my heart had quickened unpleasantly.

'Riddles? Don't be so intense.'

'I think you're the intense one,' I told her.

'I was only warning you.

'Please don't bother.'

48

'But I like to be helpful. Did you know that there are hidden shafts round here?' she asked after a pause. 'Where people can fall and never be found?'

'Yes, I've heard. About Miss Sibley, too.' I fancied she was momentarily taken aback.

'Miss Sibley was a fool,' she remarked shortly. 'If she'd taken care – '

'Well, *I* do; I usually look where I'm going.'

'Oh, I'm sure of that. I'm sure you don't take risks. How boring for you.'

I said nothing. I could feel her frustration; sense that she was trying to goad me. Then suddenly she cried, 'Why can't you be *yourself* for once in your life? *Give*. Enjoy. Don't be so smug. The wind and the rain – take them, Belinda, breathe, *breathe*. Be what you are – a part of it all. *Master* of the living – and of the dead, perhaps.'

The last sentence ended in a sibilant whisper. Her words and the expression on her face made me think she must be slightly mad. I was going to run from her down the slope when she caught hold of me again, swinging me round. 'Lift your arms to the sky, Belinda,' she insisted. 'Dance – dance!' Her clutch was too strong for me. Gyrating and gesticulating like a wild thing, she pulled me this way and that until at last, caught in a tangle of bramble, she let go. I stood facing her, breathless, trembling in every limb. She was smiling, breathing heavily. Then, quickly, it was as though all energy left her. The smile died, leaving her face a dull mask.

'Oh,' she said, with a scowl. 'Come on, let's go back.'

As I went with her down the hill, she said, 'You're not much fun, are you? Are all Canadians the same?' Her voice was loaded with sarcasm. When I didn't answer, she insisted, 'Well?'

'That's a stupid question.'

'Oh, I've annoyed you. How cruel I am. Please forgive me.'

I turned and looked straight into her hard eyes. 'Why do you want to frighten me?'

She laughed. 'To tell you the truth, I don't bloody well

care whether you're frightened or not. You're not all that important to me. I was just bored, that's all.'

It was probably the truth, I thought. Because she didn't know how to use up her excess energy she took pleasure in frightening and teasing people.

I decided that my first walk with Katherine would be my last. Yet when we entered the house no one would have believed she was the same person I'd been with on the hill. With her wet mackintosh off and her hair combed back she had a veneer of well-bred aloofness that made me wonder — which was the real Katherine? This, or the wild creature of half an hour before? I recalled her laughter, her wanton dance; yes, wanton described it. As wanton and macabre as the witches in Macbeth.

Witch? The word had been a mere flash in my mind, but it could be true. I had heard and read about modern witchcraft, of course, but had never really believed in it; I didn't believe any one person could ultimate power over another, unless the victim was a participant. But my cousin was in a weakened state of health. Whether I was imagining things or not, I was there to protect Anne, and in future I would take care not to leave her alone for too long. If Lucien wasn't near, *I* would be. I would be on the watch always, so that if danger came I would be aware of it and able to contact Martin Grey.

The next morning the mist had cleared but the wind had freshened, driving watery clouds across a grey sky which was spattered at intervals by thin sunlight. After breakfast I went upstairs to see my cousin. She was feeling better, and seemed anxious to reassure me. 'I'm sure Louis is right, really,' she said. 'I'm rundown and nervy. I told him about us going away soon for a holiday.'

'Oh? What did he say?'

'He said it was a good idea when I was strong enough,' she answered. 'So I'm going to concentrate hard on getting well, and try not to imagine things or have stupid nightmares.'

I hoped she was correct about the doctor, and that when the time came he would not succeed by some means or other in preventing her getting away.

'By the way,' she said, as I was leaving the room, 'are you going into Tregale today?'

'Probably,' I answered, knowing that if there was no one to see me go I should be off presently to see Martin Grey. 'Why?'

'I was wondering if you could get me some face powder?' she said. 'It's called "Petal Pale"; they keep it in the shop.'

Although I did not relish encountering Mrs Pender, who had received me so ominously with her cronies, the fact that Anne wanted an errand doing did give me a legitimate excuse if I ran into Louis Dendas or Katherine.

'Of course I'll get it for you,' I said. 'Anything else?' She shook her head. 'My purse is on the dressing table. If you take out a note – '

'Oh, don't bother, Anne. I've got change. You can pay me, if you must, when I get back.'

I went to my room, slipped on my coat and ran downstairs.

Lucien came out of the sitting room before I got to the door. 'Going out?' he said.

'Anne's asked me to get some face powder for her,' I replied. 'So I'm taking the chance of a walk.'

I thought just for a second that he was going to say he'd come with me; his eyes were reflective, as though considering. Then he said, 'Take care of yourself. Aren't you wearing a scarf?'

'No. It's not winter.'

'There's a wind, though. By the way – ' he brought a piece of paper from his pocket ' – I'm not a writer, least of all a poet, but when I woke up this morning this verse was running through my head. It's not very good, but I'd like your opinion.'

'I'm no authority, Lucien,' I said. 'Katherine – isn't *she* the writer?'

'Katherine wouldn't understand,' he said shortly. 'Her repertoire is limited.'

I took the paper from him. 'Not now,' he added. 'Read it later, when you're quiet and alone.'

He watched me put it away in my bag. When I looked up

51

his eyes were still upon me. I had the curious sensation of timelessness again, as though the world had slipped away, leaving me in a limbo of wonder, of things half known, only dimly perceived, but unutterably beautiful. The pause could only have lasted seconds, but it might have been eternity. Then I heard him saying, 'I'm glad Anne's thinking of her looks again. Vanity is always a sign of recuperation.'

Anne! I looked away abruptly. I should have known he was thinking of her. The poem was probably some sort of lyric inspired by her beauty and his love for her. I felt disloyal and ashamed, determined that in future I would guard against being alone with Lucien.

I met Martin on the path halfway to Tregale, and explained why I hadn't been the previous day.

'We had company,' I told him. 'Two guests, film people – Helen something or other and a man called Marcus. Marcus Raine. He's dark with a beard. I don't know how long they're staying but it was hard to get away, you know how it is. And when I did, Katherine got hold of me at the door and insisted on going along with me. So we went in the other direction.' I paused, adding, 'It was a very unpleasant walk.'

'Why?'

I told him about her strange behaviour on the hill; he didn't seem surprised. 'As I thought,' he said. 'You're enmeshed in a household of neurotics – and possibly worse.'

'Anne isn't neurotic,' I retorted quickly. 'All the others pretend she is but – '

'Yes? What were you going to say?'

'I don't know ... Yes, I do – I think for some reason they want something to happen to her. Not Lucien, of course. He's different. But Louis and Katherine. I suppose you think *I'm* being neurotic, too?'

'On the contrary. As I told you, I think you're a very sane and balanced person. There's one thing I'd like confirmed, though.'

'What?'

'In your grandfather's will, it was stipulated that if Anne should predecease you – excuse the legal jargon – you would inherit certain capital which at present is held in trust until she reaches the age of thirty. Is that correct?'

'Yes,' I said. 'Something of the sort. But who told you and why do you ask? I'd forgotten about the money ages ago. It's never been important to me.'

He smiled reassuringly. 'I'm sure of that. As to your first question — there are quite simple legal means of finding out these things.'

I felt worried and confused. 'What are you suggesting?'

'Nothing,' he replied. 'I just like my facts to be clear.'

We walked on without speaking for a minute, then I said, 'About facts — so do I. And as I'm concerned — or appear to be — I don't understand the secrecy.'

'I don't suppose you do. In your place I'd feel the same. But cheer up — maybe you won't have to wait long. The only thing that bothers me is your safety. It's useful having you there, but I still feel you should leave.'

'No. I'm not going without Anne,' I insisted. 'And whatever you say won't make any difference. You can't *make* me go.'

'Fair enough,' he said.

I walked on with my head up, not looking at him, guessing he might try again to make me change my mind. Presently we came to Tregale. I went into the shop, bought the powder, and was out again before Mrs Pender had time for any insinuations. Martin was waiting for me outside.

'How's the gossip?'

'No one in there except Mrs Pender,' I answered. 'She just got the powder, and took the money for it as though she was receiving poison.'

He laughed. 'What are you doing now?'

'I'd better get back,' I said. 'Or there'll be a search going on. Oh — I forgot one thing. We have a help now at the house, a lame girl called Mary. Mary Ellen.'

'Oh?' His glance held a question.

'I feel a bit sorry for her,' I said. 'She's rather dumb, and not at all attractive. Katherine seems to have got her knife into her already.'

'Trenoweth.' He frowned reflectively. 'Does she come from round here?'

53

'I've no idea. She's obviously Cornish. I'll find out about her if you like.'

'A good idea,' he said.

I left him soon afterwards and walked back to Ravenscarne. The wild sky had brightened, slashing the landscape with gold. When I reached the house it seemed deserted except for Mary who came down the hall with a dustpan and brush in her hand. 'It's lovely out now,' I said with an attempt at friendliness. 'I think the mist and rain have really cleared.'

She mumbled something, eyed me furtively and disappeared into the lounge, looking back once as though she was scared. I wondered what I had said to frighten her, and came to the conclusion she must be a bit simple.

I took the powder up to Anne. She was sleeping, so I placed it on the bedside table by her mirror, and went to my room. I was putting my coat on a hanger when I remembered the paper Lucien had given me. I opened my bag, took it out and read it, realising with a quickening of my pulses that this was the first note I had ever received from him, and that it was not necessarily about Anne.

In copper-plate handwriting, so characteristic of his personality, the poem ran:

I searched a billion million years,
Through space and time, and countless spheres.
From birth to death, and death to birth,
Until at last we met on earth –
To recognise, and know the pain
Of lovers doomed to part again;
Yet burning with a light so rare
That all it touched, caught unaware –
For one brief moment beauty knew
Of love divine, before it flew.

Rather similar to Blake, I thought.

I let the paper fall to the bed where I was sitting. My hands were trembling. What did it mean? And why had he given it to me? As I asked myself the question I already queried the inevitable answer and denied it because I didn't want to know. He should never have told me, I thought. He should

54

not have written that poem. I knew I should have torn it up immediately. But I didn't. I went to the chest of drawers and put it carefully away between some handkerchiefs, where no one would be likely to see it.

My conflicting emotions bewildered and weakened me, as though all will-power was destroyed, leaving me at the mercy of a destiny stronger than myself.

For some minutes I battled with my own feelings, until at last one fact emerged clear and decisive. Whatever happened, nothing must hurt Annie. Thinking about her strengthened me; I was able to put the whole thing in perspective. I decided that when Lucien asked me what I thought about the poem I would just answer, 'Interesting, quite good.'

That, surely, should put an end once and for all to any fancied bond between us. I tried not to visualise the hurt look clouding his eyes, the inevitable snub he would feel, wishing with all my heart I had never left Canada or seen Ravenscarne.

I knew now that no good could come of it, only harm, unless Martin Grey was really near to solving the evil pattern of events. And this I doubted. It seemed to me that the dark forces had become too strong, were mounting steadily with an intensity which must eventually result in some dreadful climax, the nature of which I could not foresee.

For the next two days I had nothing of importance to tell Martin, though I met him at the appointed times. The weather was showery, alternating with fitful bursts of sunshine, and the two visitors were out a good deal looking for possible sites for the film. I had avoided Lucien as much as possible, but one day when I ws standing in the lounge idly watching the clouds racing across the sky he came up behind me quietly and said, 'Well?'

I turned. 'Hullo, Lucien.'

'You didn't like it?' he asked.

'What – oh, you mean the poem?' I tried to keep my voice steady. 'Yes, I did, but – '

He shook his head slowly. His eyes weren't hurt, as I'd feared they might be, but thoughtful with a searching look in them.

'Forget about it,' he said. 'I don't want praise for what's a very poor effort at expressing the unknowable.'

'I think you did that exactly,' I told him. 'With imagination.'

'And how would you define imagination?' he asked.

I tore my eyes away. 'You should know better than me,' I replied. 'I'm only an ordinary practical person.'

'There's nothing ordinary about you, Belinda,' Lucien said. 'If you were it would be easier.'

'What do you mean?'

'Look at me.'

With an effort I stared straight into his face, trying to keep my gaze steady.

'I never thought I should say this to you,' he continued. 'It's perhaps the hardest decision I've ever had to make. And it won't happen again. But I think – '

'Yes, Lucien?'

I was surprised when he echoed almost what Martin had said to me previously.

'For your own good, perhaps you should go away.' The words were blurted out as though against his will. 'Before, when you suggested it yourself, I was dead against it. I still am, in a way. But you're getting too involved.'

'How do you mean – involved? With Anne?'

'You know the answer very well. This isn't an ordinary household. I – why don't you go back to Canada?'

'It's funny,' I answered. 'Anne has said the same thing. So did – ' I was going to add 'Martin Grey' but remembered not to.

'Who else?'

'Katherine perhaps,' I lied. 'I forget. Doctor Dendas told me to stay. And I shall.'

'Very well. If that's what you want.' His voice was lighter, easier; I knew I'd said what he really wanted.

'Later, though, it would be nice for Anne and me, and you too if you wanted, to go for a holiday,' I suggested. 'I mentioned it to Louis and he agreed. They both did.'

56

Lucien's face clouded. 'One can always make plans,' he said. 'Fulfilling them may not be possible.'

He turned without another look at me, and walked out of the room.

Later that morning Marcus said he and Helen had to go into Penzance, and that if I'd like a change I could go along with them and join them for lunch. As Anne still seemed a little better and Lucien was staying in, I accepted gratefully. To see shops and people would be a welcome break, and I would be back in time to see Martin later.

When we set off the weather had brightened, leaving the sky clear except for a few grey wisps drawn cobwebbed across the sun.

Marcus drove with Helen beside him, leaving me comfortably alone in the back seat. I was glad of that; I found them hard to talk to, perhaps because I knew no film jargon, and socially we had little in common. Once Marcus spoke to me without turning his head.

'How do you like being at Ravenscarne? Rather benighted, isn't it?'

'Yes. I wouldn't like to live there always.'

'When people spend their days in places like that they make their own interests, of course,' he answered, 'as they did in the old days.'

'Except there's television now,' I reminded him, 'which I suppose has completely put an end to old hobbies like weaving and herb growing — that sort of thing.'

'You'd be surprised. Old customs die hard.'

'Just look at that!' Helen said suddenly, waving her hand towards a sweep of high moors dotted on the sky line with several ancient mine-stacks. Gorse flamed bright in the sunshine, merging in patches to deepest purple, where heather was in full bloom, with a drift of last bluebells in the bracken.

'Wouldn't that do for the escape scene?' she asked Marcus. 'With the figures taken on the ridge, near those old stones, it would be wild enough.'

'Might,' he agreed. 'It's just possible.'

We reached the town shortly after eleven-thirty, and

arranged to meet for lunch an hour later at a small select-looking old-worldish place, apparently renowned for home cooking.

Marcus and Helen went off then on their own business, leaving me to my own devices.

First of all I had a look round a large store where I fell for some chunky earrings – always a weakness of mine. Then I made my way down to the quayside, exploring the harbour and maze of side streets, marvelling at the picturesque island of St Michael's Mount, with its fairytale turretted castle rising gem-like from the sea.

After that I climbed up to the town again, and from the busy main street wandered off in another direction, choosing the quieter streets and alleys where shops were smaller, more intimate and characteristic of Cornwall.

Among a medley of confectioners, ironmongers, and small stores selling what boasted to be the original Cornish Piskie, I came across an antique shop which looked interesting, with an assortment of relics and ancient souvenirs – some obviously genuine, others of doubtful origin – jumbled somewhat haphazardly in a rather badly lit window. As I wanted one or two presents to take back with me to Canada, I seized the opportunity of looking round.

The inside, as I had expected, was darkish, probably to enhance the archaic atmosphere, which had the distinctive musty smell of ancient wood and upholstery so charac-teristic of too many articles jumbled into too little space. A cloisonné bowl sat on a Victorian antimacassar lying on the seat of a Louis Quinze chair. A Swansea pottery jug nestled close to a rather ugly Coronation mug. There were beautiful objects among a confusion of late Edwardian horrors; yet the whole effect was tantalising and the sort of place, I guessed, where real bargains could be picked up.

I was examining a cameo brooch when a friendly looking middle-aged woman wearing glasses came forward from the back of the shop.

'Can I help you?' she asked, hope of a sale in her voice.

'I rather like this brooch,' I answered, showing it to her. 'It's genuine, isn't it?'

'Oh, yes, Miss. I can vouch for it. It came from a very

good house. The old lady had to sell up. Such a shame; but that's how it is these days, with living being so costly. The older people can't go on in the way they used to. It doesn't seem right, does it?'

'No,' I agreed.

She adjusted her glasses carefully on her nose, picked up a magnifying glass and scrutinised the brooch carefully under the light.

The price was quite reasonable so I took it, searching in my purse for the right amount. I hadn't sufficient without changing a five pound note.

'Do you mind this?' I asked.

'That's all right,' she answered. 'I'm rather short in the till, but if you wait a moment I'll see what I've got.'

She disappeared through the door at the back, and while I was waiting I had another look round.

Suddenly I saw something I'd not noticed before, pushed against the wall in one corner: an oil painting, rather crackled on the surface, in a chipped gilded frame.

I went closer and bent down to examine it. It wasn't very large, about two feet by two and a half, and it was thick with dust. I rubbed my hand over it and saw that beneath the yellowed varnish the colours must be bright still and beautifully blended. I could see no signature, but I was startled by a certain likeness in the portrait that was unmistakable. The face, clean-shaven, was surmounted by an ornate cap or hat of probably fourteenth-century design, below which dark hair cut squarely reached to the bottom of the ears. The neckline of the doublet appeared to have been heavily embroidered or jewelled. But at the time these facts meant little to me. I was aware of only one thing: Lucien's face staring at me from the cracked canvas, the mouth with its gentle half-smile; Lucien's eyes, which seemed to be watching from the shadows. I tried to subdue the quick acceleration of my heart, the creeping strange feeling that I was back in some other world out of time or physical reality. An overwhelming sensation of nostalgia swept through me, as though I had returned from a long journey to things I knew and loved. The room blurred and darkened. My hands and forehead felt cold and damp.

I could feel faintness overtaking me, which might of course partly have been due to the stuffiness of the shop. I was still kneeling there rigidly holding the painting when the woman came back.

'Sorry I've kept you waiting,' she said. 'I couldn't find my purse. I'm careless about that; my husband's always saying –' She stopped and enquired anxiously, 'Are you all right?'

I managed to get to my feet. 'Oh, yes, thank you. I'm rather tired. A headache –'

'Oh, dear. Would you like a glass of water or milk perhaps?' There was consternation in her voice as she stared at me, and I guessed I must be looking pale.

Her practical offer of help brought me to my senses.

'No. No, really. Thanks all the same. You're very kind.'

As she handed me the change she said, 'You were looking at that old painting; it's not much good now, I'm afraid. Cracked and worn. When we picked it up we thought it might be of some value but there was no name on it, and a friend of ours who knows about artists said it probably wasn't the work of anyone important. No one seemed to know who the man is either, although some thought it was Sir Lance Pendrake; they were a rich family in the old days. He was a bit of a rake though – had a name for dabbling in occult things and came to a bad end. Burned to death or something. But then, it could be rumour. People do say such things. But, anyway, the family died out, and the house isn't there any more. It was near Tregale somewhere. 'Throw it away,' I've told my husband, many times. But he won't. He's a stickler for old things. And so there it is. Are you interested? You can have it for next to nothing if you like, though I wouldn't give it houseroom.'

I was tempted to make an offer for the painting. But to have done so would only have added a further link to my mysterious involvement with Lucien, admitting something I was determined to have no part in.

'No, I don't really think so,' I answered. 'As you say, it *is* very shabby, and as I come from Canada the weight would be a drawback when I fly home.'

The woman agreed, and after a few cursory remarks about

60

the difference between the Cornish and Canadian climates I said goodbye, and a moment later was outside in the sunlight again.

I reached the cafe punctually at twelve-thirty and found Marcus and Helen already sitting there in a window-seat, at a small table for three. I went in. The interior was rather arty-crafty, obviously a social rendezvous for people of leisure; but the smell was tempting, redolent with the odour of freshly baked cakes mingling with that of savouries and home-made pastries.

'We'd finished what we had to do,' Helen said, 'so we thought we'd be on the safe side and get seats. What'll you have?'

I looked at the menu and ordered a cheese omelette.

'No vegetables?'

'No, thanks. I'm not really hungry. An omelette will be plenty.'

I was in a dream through the whole meal. Whether Marcus and Helen noticed or not I couldn't tell. They too seemed abstracted, as though they had something on their minds.

'You're sure you've got everything?' Helen asked Marcus as she toyed idly with an ice. 'Did you check the list?'

Marcus glowered. 'I'm not like any forgetful woman,' he replied. 'Look after your own business and leave other people to take care of theirs.'

'There's no need to be rude,' she retorted. 'Just because you've got things to do – '

'Oh, for God's sake!' he exploded. Then, with a quick glance at me, said half apologetically. 'Don't take any notice of us. Bickering is our recreation.'

'He was brought up on D.H. Lawrence,' Helen said over-sweetly, 'with a complex about inhibitions. You know!'

I didn't, and wished they'd stop arguing. However unpleasant it was, their joint aggressiveness had an intimacy which excluded me, making me feel decidedly *de trop*.

The sun went in suddenly, and Marcus said, glancing out of the window, 'Hmm, hope it's not going to rain tonight.'

'If it does, it will be cold with this wind,' Helen retorted, almost with relish.

'That's right. Go on, be cheerful.'

Forcing myself to take an interest, I enquired, 'Are you going somewhere then? This evening, I mean?'

Helen flung me a curiously veiled look. 'Not that I know of. Why? What makes you ask?'

'Talking about the rain.'

'It might just happen that some business or other crops up,' Marcus said. 'Our plans are necessarily elastic.'

I felt like a child rebuked.

'I'm sorry. I didn't mean to pry.'

'And what does *that* mean?' Marcus said irritably. 'You women get so intense — making mysteries of nothing, situations that don't exist. Yap yap yap! Not enough to do, that's the trouble.'

Helen smiled at me placatingly. 'Ignore him. He's irritable today. Got a liver, I expect. A real old bear. Dashing about so much doesn't agree with him.'

She turned to Marcus. 'You hate it, don't you darling? You like to be free — in other words, pick up an excellent salary without having to do the job. That's what they call having one's cake and eating it, isn't it? Besides —' she faced me again ' — he suffers from chest. And as we haven't much time to get things settled, we have to use every minute. It isn't always fun, especially if the weather turns sour. Take my tip and steer clear of film-making. It can be sheer bloody hell.'

It occurred to me that Helen was taking rather more trouble than was necessary to explain. It didn't matter to me where they went or what they did. I didn't like either of them. There was something ambiguous and misleading behind the lighthearted facade which I mistrusted, though I couldn't have said why; a suggestion also of stabbing hurtful teasing that chilled me. I could imagine them when they were children wilfully taunting others — a form of immaturity I'd never been able to tolerate. Yet they were Lucien's friends. Lucien! So different. What had they *really* in common? I wondered. Perhaps nothing. Perhaps he just accepted them on face value as people concerned in interesting jobs, or perhaps they were careful to present a different more amiable front to him. That was probably it.

Anyway, for some reason he was important to them, which was why they had taken me along; out of politeness to Lucien. Well, I wouldn't inflict myself on them again. In future, if I wanted to do any shopping I'd make my own arrangements.

The journey back was a silent affair. It was three o'clock when we reached the house, and the earlier cool breeze had already freshened to a strong wind that blew our coats against us, whipping Helen's hair and scarf gustily against her face. She put one hand up to free herself, and toppled her shopping basket with the other, inadvertently dropping a paper bag. Marcus bent forward immediately and retrieved it, glancing at her furiously. 'Can't you be more careful?'

I waited a few seconds until they'd gone on ahead, and looked back quickly, wondering if I'd imagined something had rolled from the bag to the verge of the grass and shrubbery.

I hadn't.

A faintly glowing object looking like some kind of a pendant was lying there, half hidden by the undergrowth. I picked it up quickly, slipped it into the pocket of my coat and hurried after them. It was something to show Martin, I thought; evidence of some kind which might prove important and could easily be connected with the carved relic I'd seen when I was with Lucien at Ravenscarne. I had no practical reason for thinking so; but the brief contact with the object had momentarily disconcerted me, as though my fingers had touched something evil and corrupt. With my imagination conjecturing this way and that I recalled Lucien's reaction when I'd first spotted the curiously carved emblem on the hill − the alarmed way he'd told me not to touch it. There'd been a kind of fear in his eyes. Fear for me. He must have suspected that evil things had been going on − suspected, but had no proof. Perhaps, like Martin, he was trying to find out, saying nothing to me because he didn't wish me to be worried.

My heart warmed to him again, dispelling in one quick moment my resolve not to think of him. If only I could talk to him and have things out in the open, we could have contacted Martin together; unity would have given extra

63

strength to the fight against what evil there was. But my promise to Martin prevented it. Meanwhile it was a matter of going on blindly, leaving Lucien perhaps, as well as Anne, in danger.

I couldn't understand why he didn't see through them all, sense Katherine's malice towards Anne, and recognise the doctor for what he was — a clever, evil-minded man with an interest in unholy things.

I was sure this was true and the word was right — *unholy*. From that moment I no longer had any illusions about happenings round Ravenscarne. There were sinister malignant forces at work that could very easily be those of black magic.

When we were safely in the hall, I went up to my room and took the metal charm, pendant or whatever it was, from my pocket for a good look. As before, when my hand touched it, I involuntarily shivered. It was triangular-shaped, obviously old and of ancient design, with a curious figure slightly raised from the surface — carved, probably, just as the one I'd seen with Lucien, but of a different design. This was four-leged and scaled, with clawed feet and short tail resembling the flat fork-tongued jaws of a snake. The breasts were bare and female, the head human and long-haired of no particular sex, but with features so incredibly evil I could feel my throat constricting with aversion. It had two small rings at the back which confirmed my first impression it was meant to be worn round the neck.

But whose?

More than ever bewildered, I hurriedly slipped the thing into the drawer of my dressing table. Then I took it out again and placed it more safely between underwear. I was sure that neither Helen nor Marcus had seen me pick it up, but they would be bound to discover it was missing, and I trusted none of them, including Katherine, not to have a furtive look round my room when I wasn't there. If I suspected *them*, they probably suspected *me*, too. In future I had to be on my guard.

Before going down to tea I went along to see Anne. It was obvious that during my visit to Penzance something

64

had happened to her. She was lying rigidly in bed, with a fixed stony expression on her white face.

'Anne,' I said, putting my hand on hers. She turned her head slightly. Her eyes looked frozen, dull, as though she was in a trance. But I knew it wasn't that; I guessed that in my absence the doctor must have been up and once more insidiously drugged her. Yet there was no smell, no sign of any fresh bottle of medicine or syringe lying about. There wouldn't be, of course. He would be too wily for such carelessness.

I shook her gently by the shoulders. 'Anne, dear.'

Her beautiful eyes stared up at me. Then with a great effort she said, 'Go away, Belinda, it's no good.' Her whole demeanour – voice, and the expression on her face, imploring yet hopeless – held the quality of some wounded sick creature aware of its own doom.

'Go away,' she whispered again. 'It's beginning again, can't you see? The cold hillside, and the – '

'Don't,' I told her sharply. 'That's only a dream. Forget it.'

She shook her head. 'It's true. I know. When it happens they – it's always like this – ' The words died away as quietly as the lids falling over her eyes. I waited for a moment, wondering if she would say any more. But she was obviously asleep.

On the landing outside I met Lucien coming along to the bedroom.

'Anne's not well again,' I said.

'I know. Louis has given her something to make her sleep. I'm sorry you had to see her like that.'

'*I'm* not,' I retorted decisively. 'And another thing, Lucien, I don't believe Louis knows what he's doing. Or if he does, then it's a dreadful thing. I think Anne may be right. If he goes on like this he'll kill her. And why? For what reason?'

I swept past him before he could stop me or attempt to answer. For those brief moments no one except Anne mattered to me at all. *No one* – not even Lucien.

Tea was a strained affair. Everyone seemed edgy, filling the air with a tension which the bright sunshine did nothing to dispel. Katherine was unusually silent; her mind appeared to be on other things, and once she knocked her cup over, spilling the tea down her dress on to the carpet.

'Damn!' she said angrily, getting up. She went out of the room with Lucien's eyes on her.

'I have a feeling Mary's not satisfactory,' he said. 'Katherine can't bear inefficiency. It makes her jumpy.'

'Oh, well, we all have accidents,' Helen remarked brightly. I noticed Marcus drumming his fingers irritably on the surface of the table, with his eyes turned impatiently away. He gave the impression of waiting to escape from the house, or it could have been the missing pendant upsetting him. I felt the same about leaving, but wanted the others to go if they intended to before I set off for Martin's cottage, otherwise there was the danger that one of them might suggest going with me.

As it happened I was not to see Martin that day at all, because when I *did* go out, I ran straight into Louis Dendas coming along the path from Tregale.

'So?' he said. 'You're taking the air? Good idea. Lovely day.'

I went straight to the point. 'What did you give Anne this morning?' I asked bluntly.

He looked surprised. 'My dear Miss Carn, I'm her doctor. What business is it of yours?'

'Everything. I happen to be her only living relative, and I'm fond of her.'

'Even so, that doesn't give you the right to question my medical abilities,' he replied.

'I wouldn't, not for a moment,' I told him, adding recklessly, 'I wasn't referring to *medical* authority.'

'Oh?' His eyebrows lifted slightly; his mouth twisted a little to one side, emphasising the sneer in his voice. 'Then please don't expect me to waste time answering riddles.'

'It isn't a riddle. I'm suggesting that you're damaging Anne's morale.'

He gave a short brittle laugh which had no humour in it.

'Indeed? And how? In what way have I outraged the conventions?' he said.

'I don't suppose you have. You're too clever for that.'

I turned and left him, continuing along the path, but he caught me up.

'You don't like me, do you, Miss Carn?'

'No,' I answered. 'Since you ask me, I'm afraid I don't.'

'Why?'

'You should know,' I said.

'For once I agree with you,' he said more amiably. 'But *you* shouldn't. You should learn to accept people and things at face value.'

'Including your sculpture?'

'Not mine, Miss Carn. But I'm surprised you don't appreciate such work. You may not agree with it, just as you may not agree with certain philosophers — Hegel, Kant, Freud — or the other ritualistic and mystic religions. There are so many of them — Buddhism, Laotse — such a wide choice for the intelligent mind, and why condemn any one of them? I may be a Hedonist, you may be a Christian. I say *may* be; that should not debar each of us from respecting the other's trend of thought.'

'Doesn't that rather depend on the quality of the thought?'

'The sculpture you saw in my garden has quality, surely?'

'I didn't quite mean that.'

'I'm afraid that's the trouble,' he said in a very soft voice. 'You're not sure whether you stand with the rest of nature, or what you mean when you decry it.'

I realised he was trying to tie me up in mental knots, and walked on quickly, hoping he would turn back, but instead he said after an uncomfortable pause, 'Does my company worry you?'

'I came out to be on my own.'

'A pity,' he said. 'You see, I think we should get things straight between us. I'd rather have you as a friend than as an enemy. In fact, to be my enemy would be dangerous.'

'Are you threatening me?'

He shook his head. 'Come, come! What a thing to say.'

I made no comment, and at last, realising that he had no intention of going back without me, I turned sharply in the direction of the house, saying, 'I've had enough. I'm sorry, Doctor Dendas, this is a stupid conversation. I don't go in for mental acrobatics, and I'm really rather tired.'

'Yes,' he agreed, 'I think you are. I think that's what's the matter. You've got things on your mind. Your cousin — and Lucien, perhaps?'

'Lucien?' I echoed sharply.

'Of course. Why not? He's a remarkable fellow. Very remarkable. And fond of you; why shouldn't he be? You're attractive, and he has a sick wife — '

I started to tremble. 'How dare you insinuate — ?'

'But I'm insinuating nothing — only the truth. I'm glad, for his sake. But if you think wrongly of *me*, it's going to worry him very much; because we're close friends, Lucien and I. Never doubt that. That's why, if you're wise, you won't make trouble — for any of us. Do you understand?'

I did not reply. I wondered if he knew about my pact with Martin. It was quite possible. He might have seen us meeting — might even know that Martin Grey was not what he professed to be.

'I see that you do,' I heard the suave voice saying after a pause. 'You understand very well. Good.'

Ten minutes later I was back at Ravenscarne. The house seemed deserted except for the distant sound of pans rattling in the kitchen.

I was annoyed that the meeting with Martin had misfired, but daren't risk starting off again in case Louis was still on the watch, which was quite likely. I felt at a loose end and, for something to do, looked in on Anne. She was still sleeping. I left the bedroom, went downstairs and wandered aimlessly into the kitchen. Mary was standing at the sink scrubbing pans. She turned her head like a startled animal and dropped a knife to the floor.

'I'm sorry, Mary,' I said. 'I didn't mean to make you jump.'

'It's all right,' she mumbled.

'Is there anything I can do to help?' I asked. 'You must have plenty to cope with here.'

'No,' she said, glowering. 'I've got my duties.'

The words had a false ring about them, as though she'd been well-primed what to say.

'That doesn't mean you can't have assistance.'

'I'm not to get talking,' she replied stubbornly.

'Who told you that?'

She glanced furtively towards the door. 'No one.'

'Who told you, Mary?' I insisted.

'Her — the dark one. That Katherine,' she said grudgingly. Adding, 'now don't you go saying nothing.'

'Of course I won't. I wouldn't dream of getting you into trouble. Try and think of me as a friend, someone you can confide in if you're worried.'

She stared back into the sink and continued with her scrubbing. 'Isn't anything to worry over,' she stated. I waited until she looked up at me again with an expression of self-satisfied complacency on her simple plain face. 'They couldn't do without me here. I have my use.'

'I'm sure you have,' I agreed, and wondered what it was since she obviously was not alluding to domestic work.

'I'm going to *be* someone one day,' she boasted in the manner of a half-witted child. 'You'll see!'

There was an uncomfortable pause between us until I asked, 'Is everyone out?'

She eyed me suspiciously, then said, 'I don't know about Mr Lucien. The others — those film people — have gone up over.'

'Up over?'

'The moors.'

'Oh, I see.'

She washed her hands under the tap, picked up the pans and put them in a cupboard. I watched her, wondering how it must feel to be so ignorant, unattractive and lame. Her shadow, thrown against the wall from the fading sunlight, was hunched and grotesque, resembling more that of some allegorical monster than a human being. I recalled an ancient book I had once read with illustrations of spine-chilling horror. There had been a story in it called 'The Familiar'. Mary's shadow reminded me of it. I tried to feel compassion but couldn't. Ugliness of a certain kind had always appalled me; there could be hidden beauty in deformity of the body if the spirit was straight but deformity of mind and soul was a frightening thing, and I knew suddenly that something in

Mary Trenoweth was already becoming twisted, perhaps beyond repair.

By evening the high wind had lessened, though sullen clouds still darkened the horizon, threatening a wild night. At dinner Helen had a sparkle in her eyes, a determined-to-be-lively look which didn't deceive me. Marcus, too, shed his taciturnity for a corny intellectualism, flavoured with sardonic humour which I found more distasteful than his natural aggression.

Lucien had asked Louis Dendas over for the meal. Louis was pert, whimsical, and horribly precocious. I wondered again how Lucien could stand any of them. But perhaps he had to, because there was no one else in the vicinity to converse with. Or could there be another reason? Was he in some way in their power? I discarded the idea almost immediately, telling myself I was imagining things like any foolish woman in a detective story.

More wine than usual was drunk with the meal. I didn't know what it was, its flavour puzzled me, and I took only one or two sips.

Once Louis said, 'Don't you like the wine? It's a special one from France. I brought it over with me the last time.'

'I'm sure it's unique,' I answered politely, 'but I don't much care for alcohol.'

'Ah! An abstemious little virgin. Too bad!'

I could feel my cheeks flushing, and kept my eyes firmly from Lucien, knowing he must be embarrassed for me.

There was a murmur of uncertain laughter followed by trite conversation and gradually the atmosphere eased.

Afterwards we had coffee in the lounge, and chatted for a time about films and modern plays.

'Have you decided on the location yet?' I asked Marcus.

'The high moors near the stones are possible,' he replied.

'Do you mean the ones we saw going to Penzance?'

'Oh, no. Others.'

My heart did a funny turn. 'Where?'

'On the ridge behind the ruin. A half circle.'

'A remnant of pre-Druid days,' Louis interposed.

'Probably used as a sacrificial site.' I did not look at him, but could feel his eyes upon me.

'The victim was usually a young girl,' Katherine explained, 'An – innocent.' She paused, eyeing me significantly before adding with sly satisfaction.' As brides are supposed to be.'

When I said nothing she enquired more sharply, 'Aren't you interested at all?'

'Not really.' I tried to sound casual.

'No, I suppose not. You're what Louis said, the good little virgin type, content with present day morality without a clue as to what you're missing – the lust and fulfilment of primitive life, the taste and touch of the senses, of mind and flesh. In the past it was different –'

Her voice droned on.

Bored and mildly sickened by her earthly utterances, I got up, saying, 'If you'll excuse me, I think I'll go to bed early and read.'

I went to the door, hearing Lucien remark, 'I don't blame you. Good night, Belinda.'

'Good night,' I answered and left, not looking back.

Before going to my room, I went to Anne's. She was awake.

'Are they still there?' she asked.

'Yes. Why? Didn't you expect them to be?'

'I don't know. They'll go out later,' she answered, 'when everything's quiet. They always do.'

'You mean Marcus and Helen and Louis? Is that who you mean?'

'Yes. All of them, and the others. They have meetings.'

'Why? What for? And who? Please tell me.'

She turned away, burying her face in the pillow. I went closer. 'Who exactly Anne?'

'I told you – them.'

'Those "others", you mean?'

'Yes. But I never know who they are and what they do exactly, because I never see. It's those drugs Louis gives me.'

I took her hand. 'Why don't you tell Lucien?'

She laughed softly, bitterly. 'I did, more than once. But

as I was ill he didn't believe me. Besides – ' Her voice trailed off.

'Besides what?'

'Oh, don't bother with me, Belinda. There's nothing you can do. It doesn't matter. Nothing matters. I just wish – '

'Yes?'

'I wish I could die.'

I didn't know what to think or say. I guessed that Louis had paid her a second visit that day, probably when he came over for dinner, and that she would soon be slipping off again into unconsciousness. Already her eyes had dulled, heralding the trance-like state to which I had become accustomed.

I put my two hands on either side of her face and said urgently, 'Look at me. Try and keep awake. I'm going to fetch some coffee.'

I went downstairs quietly, and hurried to the kitchen. There was no one about. Mary was probably tired, I thought, and had gone to bed. I used instant coffee, made it black and strong, and took it up to Anne without being seen. She was lying against the pillows, with a far-away look in her eyes as though she was no longer fully aware of where she was.

'Here,' I said peremptorily, handing her a cup. 'Drink it.'

I forced some of the coffee between her lips, and after a few sips she was able to life one white hand to the cup. After the coffee she revived a little, but I knew it would not be for long.

'Listen,' I said firmly, 'something's happening tonight, isn't it? I know. You started to tell me. Try and remember. Just try. I may be able to help you. I have a friend in Tregale. Anne, can you understand?'

She stared at me. I saw her making a great effort to speak.

'Yes, yes?' I prompted, with my face against hers. 'Go on – I'm listening.'

'The old house,' she whispered at last. 'Grandfather's. They'll be there. They've cursed it. By evil. It's haunted. They always go there – '

72

'What do you mean?'

'Doing things,' she told me weakly. 'Awful terrible things — ' Her hands clutched me. In a moment I thought she might scream.

'That's all right,' I soothed her. 'Don't worry. Forget about it. It will be over soon. I'll get my friend, and Lucien.'

'No!' She sat up with a sudden revival of terrified energy. 'Promise — not Lucien.'

'All right, all right. If that's how you feel, I promise. Now try and rest. For my sake and your own.'

She fell back with her eyes closed. I waited a few minutes, then lifted her limp hand and felt the pulse. It was frail but quite regular. She was asleep, and would probably not wake again for hours.

Presently, I crept away to my own bedroom. If I'd had the courage, or really believed I could reach Martin or 'phone him without being seen or heard, I'd have done so. But after thinking about it I decided the risk was too great, and that my best course was to find out what I could for myself and contact him in the morning.

The hours passed slowly that night. I didn't go to bed, but slipped my dressing-gown over my clothes just in case anyone looked in. At eleven o'clock I glanced from the window through a chink in the curtains. There was a full moon shining fitfully between massed clouds, riding like galleons over the humped line of the moors. At moments the outline of the ruined house was thrown into brilliant relief; at others it was swept into darkness. There was no sign of life about; no flicker from any of the empty windows or movement on the hillside.

I closed the curtains again, and got into bed with a book. I tried to read, but couldn't concentrate. The silence of the house seemed abnormal. No creaking of doors or voices from below, no footsteps or sound but the tapping of twigs blown against the window from the dying wind. I listened so intently that my ears began to ring.

'It's no good lying here,' I thought. I got up again and looked out once more. There was nothing to be seen but the sky had cleared considerably, leaving the landscape fully

73

bathed in the eerie blueish light of the moon which flung black shadows from the boulders, streaking in long finger shapes towards the valley.

I waited for some minutes but nothing happened. So I lay on the bed again, waiting. I may have dozed off; something – some slight sound – woke me with a start. Glancing at the luminous dial of the clock I saw it was eleven forty-five. Presently I got up and returned to the window. All was as before – silent, lonely and deserted.

For about five minutes I wandered about the bedroom restlessly, looking out intermittently. Then, just as I was deciding to give up the vigil, I saw it – a flicker in one of the ruined windows of the old Ravenscarne.

I paused uncertainly until I was sure my eyes hadn't deceived me, then got up abruptly, pulled on a brown tweed coat and wellingtons, found a dark woollen scarf and put it over my head; not only because of the chill air, but to hide any glimmer from my hair.

Tiptoeing downstairs, I wished Martin Grey could have been with me, and wondered again at the last moment if I dare telephone. But Lucien would probably hear. He'd prevent me going out, deny anything was wrong, because he didn't believe it was. Or did he? Was he turning a blind eye to certain things because he was implicated? Blackmail perhaps? Once again the tormenting questions revolved in my head. I recalled how he'd suggested my leaving, indicating that he knew very well something was afoot. Why then hadn't he confided in me?

He didn't want me involved probably, or was worried I might let out something to Anne. Anyway, there was no point in wasting time wondering. At all costs my mind must be clear tonight. I was careful to slip up the latch of the door as I went out, knowing that my own safety could depend upon getting back before the others returned.

Outside, I found the sky had dimmed again, and in the protective darkness I hurried up the path to the road, using my torch as little as possible. On my reaching the moors, the clouds disappeared as quickly as they had arisen, and the hillside became suddenly alive, as though charged with a new and strange vitality. Shapes that had slumbered in shadow

74

leaped into clarity – the clutching branches of bramble and gorse reaching hungrily between great boulders like giant claws against the eerie light.

The air had become colder, shivering through the bracken with a whining sound, moaning and sighing dismally on the thin wind. I was glad of my warm coat and scarf. But it was not only physical cold I felt. A sense of spiritual desolation emanated from the landscape, as though things dead and forgotten – dark evil things – were reborn, temporarily taking possession of nature.

Climbing, I noticed obscene groups of yellow and spotted fungi peering luminously between stones. Their pungent odour was thick and cloying, redolent of decaying life. Revulsion and fear deepened in me but I knew there was no question of going back, not only because of Anne but for the sake of decency and my own conscience.

When I reached the ruin the lights were still leaping fitfully behind the sightless holes of windows, as though from torches or the wan flare of candles.

I bent down and half crawled to the door, keeping well in the shadow of the wall so I wouldn't be seen. Across the nearest gap shadowed silhouetted shapes of hooded figures passed. I paused, crouching by a stone, and listened.

The low murmur of voices rose and fell sibilantly in a kind of chant, then died into silence. After a moment it started again. I crept nearer, stood up and flattened myself against the broken pillar of the porch where I could see and not be seen, waiting rigidly.

Looking back now I wonder how much of the weird scene was really fact, and how much some sort of elemental mirage.

At one moment grey coils of swirling mist took everything into a sullen wave of writhing shadows. The next – as the greyness was swept into a brilliant flash of green moonlight – the moaning and wailing rose to wild screaming-pitch. Pale waving arms moved in a rhythmic circle round a tall standing stone. No one was recognisable, hoods and masks veiled all trace of human features, but at the foot of the rock a naked woman lay shuddering yet writhing with orgiastic desire. Mary, was it? And who was the tall horned one, the leader obviously, who took her to the brink of evil fulfilment and ultimate sadistic rejection? Who? *Who*? Even as the question seared my mind, I didn't want to know. I tried not to look, but my will was defeated – and I remained static, pressed against the hard granite, eyes rooted and hypnotised by the spectacle.

At moments the very earth seemed to shudder, and it was then that further terror came – something too horribly grotesque for mere words to describe. It was as if the ground opened, revealing pale bald heads pushing mushroom-like through dust and soil, with spectres of beings long-dead gesticulating obscenely from decayed limbs. Empty eyes gaped, skeleton jaws became mechanised to life. There were monstrous primeval ugly things, and some pitiful and sad, wrenched from their rest to float wraith-like at terrifying corrupt command. There was an instant when sudden intense darkness obliterated everything into negation and blackness, slowly resolving into a hovering cloud of gigantic malevolence. The vileness intensified, lighting the sky momentarily to sickening lurid crimson – a lowering glow turning the earth to the colour of blood.

And then I knew.

Blood or flame, what did it matter? The dark god was there, epitomised in every movement, every symbolic shadow of that dreadful night.

I closed my eyes, trying to dispel the vision. But even when shut the macabre pattern zig-zagged against the lids, impelling me to look again.

The inky form was gradually disintegrating leaving the landscape much as it had previously been – a sinister sickly green, with the deadly crimson dying into shade. Mary, if it *was* Mary, was huddled near the altar – for altar-to-evil the stone must have been – and as I watched, two of the masked shapes stepped into the broken circle and between them lifted the cowering girl high above their heads.

The rest of the figures stood up, arms raised.

And then, suddenly, with her first scream, I had the power to move.

She was still screaming as the hooded forms turned and

came towards the shell of the door from which I fled into the shadows cast by a quickly clouded moon.

I knew they were after me, but somehow, owing mostly to the intermittent light, I managed to reach Ravenscarne.

It was then that reaction set in. There was a chair just inside the hall; I slumped into it with my head in my hands and waited for a few minutes until my heart and breathing eased, dispelling giddiness. Then I got up, still shaking, and forced myself upstairs.

I didn't pause to look in on Anne as I passed her room, not daring to disturb her or risk delay.

It was only after I'd locked my own bedroom door and fallen on the bed that I realised my torch was missing. My stomach lurched. If they found it, *they* – whoever they were – including the doctor and Katherine, would know, or at least put two and two together.

So I went downstairs again, and in a kind of panic searched the passage, which was lit intermittently to a pale clarity from the tall window where wan light streaked, casting elongated fitful shadows across the floor. There was no sign of the torch. I must have dropped it, somewhere on the hillside or nearer to the house perhaps. If by chance anyone found it and asked me about it, I would have to lie and deny it was mine. Katherine wouldn't believe me, but she could prove nothing. *Nothing*, I told myself as I went upstairs again.

But I was very afraid.

When I'd returned and locked myself in the room, and put a chair against the door – quite a heavy one, which would warn me of anyone trying to enter – I lay down and tried to rest. But I couldn't sleep. About three o'clock there was a muffled murmur of voices below, and the padding of footsteps – furtive, like the soft tread of jungle creatures. Presently quiet feet passed outside the door. No word was spoken; no sound of whispered conversation – just a vacuum, a cessation of all movement, more chilling in one way than actual confrontation. Hardly breathing, I lay there waiting, listening to the silence. And then, at last, the soft tread of feet started again, presently dying away.

My body relaxed gradually, but I was still far from sleep

and lay there for perhaps half-an-hour, then got up and had a wash. My face didn't look too bad. A few scratches here and there, and of course my eyes were ringed. But I had some good make-up, and when I'd used it carefully, the effect would be better. This fact helped my morale. As a youngster, like most girls with any looks at all, I'd fancied myself an actress and had been considered pretty good in school plays, so when I went downstairs in the morning any remnants of talent I still had would be put to full use. I'd have to play for my life — perhaps Anne's as well; put on an act which I hoped would fool even such experts as Marcus and Helen.

With this decided I went back to bed, and presently fell into an exhausted sleep.

As I slept I dreamed.

It was no ordinary dream, but intensified by a clarity that took me far away from the normal physical world to a region that was at once familiar, as though stamped on my memory from another bygone existence. I was walking along a moorland ridge with Lucien. The sky behind us was a dying twilit green above the distant hills; my dress was white, blown in the wind from a kirtle, and my hair was free. Lucien's arm was round me, and a nimbus of light encircled us, sending elongated shadows skimming down the slope. The peculiar thing was that although I knew the girl to be myself, I could see her objectively. It was like looking at a photograph stamped on Time. There was yearning in me, and great happiness; also terror, because I knew when darkness fell there would be inevitable separation and something else; something that yawned and gaped ahead, predicting doom. Yet we went on walking, and as the sky faded a massed blackened shape protruded over the horizon, gathering slowly in size and purpose. There was a sudden screaming and roaring, with the thunderous sensation of earth crumbling and opening beneath our feet. The hungry cloud burst into an unending scrambling army of beings swarming in our direction, with the lurid flame of torches and searing heat as we struggled for air. Hands clawed and tore at our flesh. Voices shrieked. In that dreadful moment all the fiends of hell seemed let loose.

78

Lucien was the first victim. I saw him writhe for a second like a blackened puppet, with toy arms and legs jerking convulsively before extinction.

Then I fell, and as darkness claimed me heard unmistakably just one short sentence: '*Her*, too. Get her — devil's daughter!' It was over.

I woke from the nightmare with perspiration soaking my body, and my heart pumping painfully against my ribs. For some minutes I lay quite still, while the blurred outlines of the bedroom came into focus.

I could see from the light penetrating the curtains that the sun was already risen, and guessed someone would be about downstairs. So I got up, had a quick wash, used cream and a minimum of make-up, then arranged my hair carefully, hoping the faint bruising on my face wouldn't show.

I pulled on a blue shirt and jeans, and took a good look in the mirror. The overall effect was reassuring, sufficiently so to give me the confidence I needed. Mustering a casual air, I went down the stairs and found Katherine at the bottom, carrying a tray with tea and toast on it. She was wearing a housecoat and was obviously taken aback at my appearance. Her mouth was sullen, her eyes tired, when she said a little maliciously, 'How bright you look. Very surprising. I was bringing you a cuppa. And something else — ' She paused, and balancing the tray on one arm, took the torch, handing it towards me and continuing, 'Your torch, I think, Belinda? You must have dropped it. That was careless of you.'

I shook my head. 'What are you talking about? That doesn't belong to me. Mine's got a red ring near the bulb. Hadn't you noticed?'

She was quite taken off her guard by the lie.

'But — '

'I don't suppose you did,' I said over my shoulder as I passed by and went on to the sitting room. 'Why should you? What's so important about a torch, after all?'

For once she had no answering thrust. But I could feel the menace of her hard eyes boring through the back of my skull with threatening intensity.

A little later I went up to see Anne. To my surprise

she appeared refreshed and looked better than she had for many days.

'I had a marvellous night,' she told me. 'Louis is quite right, you know, about some things anyway. I *do* need rest and plenty of sleep. Maybe I misjudge him sometimes.'

'I don't think —' I broke off, realising how dangerous it could be to put my own opinion of the doctor into words just then.

'Well?'

'I was going to say, perhaps we ought not to bother about him so much,' I said. 'If you're really better, that's all that matters.'

'And I am,' she affirmed with undue emphasis. 'I know I am.'

A bright colour was already staining her face, intensifying the awakening over-brilliance of her eyes. A moment later the door opened and Lucien appeared with coffee and biscuits. Anne reached over to him. He gave me a brief glance, no more, and went to the bed.

I left quickly, wondering what his eyes had been trying to say to me; wondering, yet knowing, and feeling strangely bereft because of it.

The morning was blurred with fog, holding a furry darkness blown on drifts of thin wind against the windows and walls of the house, draping the bushes in cobwebbed clutching shrouds of grey, overhung by fitful macabre shapes which cleared intermittently then thickened again.

Not really a morning for walking, but I knew I had to go. Knew if further horror and culminating tragedy was to be averted, I had somehow to reach Martin Grey's cottage, and the sooner the better, before the household was properly astir.

I went up for my coat and headscarf, and when I came downstairs saw Mary eyeing me furtively from the back of the hall. She looked hunched and ponderous, her wide face a mere blur — vacant, almost featureless in the poor light. Yet I sensed a cunning quality about her — a certain smug triumph that repulsed me, because I knew she was now identified with vile things, and had become during those few night hours the instrument of her seducers who were also the destroyers and corrupters of life.

I turned away abruptly and went out, trying to shut her image from my mind. But as I walked towards the path leading to Martin's cottage, it seemed in my tensed state that her eyes followed me; small, pig-like, pebble-eyes, concentrated now with the unholy energy of unified evil.

'Imagination,' I told myself with an effort. 'That's all — ' just the fog, and having no sleep. Keep going. Whatever happens, don't think and don't look back — just *go on*. Martin's there. *He's* all right. You know that.'

But did I? *Did* I? Just for a moment the grey world seemed to spin into a vortex of darkness and doubt. I knew nothing about him really. I was depending only on instinct. Suppose I was wrong? Suppose he, too, was somehow concerned in the sinister pattern which might even now be tightening its threads, with every step I took?

I paused, trying to get my thoughts clear; and as the wild sudden hammering of my heart eased, I knew I had been wrong to doubt.

The fear remained though, with an uncanny creeping sensation, that I was not alone. Enshrouded in the mist, someone or something waited.

I stood there listening, realising for the first time that silence itself was a living thing, filled with the hidden thoughts, perhaps, of countless beings long since dead and gone, and of others still about, impressing the very ether with their own dark purposes.

When the mist cleared momentarily, I moved. And then, suddenly, there was a crackle of twigs behind me. I stopped again, chilled and tense, as a cool, malicious voice said from close by, 'Good morning, Miss Carn. How lucky we should meet.'

I turned quickly and saw Louis Dendas watching me from a clump of furze and rock. He was smiling, although the smile itself was a travesty of anything human, holding only vicious smug triumph.

81

From a tight throat I managed to say, 'I didn't hear you following me, and you must have done. Why?'

'My dear young lady! Surely I should be the one to ask questions on such a morning as this.'

'What I do is my own affair,' I told him. 'I'm tired of being quizzed and questioned. Can't I *ever* be left alone to take a stroll?'

He thrust his pale face close against mine, satyr-like with his pointed beard and sly eyes.

'No,' he said softly. 'It is my duty to see you come to no harm if you will persist in taking foggy walks.'

'Very well,' I said, turning. 'I shan't go.'

'Dear, dear,' he sighed. 'You do dislike me, don't you?'

'Yes,' I answered. 'I don't like being followed.'

I turned automatically, realising that for the time being all chance of seeing Martin was gone. As we walked back to the house he said, 'You're afraid of me, aren't you? I wonder why?'

'Afraid?' I said. 'No, of course not. You don't frighten me at all, Mr Dendas.'

'That's good. Because I am really a very ordinary sort of creature, and I find you rather — unique.'

'Oh?'

'You have depths and imagination. Probably Uranus figures largely in your horoscope.'

'I don't go in for astrology,' I said abruptly. 'And now if you'll forgive me — ?' I was turning to go into the house when he stopped me.

'But no. You came out for a walk. I should dislike very much to deprive you of it. Why not stroll along to the cottage with me and have coffee?'

I was about to refuse vigorously when he added quickly, 'Lucien is coming. You will be quite safe.'

Almost simultaneously with his last remark I heard the front door of Ravenscarne open, and saw Lucien coming towards us.

He appeared cheerful and relaxed, and agreed readily to the suggestion. So having no legitimate excuse, I acquiesced, and we set off, walking in single file along the narrow path. It did not take long, and when we got inside the cottage I was impressed, though not entirely surprised.

The interior was very old yet luxurious, holding an atmosphere more of some museum than a home. Historical relics of various ages from different continents and countries were displayed in nooks and corners, where the light from the mullioned windows and hidden illuminated recesses caught them at bizarre angles, imbuing them with extraordinary life despite their age.

Most, I guessed, were Eastern in origin, yet they were so skilfully placed that they quarrelled in no way with the expensive glass and modern accessories which blended perfectly with the Persian rugs and brocade curtains.

Exotic orchids were arranged on the walnut table in what appeared to be a genuine blue Venetian glass vase. There was a great deal of beauty here, but in some way it repelled me, because it did not convey a man's taste. Even the strange flowering succulents had a clutching, sexually feminine quality, trailing as they did from Chinese pots held by wrought iron holders on the walls. One particularly, with thick juicy leaves and spotted flowers, mildly disgusted me, though I could not have explained why; perhaps because it was so sensually alive and foreign, exuding a musky perfume which was slightly nauseating.

Louis was politeness itself, almost as though we were meeting for the first time. He insisted on my sitting in a low, tall-backed Louis Quinze chair, beautifully upholstered with handsewn tapestry, and arranging a cushion at my back. I hated such attention from him, but accepted with as good a grace as I could. Then, after going through to the kitchen to see about the coffee, he came back, went to a smallish glass-fronted cabinet, and brought out a carved ivory figure.

'I picked this up the other day at a sale,' he told us. 'Quite rare, though I'm not precisely sure of the dynasty. Chinese, of course,' he added for my information.

His hands caressed the smooth surface of the figurine lovingly, and the movement of his pale hands repulsed me; I could not help picturing their part in the orgy of the preceding night, knowing that he must have taken a full share of lascivious pleasure in the dark happenings.

'It's very beautiful,' Lucien agreed. 'You've certainly got a nose for bargains. Katherine mentioned it the other day.'

Katherine! The mention of her name reminded me that except for Mary she was alone in the house with Anne. I tried to think of an adequate excuse for leaving, got up and said quickly, 'Do you mind if I *don't* stay for coffee, after all? I've forgotten something – something very important that I must get into the post. A letter to Canada –'

'What a pity,' Lucien said. 'But if –'

'Nonsense!' Louis interrupted, before Lucien could finish. 'The post doesn't go till twelve-thirty, and it's seldom punctual. The coffee's about ready. You've time for a cup, surely?'

I sat down again helplessly. 'All right, but it seems rather rude leaving immediately afterwards.'

'Rudeness between friends is permissible,' the doctor said lightly, 'as we have discovered, haven't we?'

I could feel the warm blood staining my face, knowing that Lucien was looking at me closely. When I did not reply Louis went through to the kitchen, and returned shortly afterwards with the coffee on a tray.

As I drank from a delicate bone-china cup, I wondered what blend it was. The flavour was unfamiliar to me; rather exotic, and when cream was added, tasted extremely rich. But it was good, and made me feel better. Instead of enlivening me, which coffee usually did, I felt relaxed and contented, and did not leave as I had planned, but waited for another half hour, in which time my feelings towards the doctor mellowed considerably. When I tried to recollect later what we had talked about, I couldn't. All I remembered was the glint of firelight, Lucien's voice and the gentle glance of his eyes upon me. This, combined with the warm atmosphere and richly macabre surroundings, encompassed me with a strange dream-like quality that made me listless and at peace, forgetful of the need to get back to Anne.

It was only much later that I realised I must have been drugged.

When I left, Lucien accompanied me. 'It was nice having

you there, Belinda,' he said as we walked along. 'Did you enjoy it?'

'Yes,' I admitted, still in a hazy glow of contentment. 'Although I didn't expect to.'

'Oh?'

'I find Doctor Dendas – Louis – rather an enigmatic person, and I don't like having to puzzle things out,' I told him.

'I thought you did. You've got a particularly agile mind. That's one of the things I – '

'Yes?'

'Admire about you,' he said quietly, as quietly almost as the soft lap of fog against our faces. 'But admiration, of course, isn't all – in fact it counts very little really. The other things are so much more important.'

Against my will I couldn't help asking, 'What things, Lucien?'

'You must know, surely?'

He didn't take my hand, didn't even look at me, but in some strange hypnotic way, the moment was one of deepest intimacy.

Trying to be prosaic and practical, I asked, 'Do you think the fog will clear today?'

'It's doubtful.'

'This sort of weather can't be good for Anne.'

'No.'

'It would be nice for her to get away, wouldn't it, Lucien?'

'Yes. But even if we made arrangements she'd probably back out when the time came.'

'Why should she? She seemed quite exited at the idea.'

'At the moment she may be. But you must realise how her moods change.'

'Are you sure it's not the medicine?'

He turned his head sharply. 'Belinda, please don't bring all that up again. We've had so much of it. I wish – '

'Yes?'

'I wish you could trust Louis. See him for what he is – a very remarkable and intelligent doctor.'

I didn't reply. I wanted to agree with Lucien; wanted

to have trust in Louis just then, because I was still in an entranced state of friendliness following the visit to the cottage. But I couldn't. Even Lucien's pleading failed to affect my inner judgement where the doctor was concerned. Though active antagonism had temporarily passed into tolerance, I knew, deep down, that my dislike was founded on fact. He had a nasty mind with evil aims. I had been able to put up with him for a brief time, and that was all.

So I walked on silently with Lucien beside me, a curious lightness in my head which gave an impression of floating through fog, as I'd floated in my dreams when I was a child.

The tenuous branches of the bushes became phantom-shapes, together with the hunched stones and wraith-like curling fronds of bracken. I could imagine the humped forms of strange beasts watching slyly as we passed. But I was no longer afraid. For the moment at least we were apart from the real world, encompassed in another dimension of space and time. Space and time! My heart missed a beat. I recalled the first two lines of Lucien's poem:

I searched a million billion years —
Through space and time, and countless spheres —

Despite my numbed senses the words beat vividly on my brain, bringing as well another memory of the dark antique shop where Lucien's face had stared at me from another far-off century.

Instinctively I quickened my pace, and with a queer mixture of relief and a sense of loss, saw the misted outlines of the house emerging only a short distance away.

As soon as I got in I went upstairs to see Anne. As I had feared Katherine was with her, but my cousin appeared better, and was obviously stimulated by the girl's company.

'Katherine says Lucien took you to see Louis' cottage,' she remarked.

'Yes. It's quite sumptuous, isn't it?'

Katherine laughed. 'I'd have used another word. But he's certainly got a collector's eye.'

I was surprised by the malice in her voice because I'd

imagined they were birds of a feather. They had always appeared friendly.

'I suppose that's his hobby,' I pointed out.

Katherine's eyebrows arched with surprise. She shrugged her shoulders and remarked acidly, 'He's won you round, hasn't he? It's wonderful what wealth can do.'

'Wealth has nothing to do with it,' I retorted angrily. 'And my feeling towards Louis Dendas hasn't changed at all.'

'Oh? You could have fooled me,' Katherine said.

'I don't know what you're talking about.'

She laughed. 'For once, Belinda, you look quite alive. Oh, well, maybe Lucien was the tonic.'

My head began to ache quite suddenly and violently. All I wanted just then was to go and lie down.

'It wasn't Lucien, and it wasn't Louis,' I said coldly. 'It was the coffee.'

'Went to your head, did it?' Katherine said. 'Perhaps. Louis is quite an epicure over food, drink — everything.'

'I realise that.'

She smiled. 'Well, don't take it to heart. Louis must have his little games.'

'And you?'

'Of course.'

I got up, touched Anne's hand, told her I'd see her later and left the room. As I walked along the landing the walls and ceilings seemed to converge, while the floor rushed up to meet me. I steadied myself until the giddiness had passed then went into my room and flung myself on the bed, closing my eyes against the quiver of spots and dancing flashes of light that threatened migraine.

I did not go down to lunch that day, and no one called me. I fell into a heavy sleep, and when I woke up I saw by my watch that it was already four o'clock.

I lay for some time, thinking back, realising there was absolutely no question that Louis Dendas had put something pretty strong into my coffee. My head still ached and I could easily have slipped into sleep again, but I knew I mustn't, because later that afternoon by some means or other I had to contact Martin.

When I went down presently, Marcus, Helen, Katherine

and Lucien were just finishing tea. I knew they were surprised to see me.

'I looked in on you,' Katherine said, 'but you were asleep.'

'And you missed lunch,' Lucien said rather pointlessly. 'We've been worried. You shouldn't get so exhausted. You're supposed to be on holiday. If I thought you'd agree I'd get Louis to have a look at you. You might need a tonic. But I suppose that's no good?'

'No,' I answered emphatically. 'I'm quite all right. But another time if I oversleep, I'd be glad if you woke me.'

'We thought perhaps you'd had a bad night,' Katherine remarked over-casually.

'Insomnia was never my problem,' I told her.

'Well, would you like a lunch-cum-tea now?'

'No, thanks. Just a cup of tea.'

As I drank it my eyes went to the window. The fog, if anything, was worse. Obviously there would be no excuse for going out for a walk. I should have to contrive somehow to slip out of the house unseen, and I guessed this would be more difficult than ever now.

Since the previous night's events Katherine would be on the watch, I'd already seen that the doctor was and Lucien wouldn't want me to risk breaking my neck or falling down a shaft.

I didn't like having to lie and pretend, especially to Lucien, but there seemed no other way. So when tea was over I put my hand to my head, explaining that it ached rather badly and that I thought I'd go upstairs again.

'Sorry to be so stupid,' I apologised, going to the door. 'I don't usually have headaches, and why I'm like this I don't know. But I feel as if I could sleep still. So perhaps — '

'The best thing you can do,' Lucien agreed. 'One of us will look in later and see if you're all right.'

'Oh, you needn't bother,' I assured him. 'I'm certain it's nothing serious. And I have some aspirin. I'll take two. That'll cure me.'

When I reached my room I lay down with a book, determined not to doze off. If I did it might be for too long, and spoil my chance of escape. The house was quiet, except for occasional distant sounds of footsteps and closing of doors. I got up once and went to the window, wondering if anything was happening on the moors; but the hillside was a mere wall of fuzzy greyness pressing against the glass.

It would be an evening for further dark things to happen, I thought, realising suddenly how I longed for the comforting, normal presence of Martin Grey.

I waited for about forty minutes before putting on my coat, scarf and wellingtons. Then I went to the bedroom door and opened it, with ears on the alert for any sound. There was the murmur of voices from the lounge below, which told me they were all in conference about something.

I crept along the landing, pausing at Anne's door; but all was silent inside, so I went on, picking up a torch which had been conveniently left on a small table in an aperture.

Then I went on, moving slowly and as soundlessly as possible, towards the back stairs. I descended with care, making sure not to tread on a certain step which I knew had a loud creak. The stairs came out at the end of the hall near the kitchen where a short corridor branched off to the side door. I had just got there when there was a sharp click from the kitchen door. I looked back and saw Mary's dumpy form moving in her lumbering way past the passage in the direction of the lounge. There was a fleeting glimmer of her pale moon-shaped face as she glanced over her shoulder. I didn't know whether she had recognised me or not, possibly the bad light had confused her, but I hurried out and ahead as quickly as I could, and was soon cutting away from the garden towards the cliff path in the direction of Tregale.

Progress was slow, more of a scramble than a walk, and the fog seemed to thicken as I took the first bend towards the cliffs. This was less than a hundred yards from the house, and it had taken me quite five minutes to get that far. I had a torch with me, and occasionally switched it on so I wouldn't miss the ribbon of path or take a false step over some treacherous unguarded shaft. The faint glimmer revealed stones and the pale track of short worn turf; but after pushing ahead for about ten minutes I realised suddenly that the path could be any one of the numerous tracks made by sheep or farmers.

I stood still at one point to locate my whereabouts accurately. Normally I had a good sense of direction, but in the swirling writhing mist it was difficult to assess my bearings correctly. The faint salt tang indicated that I was somewhere on the cliffs above the sea, and I knew that if I kept on bearing to the right I must eventually come to the hamlet. That was, if I didn't take a wrong step which could send me hurtling over the precipitous rocks to my death. There was no landmark to judge by, nothing but the sinsiter clutch of the bushes and looming shapes of rocks and furze.

Trying to keep a grip on my nerves, I thought, 'This is just a wild piece of Cornish coast. These are ordinary windblown bushes. These are just large rocks −' And all the time fear deepened, because I had the feeling of being followed, of watchful eyes staring unseen from the fog; waiting until the time came − for what? My death? Or for the unspeakable to happen? The ultimate horror of being subject, like Mary, to satanic influence and submergence of self, both physical and moral?

I struggled on, rubbing my eyes and peering hard for any sign of Tregale, but could locate nothing. There was no sound above the sighing of the wind through the undergrowth, but a nightmarish conviction persisted that from somewhere quite close other footsteps kept pace with mine; evil, sly footsteps, bound on a mission of destruction.

My heart was pounding. Once I fell, and had to wait with my head down until a sudden feeling of faintness had passed.

When I got up again there was a warm trickle of blood coursing from my temple to chin. 'Perhaps this is how it will happen,' I thought. 'I shall just go on and on, wandering in circles until I'm so cut and exhausted I'll just collapse. Perhaps that's how the forces will work. They'll kill me that way.'

Then, with a sudden wave of determination, I made myself continue with hands in front, pressing back twigs, tripping a second time on one of the treacherous stones made slippery from mist, or treading on the squashy heads of the malevolent fungi.

Just for a second or two the mist cleared and I discovered to my dismay that paths branched in three directions, and I was not certain which to take.

Ahead, surely? I thought desperately. But the air was still too thick for me to distinguish any landmark. Peering closely at my watch I saw an hour had passed already. I should have been at Tregale long before this.

However, there was nothing for it but to follow the path ahead which should, I judged, lead eventually to the hamlet.

And then I heard it – a thudding and pounding from the left which grew louder every moment. I paused, my heart beating heavily. There was nothing discernible but the distorted shape of a gorse bush nearby, but I knew without any doubt at all that I'd taken the wrong track and that the pounding below was the sound of the waves breaking against the rocks. I must be near the cliff edge.

I stepped back, intending to take another direction, wanting to run but finding it impossible. The undergrowth prevented me – and something else! – something which emerged and took shape before my eyes, a hooded form which seemed to gather substance from the fog, curving down from what appeared to be an immense height towards me.

I couldn't move; terror froze me to immobility. I just stood with my whole body rigid, unable to speak or scream, while hands stretched claw-like from the darkness, reaching towards me.

The figure moved purposefully, slowly, with malignant stealth. I took a step aside – two, three ... Sensing no ground for the fourth, I swayed dizzily for a moment, brought one foot back to the other, then cut away for a few yards.

In a second the hands were on my shoulders, forcing me back towards the deadly drop. I screamed and fell, with only inches between my body and the greedy cliffs. The grip tightened. The mist cleared briefly, and as I stared up the hood fell back, revealing a distorted visage with twisted lips and blazing baleful eyes.

'You *would* interfere, wouldn't you?' a cold sneering voice hissed against my ear. 'You had to pry and trespass. You should have *known*! You could have lived a little longer if you'd wanted – you could have become *one* of us, sharing and fulfilling, until your body was glorified in sacrifice. Sacrifice to the great god of darkness. But you had to oppose us. And so –'

There was a pause. I waited until the voice continued more quietly in completely different tones, 'Such a pity, Belinda. Such a very great pity.'

I couldn't believe my ears. *Lucien*! I stared wildly up at him, and as we faced each other in that timeless pause, his expression changed; the evil in it gradually faded. Malice slowly died from his eyes; his mouth opened, his hands fell away from my shoulders, and one went to his head. He straightened up, shuddering violently. I went forward, arms extended, imploring. He covered his eyes, pushed past me, and rushed to the cliff edge, crying shrilly, 'Another age – another time – remember me!' Then there was a terrible high-pitched scream and his body went hurtling through the darkness to the great rocks below.

It was some time before I had sufficient control of myself to get to my feet. My teeth were chattering. I was dead to thought or emotion. All that remained to me during those terrible minutes was the instinctive desire for survival – to reach some place where I could rest and recover from the shock. I moved away automatically from the cliffs, taking the path inland.

A wind was rising, curdling the mist into spiralling shapes which cleared more frequently than before, giving considerably better visibility.

After crawling and groping for perhaps a quarter of an hour, I obtained some indication of my whereabouts from the jagged ruined shape of an old cottage straight ahead. I was off the proper path, but I'd seen the place on previous walks, and from there managed to get my bearings and so make my way towards the road.

Then, as though from nowhere, the indeterminate figure of a man emerged from a clump of windblown trees moving towards me. 'Martin,' I thought. 'It must be Martin.' Relief filled me. The nightmare was over now. All I had to do was to go back with him, and let him 'phone the police so that Anne, too, could be brought to safety.

I put my hands to my mouth and called thinly, 'Hullo-o-o – Martin – it's me!' My own voice was a ghost cry in my ears. But he heard, and came hurrying towards me, striking at the bracken and bushes as complete exhaustion threatened me. His arms were out; I lifted mine – and then I was stricken by horror. It wasn't Martin at all. Pale and inscrutable through the fitful light, the face of Louis Dendas leered malevolently upon me.

After a paralysing moment of terror I turned to run. But his hands gripped me, swivelling me round to face him.

'You!' he said harshly. 'You have always defied me, haven't you? Always, always. And now he's dead. The master's dead, and you've killed him.'

The horror of Lucien's end, his betrayal of himself and all that was good, and the final terrible retribution, flooded back in a wave of memory.

'I didn't know,' I managed to say, shivering. 'I didn't know – he was one of you. How could I? I didn't kill him. He –'

I was going to say, 'He was trying to kill *me*!' then, recalling against my will Lucien's last glance at me, the desperate look of longing which had swept the beastiality from his face, I kept the words back.

'You killed him, Belinda Carn,' Louis said. 'And I am your Nemesis. It's your turn. We couldn't allow you to live, could we, after that? You would gossip and talk. With our leader gone, you'd never rest until his followers also were destroyed. That would never do.'

I couldn't control the sudden trembling in every muscle of my body.

'But never fear,' he went on in soft, almost gentle, tones, 'I'll be more merciful than you were. We'll wait till the moon rises, and you shall die as they died in the past – sacrificially – those who defied the great dark one. His curse remains. His curse took the vicar – did't you know? And that silly Sibley woman. But this time no body will be found. No screaming heard. There is a place on the moors, deep down in the dank ground, where you will lie till the winds and rains have washed your bones clean – '

I knew then that he was mad. I began talking rapidly, trying to soothe him, playing for time.

'You can never be sure of a body's not being found,' I said, 'and the police are already watching Ravenscarne. They know things. Wouldn't it be wisest to leave me alone? It would be safer for you. I'm in your hands, as they say. You could pin Lucien's murder on me. You saw him fall, you must have or you wouldn't know. How could I deny it? You could put yourself in the right, you're clever enough. But it would be easier for none of us to say anything at all. If I promised you to go back to Canada – leave tomorrow – '

I stopped abruptly, because I knew from the look of his face that all I said was quite useless.

'You're talking nonsense, you know,' he said. 'Come, sit down beside me, my dear. I want your last hours to be comfortable.'

He eased me down and I sat automatically on the spot of smoothed bracken, wondering wildly what to do, how to get away. The fog was still thick in parts. If I could shake myself from his grasp I might have a chance. Subterfuge was the only way. I bowed my head and sat motionless, until he said quietly, 'Such a shame you have exhausted yourself. We could have prepared ourselves together – waited until the final glorious moment – '

I didn't reply. He peered closely into my face. 'You're faint. No wonder, after your stupid scramble. I have a tablet. It will help.'

'Help,' I thought. What a ridiculous word for a potential murderer to use.

I made no movement as he fumbled with one hand in his pocket; then, taking him completely off guard, I wrenched myself free and plunged wildly into the under-growth, oblivious of thorns and stones; rushing, jumping, falling, picking myself up again and going ahead, knowing he was behind me from his demented cries, yet never stop-ping as I twisted this way and that, intuitively heading where the fog was thickest.

I had to pause at last to get my breath, and crouched down, listening. I had evaded him; I must have − there was no sound but the moaning of the wind, although I knew that somewhere not far away he would be lurking, waiting for the first sign of movement from me.

I stayed there, taut, knowing for the first time how a hunted animal felt when its pursuers were hot on the scent. My muscles were cramped and numb. Presently I edged cautiously forward a few yards and to my relief found I was close upon the ruined cottage. Crawling on my stomach, with my hands clutching the bracken, I dragged myself along, feeling after a short time the cold smooth surface of slabs beneath my icy palms.

I went through the gaping doorway into the shell of tumbled walls and loose stones. It was very dark inside. Once a mouse or rat scurried past my cheek, and I stood up sharply, pressing against a corner of what once had been a room but was now no more than a sanctuary for wild creatures.

I closed my eyes, feeling for the torch, but it was not there. It must have fallen somewhere during my wild rush for freedom.

I sat down again weakly, wondering how long I'd have to stay there, how soon the fog would clear, and whether or not Louis was still searching for me. He would be, of course. He had gone too far to give up now. Unless he managed to dispose of me − I shuddered at the thought − he would inevitably face prison or a mental home. His whole future depended upon my inability to give evidence against him. I was therefore still in deadly danger, with no means of defence, no weapon to fight with, unless ... a stone! My fingers fumbled among the debris of old bricks. There were some loose on the ground. They were rough and hard; I found one which had an edge to it, knife sharp. Clutching it, I waited, praying that he wouldn't come. But he did. Even before his sly misted face emerged at the gaping door, I sensed he was quite close.

There was the snapping of a twig, then I saw him dimly, heard him say, 'What's the use of hiding, you naughty girl? Don't think you can escape. You shouldn't have interfered −'

95

He came towards me. I flattened myself against the wall and as his hands reached out for my shoulders I lifted one arm high and brought the stone crashing down upon his head. He gave a sharp cry, and staggered once, before falling at my feet.

Shuddering, sick with shock and nausea, and without looking at him, I lurched ahead into the lifting mist, unaware of direction or purpose, driven only by a blind instinct to be away, anywhere, from the horror of the cottage.

Once, as a broken branch waved its twiggy arm ahead of me, I thought of Katherine's windblown locks waiting to entrap me, and the soughing of the air as her insidious taunting voice.

There was a break in the mist, and pale light glimmered, throwing a gleam upon my face. The shadows were black holes of eyes. I knew I could go on no more. They had got me. The dark powers had won.

With which thought, unconsciousness mercifully claimed me.

I was in a dark world, and Lucien was standing by me, shadowy and unreal, in grey robes with a tall candle in one hand. I looked at him in anguish as he tried to speak, but no sound came from his lips.

He shook his head. His wonderful eyes — as I had first known them — were clouded by a strange all-consuming sadness. He was trying to contact me but imeasurable distances were between us, immersed in cloud which gradually took the shape of a picture in a frame — a portrait from another period, that crumbled and became dust before my eyes. I struggled and cried out. For a second he was clear again, only to be drawn away into the world of nothingness and negation. I realised then that I could not really have seen him physically; my eyes had not opened. They were still tightly shut. I tried to open them, but the lids felt glued together. Through my efforts to wake, a voice penetrated, saying, 'It's all right, Miss Carn. Just rest; you're safe.'

Safe? What did "safe" mean? And where was I? Almost

96

immediately memory rushed back and with it renewed terror.

I sat up suddenly, drenched in perspiration, trying to rise. Hands held me down.

'Miss Carn – Miss Carn, dear – ' The voice was compassionate, kind, and overwhelmed by returning weakness, I fell back against the feathery softness which had the gentle quality of white clouds against a warm summer sky. Perhaps that was it: perhaps everything else was illusion and I was already dead, floating in an infinity of space and peace. I was content for it to be so; content just to relax and know nothing more, because only terror waited for me in the world I had left. But against my will consciousness reclaimed me. I looked up, and as my eyes began to focus, objects slowly took shape.

The face staring down anxiously was not Lucien's, Louis' or Katherine's, but a friendly stranger's surmounted by a white cap. She was smiling and holding a small glass to my lips. 'Drink this. It will revive you.'

I swallowed the stuff, and almost immediately felt stronger and more composed. Reality emerged from the nightmare – the reality of a hospital room with flowers on the small table beside me.

I didn't speak for a few minutes, then asked, 'How did I get here?'

'Inspector Grey 'phoned for an ambulance,' the nurse replied. 'He found you on the moors near Tregale. You were badly shocked and cut about, but no bones broken. You'll be all right after a few days.'

I moved my bandaged arm which felt heavy, and touched the dressing on my head.

'What time is it?'

'Two o'clock,' she answered.

'At night?'

'No, look at the window. You've had a good long sleep. And when you've had something to eat, the Inspector will be in to see you, I expect.'

'The Inspector? Yes, of course,' I echoed vaguely. I knew there was something I had to tell Martin, something terribly important, but for the moment I didn't know what it was. Then, with the sharpness of a knife stabbing my brain, I remembered. Anne – Lucien – the doctor!

'I would like him to come now,' I said urgently. 'Quickly, please. There's something he's got to know. It's very important. It's – you see, I've killed someone. And there's my cousin –'

The nurse frowned slightly, staring at me unbelievingly. 'You've had a bad dream, dear,' she said gently. 'And you really should wait a bit before you talk with anyone.'

'No. It can't wait,' I persisted. '*Please.*'

'Very well,' she agreed grudgingly. 'I'll fetch him.'

'He's here?'

'Oh, yes. He's been on the premises most of the time. But you must have a wash first. It will freshen you up.'

She sponged my face and hands and adjusted the bandages, then gave me a mirror. I looked awful. My face was grazed under the eyes which were swollen beneath. There was a cut covered by plaster running the length of one cheek.

I shook my head helplessly. 'I haven't even any *powder*,' I exclaimed. 'If my nose wasn't so shiny it would help.'

The nurse laughed. 'Wait a moment. As you say, your nose could do with toning down. I'll see if I can find some cosmetics.'

She went out of the room, and was soon back with a compact. The powder wasn't my shade at all – too dark and yellowish – but it was better than nothing. My face didn't feel quite so naked when I'd given my one normal feature a good dusting.

Martin came in shortly afterwards, and my heart lifted; he looked so wholesome in his tweeds.

'How do you feel, Belinda?' he asked, sitting on the edge of the bed.

'A bit of a wreck,' I admitted. 'And I know I look it. But I gather I'm expected to pull through.'

'You bet you are.'

There was a brief pause before I commented, 'I guess you'll want a statement.'

'Later,' he answered.

'But I've got to tell you now. Because of Anne.'

98

He smiled reassuringly. 'Your cousin is perfectly safe. She's here, in hospital. We fetched her last night after you collapsed near my cottage.'

'I don't remember that.'

'No. You will in time, I expect. Luckily you managed to speak – that's how we got hold of Dendas.'

'The doctor – but – I – he –'

'Now, now, just forget him for the moment. I was telling you about Mrs Wilding.'

'Is she all right?'

'She soon will be,' he said. 'The doctors tell me she's a very healthy young woman with a strong constitution, perfectly normal in every way, except that she's been drugged over quite a long period of time. But with treatment she'll eventually recover.'

I lay back, trying to absorb what he was saying, knowing it to be true yet unable to comprehend the implications.

'It was the doctor, wasn't it?' I said at last. 'Louis Dendas? I knew it was him. From the beginning I knew.'

'Not only Dendas,' Martin said, and I thought with a stab of misery, 'Lucien. If only it hadn't been Lucien.'

After a pause, I stated dully, 'They're both dead. Lucien went over the cliff, and Louis – I killed him with a stone.'

'No you didn't,' Martin assured me. 'He was stunned and cut, and a good thing too. But he'll live.'

I was relieved. Whatever justification I'd had, I knew that if I'd been responsible for his death, it would have been on my conscience for the rest of my life.

'Try not to dwell on unpleasant things,' Martin went on, 'for the present anyway. When you're stronger – tomorrow, perhaps – we'll get facts down.'

'All right. But I can remember everything clearly. *Everything*. It doesn't frighten me any more. Except –'

'Yes?'

I didn't answer at once. I knew there were some things I would never be able to explain properly, even to myself; realised also that there had been qualities in Lucien that Martin would not accept, knowing nothing of the long battle between good and evil which had worn him down so utterly, resulting inevitably in his death.

'What were you going to say, Belinda?' Martin queried again.

'Nothing much,' I replied. 'I was just wondering.' I waited before asking, 'It *was* black magic, wasn't it?'

'Something like that,' Martin agreed. 'And other things, as you must know. Drugs — quite a traffic in them going on between this part of the coast and Brittany. Lucien Wilding was at the centre of it.'

'Lucien?' I echoed incredulously, though I guessed then it must be true.

Martin gave me a long look, as though testing my capacity for facing facts before he explained in calm, clear tones, 'When he met your cousin and married her, he was already a complete addict — LSD at that time, then cocaine, heroin, the whole lot. An experimenter, I should say. He'd been convicted twice for serious offences. Then he linked up with Dendas, another of the same type.'

'No,' I interrupted. 'They weren't alike. Louis was *bad*.'

'Wilding was the more subtle,' Martin stated inflexibly. 'He'd gone further; too far ever for a cure. And with Dendas being a doctor, the stuff was more readily available. Between them they worked up a steady and remunerative trade, with sufficient also to supply their own insatiable needs and the money to pay for it. You see, drug addiction of that kind can lead to a particularly dangerous type of insanity.'

I shivered. 'Yes. I'd known for some time that Louis was mad. But *Lucien*! He was so different. He was so gentle, until —'

'Until what?'

I described as best I could my last dreadful meeting with him on the cliff, then going back to the orgy in the ruin, omitting nothing — the rape of Mary, Katherine's involvement, and my suspicions concerning Marcus and Helen. Just one thing I held back — although Martin must have been aware of it — the terrible fact that Lucien had been wearing a horned mask when he attacked me: the mask of the leader. I could not accept fully, and knew I never would, that *he* had been the weapon of Mary's debasement.

100

When I'd finished Martin remarked quietly. 'It all links up.'

'What?'

'The drugs. The demonology. Satanism. They're part of the same thing: a sense of power; inflated lust for evil − call it what you like. But it's over now; round here, anyhow. We have all the ringleaders, including Katherine, under lock and key, and you helped quite a bit, let me tell you. If I know my job, they'll be safe from human society for some years to come. Dendas will probably spend his life in an institution for the insane. If Wilding hadn't died, he'd have done the same.'

There was a pause until I said, 'I'm glad, then, that he's dead.'

I looked away, knowing that Martin's eyes were watching me closely. Presently he said, 'You liked him, didn't you, Belinda?'

'It wasn't a matter of liking,' I said slowly. 'He was just different. He could be so kind. The real Lucien wasn't what you think.'

I felt his hand close over mine. 'I'm trying to be generous,' he said gruffly, 'because I − because I'm fond of you. So go on thinking of him in *your* way. A dual personality. Sometimes it's possible; maybe there can be two people in one body, although for a policeman that's hard to accept.'

'Have they found his body?'

'Yes. It was recovered from the rocks this morning. He's already been identified − I did that myself, to spare you, in your condition. He wasn't a pretty sight. But of course you'll have to attend the inquest.'

'When?'

'As soon as you're fit enough. The sooner it's over the better. You're the only witness. Dendas may or may not have known exactly what happened. In any case, he's unfit to answer questions, and it's on the cards he'll remain that way.'

'I see.'

'Belinda −'

'Yes?'

'I have to say this: don't fret too much about Lucien

Wilding. See things in perspective, if you can. There's one thing you should be clear about. However gentle one side of him may have been, the other was completely homicidal and unscrupulous. The fact was — if I'm not much mistaken — that he had been meaning to get rid of you from the beginning. He had a very good reason for urging his wife to get you to Ravenscarne. Your cousin's fortune, or at least part of it — a considerable share of the capital — went to you, didn't it, if anything happened to her? Well, then, if you were out of the way when she died, Lucien would inherit. Do you understand?'

'You mean that he planned to kill me, from the start — is that what you think?'

'Of course. A fall over a cliff — a reckless walk on some foggy night — nothing could be simpler. Meanwhile, everyone in the district practically had heard that Lucien had a hysterical sick wife who had been mentally deranged for some time. When you were out of the way, disposing of Anne wouldn't have been difficult with the assistance of Louis Dendas, even though there'd have been local opinion against them. That's where they went wrong — going in for all that nasty jiggery-pokery so near to Tregale. They even used a boat sometimes for the drug running. The postman reported the crabber.'

The boat! I'd forgotten. I told Martin I'd seen it. 'I thought it funny at the time,' I said. 'Then I forgot about it.'

'For wily customers like Dendas and Wilding, it was a rather schoolboyish way of tackling things,' Martin observed. 'But that's how it happens often; these maniacs get too sure of themselves, and believe they can get away with anything.'

I tried not to be hurt by this reference to Lucien, did my best to appear unconcerned.

Martin got up. 'Well, I'll leave you now. Have a good rest. I'll be back tomorrow to see how you are, and for the official statement.'

'What will the charges be against the others?' I asked.

'Oh — drug offences, complicity in rape, possibly intent to murder. We shall see.'

'I still can't believe it, not absolutely,' I said. 'It's unthinkable somehow. Lucien may have plotted to kill me, but he wouldn't have in the end. He didn't.'

'No.'

'Don't ask me to explain, but at the last minute he changed. You said he could be two people in one.'

'I pointed out that it was a possibility.'

'Well, Lucien's good part was the real him,' I insisted stubbornly.

He didn't ask me why I thought that. He probably realised that in any case I wouldn't tell him.

As he reached the door Martin turned and asked, 'What did you think of the Walsh girl?'

'Not bad,' I answered. 'Better than Marcus.'

'Then you'll probably be glad to know we've nothing against her,' he told me. 'The other woman will probably get off lightly on the drugs charge, with a plea of "undue influence". She was obviously a warped, nasty character but there's no legal crime in lesbianism, or occultism for that matter. It's Dendas who'll take the rap − and Raine.'

'What about Mary?'

'She'll have care and attention,' Martin replied. 'Try and get her off your mind. By the way −'

'Yes?'

'Have you any idea who the others were at the meeting that night?'

I shook my head. 'Not an inkling.'

'Hmm. Never mind. We'll get them. One's at the station already − a respectable solicitor from the other end of the county. You'd never believe it, would you? Nice wife, too, home, kids, a future before him − yet he has to get involved with drugs and satanism. We've a hunch another may be a local. Whatever the outcome, there'll be no more of their wretched practices in these parts. The locals will have no pity after all this comes out.'

I knew that was true. Stone throwing and abuse would be only the beginning.

When Martin had gone I lay back, trying to rest. The nurse came in presently with some food. I ate automatically, hardly tasting it. Even then I found it hard to decide what was true and what was false. Perhaps because I didn't entirely want to. Later I slept.

This time the dream was different from any I'd had before.

I was drifting over dense black earth filmed by pale mist that billowed in coils round my feet. I couldn't feel the ground; the sensation was that of treading air. I wanted to lift my arms and fly like a bird, but couldn't. Every time I raised my hands it was as though chains pulled them down again.

In the distance a tall grey shape gradually emerged – a towering column I knew I had to reach but that filled me with rising dread. I wanted to get there, at the same time knowing I should turn and go back.

The air was cold, and as it cleared intermittently I saw strange shapes stirring and taking form from the blackened earth – humped grotesque beings reminding me of legends I'd read as a child. There was a whining wind, that presently soughed and echoed with my name, 'Belinda – Belinda –' as though from another world far, far away. Stunted trees like deformed arms clawed skeleton-like at my ankles, but I felt no touch; was aware of nothing but the column ahead growing larger as I approached and more formidable.

Nothing seemed to be moving there. It's hard now to describe the increasing fear I felt, to understand how a mere stone edifice should have such power to terrify. Yet I knew it was a challenge I had to face. So I forced myself on, treading the insubstantial terrain, floating as one so often does in dreams. Yes, in a strange dim way I knew I was dreaming, realising at the same time that if I chose I could go on forever and never wake up. Was the sea there in the distance behind the looming shape? I couldn't tell. But as the vapour suddenly cleared the scene assumed the startling clarity of black glass, glittering and icy under a frozen sky.

At that point all movement died in me. It was as though an unseen barrier halted my progress.

I waited, the bitter air searing my face. Then, unpredictably, everything became uncannily still. There was no sound, no breath or movement. I simply stood perfectly motionless, waiting. And very gradually my mind seemed to be drawn from my body and I saw myself from the outside as though I was looking at a painting.

The column, starkly clear against the glittering dark background, was paler now, each detail clean-cut, with steps leading from its base. The girl whom I knew to be myself was standing rigidly with palms outspread, head tilted back, looking towards the long window at the top. A figure stood there silhouetted against a beam of light, and I knew it was Lucien. His arms were outstretched towards her, but his features were indeterminate as though veiled. I knew the girl had only to take one step and the veil would fall on her also. The picture would become reality and she would be absorbed in it forever.

Time died.

How long the confrontation lasted there was no telling. It could have been seconds or eternity. Lucien's familiar form held the unearthly radiance of a cold green moon. I realised that his static poise was rigid with the chill of death, and shivered with aversion, longing for life.

With a shudder, the dark earth beneath started to tremble and part. A great wind rose suddenly, and the column crumbled and fell. There was a cry of anguish as the girl turned and rushed away, flying over stones and blackened debris, leaping from rock to rock until her identity was my own again and I was there alone, kneeling in that vast wasteland of despair, waiting for the morning and for the light.

Before consciousness properly returned, there was a glimmer in the distance, and a tremendous whirring of great wings. They were outspread and tipped with gold, rising triumphantly from the blackened earth to the clearing luminous sky.

From ashes to life and beauty.

The Phoenix rising.

My hand went automatically to my breast. Perhaps I prayed, I do not know, but a great peace gradually enveloped me, and took me into a warm and comforting oblivion.

The next day I was allowed to see Anne. She already looked a little better, though her eyes were dazed and unhappy.

105

They had told her of Lucien's death, but not all the details. So I was surprised to hear her say, 'It was suicide, of course, wasn't it?'

'What makes you say that?'

She smiled. 'Don't try to spare me, Belinda, and don't prevaricate. I know. I think I've always known from the very beginning.'

'Known what?'

'He didn't really love me,' she said without emotion. 'I made myself believe he did — or tried to. He was so — sort of — different. And could be so devastating. I adored him, and of course he had to have money.'

'Don't, Anne. Try and forget.'

'Oh, no. It doesn't matter now; it didn't worry me, even then. A person like Lucien had to have things other people didn't.' She paused, then continued, 'If he hadn't got so friendly with Louis Dendas everything might have worked out. Lucien wasn't all — wrong. I knew he took drugs, of course, I soon found that out.'

'Why didn't you tell me this earlier?' I asked.

'I didn't want to harm him,' she said simply. 'And the stuff Louis gave me made me so confused. I couldn't have explained properly, and if I had — would you have believed me anyway? About Lucien, I mean?'

'It would have been difficult,' I admitted. 'He seemed so kind.'

'Yes.'

'He was with you on the cliff, wasn't he?' she asked presently. 'He followed you.'

'I suppose so,' I replied, not looking at her.

He was always searching for something — that's what he used to say before I was ill. 'Life is a search.' He just went too far — and so he died.'

How truly she spoke, I thought.

We chatted for a while, discussing plans for the future.

'I'd like you to come back with me to Canada for a holiday,' I said before I left. 'Will you do that, Anne?'

'Of course,' she answered. 'That's what I want — a good long change from Cornwall. But I shall make arrangements to sell the house first.'

106

'Yes. It would probably be best. It won't take long. When you're better we'll go over together and decide what you want to keep.'

'Nothing,' she stated emphatically. 'Nothing at all except a few clothes and knick-knacks. You know, small personal things — presents from Grandfather, a few souvenirs. The quicker the rest's got rid of the better.'

'Perhaps someone will buy the place, lock, stock and barrel,' I suggested.

'Perhaps.'

That evening I wrote to my firm in Canada, explaining that I had been ill and would be returning as soon as possible. Then I booked in at a hotel near the hospital so I could see Anne every day until she was well enough to join me. During that time I knew there was something I had to work out for myself — something unfinished that still had to be resolved. Although outwardly normal and able to face the everyday world with apparent composure, deep down in the recesses of my mind I was haunted, as one is haunted by a nostalgic tune which returns at unguarded moments with aching intensity, to torment and bewilder.

A week later Martin drove us both over to the manor one afternoon to collect Anne's possessions and the few clothes I'd left behind.

The weather was fine and windless, splashed with warm sunlight flooding the moors to gold. As we left Merrinporth for Tregale the vista appeared welcoming and dreamlike, the hamlet itself a typical Cornish scene with its huddle of cottages bathed in the late afternoon light.

My grandfather's old home against the hill had a dejected, tired look, as though ready now for sleep and complete extinction. I felt I should never go there again. Its original life had gone forever. I would some time, somehow, erase from my mind the evil purposes it had recently served, remembering only my fleeting impressions of childhood and the kind old man who had lived there and loved it, imbuing its four walls with goodness. Such things could never be entirely erased.

Noticing both my silence and Anne's, Martin said, 'Cheer

up, it will soon be over. There'll be no need to return.'

I turned my head; he was smiling his out-of-doors friendly smile, but with a new intimacy, something deep and warm holding a glowing certainty that said, 'This is reality. This won't change.'

Reality. Yes, I had to cling to that. It was my lifeline, and life had to be lived. The quick lift of my heart told me suddenly, that I wanted it that way − a normal, natural existence without shadows or confusion of the spirit. With Martin, perhaps? Reliable and sane. Someone to share and laugh with. Someone of down-to-earth flesh and blood.

Yet, as we went into the house, I shivered. I couldn't for that fleeting hour help remembering how, on that first day, Lucien had come into the hall to meet me, held out his hand and given me his gentle smile, spoken to me in his warm rich voice, with his marvellous eyes turned upon me. His magic had been with me from that first moment. I wondered now what kind of magic it had been. And the ghosts! Those risen dead − had they after all been some kind of delusion? Oh, I hoped so. Yes, that was surely the answer.

It didn't take us long to collect what we wanted. Like me − even more so − Anne must have had nostalgic memories, dark though they were. She was still too near to suffering not to feel lost and alone. I was glad she'd been spared the agony of seeing Lucien die, or having to attend the inquest which I'd got through automatically, answering questions only briefly, keeping the worst part to myself, so that the verdict had been 'death by mis-adventure'. I had no conscience about that. Drugged as he'd been, it was the truth and all that Anne needed to know.

When we left, the setting sun was already low over the horizon, slipping like a ball of fire behind the high ridge of the moors where the ruin stood, a lonely shape against the sombre landscape.

'Well,' Martin said later, in the lounge of the hotel, 'that's that then. The next thing is to put the whole property, including the old relic, into the hands of an estate agent who'll take charge and get rid of it as soon as possible.' He glanced at me. 'You'll both be staying, I suppose, until it's settled?'

'I don't see there's any need,' Anne interrupted before I could reply. 'I don't care who has it, and if a buyer doesn't turn up that won't worry me either. I just want never to see it again, that's all.'

As it happened, Ravenscarne was only advertised for three days before an American couple enquired, went over, had a look at the house, and settled that same afternoon for a considerably higher price than had been expected.

Anne and I made plans to leave for Canada the following week. But before that something happened. In spite of my own earlier conviction that I wanted never to see Ravenscarne again, I had a compulsion suddenly to visit the old place once more; so on the Friday afternoon, when my cousin was discussing business matters with her solicitor, I hired a taxi to Tregale and on the outskirts of the village got out, telling the driver to wait until I returned.

The sky was already lowering above the yellow and brown moors as I took the path up the hill; the autumn air was heavy with the nostalgic smells of dead leaves, bracken, and distant woodsmoke.

A few gulls wheeled overhead, screaming mournfully. Only a faint wind stirred the dried branches of heather and gorse; everywhere and everything seemed desolate and bereft of life. It was as though all my earlier terrifying experiences were nothing more than a bad dream.

Yet I knew what I'd witnessed and gone through had been true. Retold as a tale, or written down as it is now, probably no one will quite believe me, and if I could have done I would have erased the memory as merely the hallucination of an over-active imagination. I didn't *want* to think back. But some force – instinct or inner sense, call it what you like – told me the story was not yet quite over. There was still an element of the past hovering about Ravenscarne needing to be exorcised; an aura of bygone times not yet fully extinct which for some irrational reason I had to prove for myself.

I was unaware of physical danger while I mounted the hill, ever nearer to the deserted shell. But the pungent smell of smoke increased, curdling the air with a mistiness that I suddenly realised was more than that of an autumn bonfire.

I paused by a leafless thorn and watched as the writhing greyness thickened and blew in twisted coils from the gaping windows, becoming darkened and black, streaked with lurid leaping crimson. My arm grew taut round the tree's trunk; my heart lurched as the heavy sky turned to dull veiled red. But I couldn't move. Even through the crackling of undergrowth and distant thud of falling bricks my limbs seemed to have lost all volition and power to run. From below me, somewhere down the slope, I heard a man's voice shouting, followed by others, but the voices didn't properly register. All I knew was that Ravenscarne — the old Ravenscarne of early childhood — was burning, and would soon be no more than a charred mass of tumbled wood and masonry. A conflict of emotions swept through me, including a strange sense of relief. Soon it would be gone, leaving no reminder of the recent evil happenings which had so violated a part of my life, and of Anne's. Yes — especially Anne's.

How it had happened probably no one would ever discover — some tramp or hiker could have left a half-smoked cigarette there, or perhaps the unseen powers of good had themselves taken a hand and stepped in to even the balance. It didn't matter. Ravenscarne was already beyond any human aid. Even as I watched I saw the tallest tower and roof crumble and fall. For a moment it seemed to me strange distorted shapes leaped from the darkness against the crimson sky, and above the moaning and creaking of wind and furze a thin wailing scream arose, as though a being in torment was at last being taken into extinction.

Then all died in one tremendous roar as the whole structure of the building fell, sending a hurricane of stones and bricks tumbling down the hill.

I turned then, and with the heat already penetrating my clothes, hurried back the way I'd come, passing a small crowd of men, mostly farm-hands I guessed, ineffectively equipped with sticks and what other means they had of fire-fighting.

They didn't seem to notice me and I was grateful for that. No contact remained now to link me with the past.

In time gorse and bluebells might flower again, stirring the blackened soil with new growth. The old adage that time healed all things had some truth in it after all. The wrong that human beings did must inevitably fade when the earth, purified, came into its own.

And it would be so with Anne, I was sure. For a time there would be. sad periods, perhaps even moments of fear. But the future stretched before us both, the one important thing we shared.

As the taxi carried me back to Penzance my thoughts strayed to the unfortunate Mary, and to Katherine. With treatment, Mary might become again her normal simple self. But Katherine? I wasn't sure. In her way she'd been a magnetic, colourful individual. But I doubted that she'd cared for anyone in her life except herself, and found I could spare her no pity.

The next day Martin called to see me at the hotel.

'I hear you're leaving on Wednesday.'

'Yes, I think so. Unless they want me here for any enquiries about the fire.' I paused, then continued with my eyes directly on his, 'It was nothing to do with me, you know. I went to the station and reported all I knew – how I'd gone for a last look and then the smoke appearing. But you know about it, don't you?'

He nodded. 'Of course. There's no question of your being involved in any way at all. These moorland fires start easily; I don't even think the question of arson will arise, although between you and me I wouldn't particularly blame any local for putting a match to that old relic.'

'That "old relic", as you call it, was part of me once,' I reminded him a little drily.

'Life changes,' he said. 'And circumstances; people too. Sometimes it's better just to put the whole of the past behind you, except a few good memories, and make a fresh start.'

'Maybe,' I agreed.

'Is that what you're going to do?' he asked in a voice meant to be casual but not entirely succeeding.

'I'm going to try. I've a good job waiting in Canada. Actually I'm lucky to have the post still.'

'I see. A career girl.'

'If you want to put it that way, yes.'

'There are other things,' he pointed out. 'Such as — '

'Go on. I hate unfinished remarks.'

'Marriage, having kids, all the everyday usual things most women aim for.'

'I realise that,' I told him. 'I'd be an idiot if I didn't.'

He laughed. 'Which you're certainly not.'

'Which I'm certainly not.'

'Well, then — what about it?'

'What about what?'

'This,' he said, and before I could do anything about it my face was suddenly between his two hands, his lips firm and urgent upon my own, yet at the same time so gentle and tender my heart quickened. Then he released me abruptly. 'Let's not fence any more,' he said. 'You know darn' well what I'm talking about. And it seems to me the prospect doesn't exactly chill you.'

'No.'

'Good. Then suppose we get down to things right away.'

I shook my head. 'Martin — you mustn't force me. There's Anne to consider, and I don't have everything completely in perspective yet. Neither do you.'

'Thank you, but as I've so far escaped the marital net I'm hardly likely to make a mistake now. I'm not that kind of man, Belinda. Understand?'

'Yes, I think so. All the same, you've got to give me time. I just want to get away from things for a bit, "recover my bearings" as they say. It's not that I don't feel as you do. I hope — I'm *sure* — that when I come back everything between us will be good. It's important, though, I have a chance to prove it to myself. Surely you see that?'

'No, I don't exactly. But then, as women have always seemed to me the most extraordinary, exasperating creatures on God's earth, I guess I've got to accept it.'

'It would be better if you did, and far easier for me.'

'Okay,' he said grudgingly. 'But don't stay away too long. I'm not the most patient of men by nature.'

'You'd better be,' I told him with a flippancy I was far from feeling. 'With me you'll need more patience than any woman has a right to expect.'

112

'I'll take the chance,' he said. 'So it's understood, is it?'

'Oh, you're hopeless,' I answered. 'I don't believe you've taken in a word I've been saying.' He walked away and stood for a few minutes with his back to me, then turned, came back and said, 'All right, love, you win. Go to Canada, settle your affairs there – or not as you choose. Then, when you return – and notice I say *when*, Belinda – I'll be waiting. Have you any idea how long you'll be staying in the great open spaces?

'Not more than a month or two,' I told him. 'Anne's going to art school, you know, in London, and I shall probably come back with her then – if we still feel the same, you and I.'

So the matter was settled, for the time being. I knew that before I gave any ultimate promise there was one last thing I had to do.

'Ring me on Tuesday evening,' I told him. 'Or call if you're still here.'

'Very well, Belinda,' he gripped my hand. 'I'm not going to go all sentimental again or even kiss you. I'm not trying to tie you down on any emotional rebound. I haven't an inkling what new thing you've got in your head – what's going to make up your mind for you. But I can see it matters to you; that it's something you've got to go through on your own. That true?'

'Yes. You're right.'

'Okay, till Tuesday then.' He gave me a brief reassuring grin, and was gone. I felt a sense of loss, as though a little of the sunshine had died from the sky; but relief, too, because I was free to explore the last link in the chain.

For the next few days Anne and I spent our time shopping, concluding all the necessary arrangements for the journey, seeing more of the countryside than I'd had a chance to do before, and idling about the quieter beaches, where we lay in the sun, dozing, reading, or reminiscing about our childhood.

We seldom referred to Lucien, and when we did it was briefly, hardly looking at each other, as though something remained unspoken that had still to be dispelled. Anne must have realised that I had withheld from her many of the dark details surrounding Lucien's death, but she never enquired, and I respected her silence. One day, in Canada perhaps, she would ask and I would be able to answer her frankly, without inhibition, because then I should have regained a sense of perspective.

My cousin had arranged to see friends on the Tuesday morning, which left me free to do as I had planned.

The weather was hot, and in Penzance the pavements glittered under veils of thin steamy mist which quivered over the harbour and distant Mount, merging overhead to clearest blue.

I went out early, before the streets were too crowded, but even then I had to take off my cardigan, feeling a sultry oppressiveness hinting at thunder to come.

I stood at a corner of the main road trying to recall which of two streets had led to the threadwork of smaller ones where I discovered the antique shop huddled in its maze of buildngs. I took a turn to the left, but after walking a short way discovered I was wrong, went back, and turned in the other direction.

I was wandering about for quite quarter of an hour before I found the shop, dimly lit, with a side window boarded up. I paused for a few minutes before going in, wondering what had happened. The door tinkled as I opened it and my first impression was of the faint pungent odour of scorched wood. I looked round. There was dust on the floor; one of the rugs had been rolled up and pushed to one side. Otherwise everything looked very much the same except for the deadened light due to the blocked window.

As no one came out at first I went back, opened and closed the door again. The second tinkle brought the woman I had met before.

'You *are* open, aren't you?' I asked. 'I hope nothing's wrong — that window, I mean, and the smell.'

She pushed a strand of hair back from her eyes. She was obviously tired and hadn't expected anyone to call just then.

'We had a bit of a fire last night,' she explained. 'Nothing much really; no damage done to the stock to speak of. But it was a shock. The wood round the window somehow caught alight, and the glass went. We're insured, of course. All the same it was funny – how it started, I mean. Someone must have dropped a lighted cigarette. Visitors are careless sometimes.'

When she'd got that off her chest she went on, 'Well, madam, what can I show you – ?' She broke off, continuing quickly, 'It's the young lady who came in before, isn't it? You had the cameo brooch.'

'Yes,' I answered. 'You must have a good memory for faces.'

She shrugged. 'We don't get that number of people in here. Too out of the way, you know, and the visitors like Piskie charms – all that phoney stuff.'

'Yes, it must be aggravating when you stock genuine antiques.'

'Oh, yes, everything in this shop is genuine. Some things are better than others, of course. We have to cater for all tastes and price brackets, but there's no trickery.'

'I realise that. You were very honest about that old portrait I asked about when I was in before – about its not being valuable or knowing who the artist was.'

'You mean the Pendrake one?'

'You weren't certain, but you thought so. Anyway, I'd like to see it again if I may.'

'That's a funny thing, too,' she said. 'The fire hardly touched it at all; but when I picked it up, it – well, it just went.'

'What do you mean?'

'The colours; everything. You'd hardly recognise it. I'm sure you wouldn't want it now.'

'Could I see it, though?' I persisted. 'It's of interest to me. I have a reason.'

'Oh, well, if that's the case. I've put it out for the dustmen, but they haven't been yet. I'll see if it's still there. My husband may have broken it up.'

She went out through the back, leaving me alone with a strange feeling of disquiet. I told myself it had been a mistake to come, knowing all the time there'd been no choice in the matter; driven by a desire beyond my control, I just *had* to see the portrait again, take one last look before my future could be resolved.

The woman seemed a long time returning; minutes must have passed, and as I stood there a feeling of unendurable loneliness overcame me. I felt quite faint. Objects dimmed and swam before my eyes. I clutched at the hard surface of a table for support, while words rushed and rang through my brain, accelerating my pulse with their vivid emotional intensity:

I searched a billion million years
Through space and time and countless spheres −
From birth to death, and death to birth −
Until at last we met on earth.
To recognise, and know the pain −
Of lovers doomed to part again −

I closed my eyes. I was about to turn away in an effort to drag myself from the shop when the woman came back. Her brisk voice jerked me back to reality; my heart steadied. I was able to straighten myself and face her, grateful that she was not looking at me but at the picture she was holding towards me in both hands.

'You see what I mean?' she said. 'Just look at it.'

I stared. The face in the scorched frame had faded and cracked almost beyond recognition. Where once Lucien's eyes had looked at me from the ancient canvas, there were only smudged holes. The smile on the lips was almost completely erased, and what paint remained was crazed and dull.

'How strange,' I whispered. 'For it to go so quickly like that. It's incredible.'

'Yes. But you never know with old things. As I said, it was never much good. A copy probably.'

I did not think that. But I knew that whatever it had been in the past, its value had now gone. I took it from her for a final look, feeling the texture with the tips of my fingers. Where I touched the surface the paint crumbled and completely disintegrated before my eyes, leaving only dust and an outline of shadow where the face had been. At the same moment a fitful gleam of sunlight penetrated the chinks of the boarded window, spilling the frame with an aura of golden light. Then as quickly it faded.

Suddenly I felt better. My heart lifted, and I fancied that a wave of fresh air swept through the shop, as though dark gates had swung open to freedom.

'Well,' I heard the woman saying, 'I've never seen anything like that before. Never.'

I smiled at her brightly. 'As you say – it couldn't have been very good. Anyway, it's no use now, but thank you for letting me look at it.'

I bought one or two small gifts before leaving, and shortly afterwards was out in the street again. The closeness had gone, and a gentle summer breeze fanned my face as I walked down to the harbour.

Martin didn't call in at the hotel that evening, but he 'phoned.

'Sorry I couldn't get back,' he apologised. 'A policeman's life's a bit unpredictable.' He paused then added, 'Well? What's it to be? Still going?'

'Yes. Tomorrow,' I told him. 'There's no point in delaying things.'

'Sudden, though. I rather thought we could have a few more days.'

'Interims between hotel meals and police calls?' I queried.

'Better than nothing, I'd have thought.'

'Oh, Martin, it must be much more than that,' burst from me explosively. 'We must both *know*. I've got to – to adjust –'

'Damn it, Belinda, how many times have you said that? And to what, for Pete's sake?'

'Things,' I said vaguely, after a short pause. 'The change –'

'The upheaval and shock. From Ravenscarne, I suppose.'

But I didn't mean only Ravenscarne, and I felt he knew it.

There was a faint crackling on the line, a moment's silence between us, then he asked loudly, 'Are you trying to tell me to get off your back? If that's it, I'd rather know now.'

'Of course not,' I almost shouted, a bleak vision of life without Martin Grey chilling my mind. 'I just want you to try and understand. I know it's difficult. I can't quite

117

fathom things myself yet. But it'll work out in the end. Everything will be all right, I'm sure.'

'For who?'

'Both of us. I shall get up second wind, and be back before I'm expected.'

'Hmm.'

'Martin —'

'Yes?'

'I'm — I do need you, you know — well, much more than that — but it's difficult on the 'phone — ' My voice trailed off.

'Thank you.'

I waited for him to add something else, but he didn't. The crackling on the line increased, then died again, enabling me to say more loudly and firmly than I'd meant, 'Well, I must go now. I'm wasting your call. Thanks for ringing. And — and Martin —'

'Yes?'

'I *will* be back.'

'See that you are.' The tone was gruff, as though someone else was speaking.

'There'll be time then for everything,' I cried. 'We can sort it out — '

The crackling started again and became a jarring sound.

'Oh, damn!' His voice rose above it explosively. 'The bloody line's going.'

I laughed. 'Never mind — 'bye for now. We can talk some other time.'

Yes, I thought as I put the receiver down, there'd be plenty of opportunity of talking and other things later.

And then I wondered.

Once back in Canada, *would* I come back to find Martin waiting with his arms out for me, just like that? Had I taken too much of a risk?

I realised as the question formed how bleak and empty life would be without him.

Then what was the answer?

Doubtful, feeling suddenly insecure and unsure of myself, I went out later, unknown to Anne, and as though drawn on invisible strings, wandered down to the harbour. Though it was very late a few people were still strolling about. The sea was calm, and deep glassy green, almost black, rippled by glittering gentle waves from the luminous light. St Michael's Mount, pin-pointed silver from the moon, rose ethereally from the water. I was sad suddenly to be leaving Cornwall, knowing it might be for good, and that the strange mystery of Lucien and the past could never be entirely solved. Somehow I had to accept the fact and rid my heart of it forever.

The shadows of that last night were elongated and transient, moving strangely in the gentle wind over the sea and beach. People passed at odd intervals — strangers unknown to me, but holding somehow a queer significance because they belonged to a scene in my life which was so quickly to fade.

I remembered an old saying — 'Ships that pass in the night' — and thought, 'That's what *I* am — a temporary shape passing. Like all the strange visions and illusions, perhaps, of my period at Ravenscarne.'

A little shiver shuddered down my spine. Through the moonwashed night, Lucien seemed suddenly everywhere — in the rhythmic cadence of the waves breaking, over the pale sand and shingle, in the transient ever-changing light. For that brief time part of me seemed drawn from my body beyond material things, revealing a pattern of love and revenge for former wrong.

I wandered on bemusedly, and presently became aware of a small cafe place with lights streaming from its window over the promenade.

I went in and ordered a drink. There was a sailor sitting at the next table, and a long-haired youth and girl in the corner with their heads close together. The air was steamy, redolent with the tang of coffee, beer and cigarette smoke. As I took my drink I glanced through the window and saw an elongated shadow streaking the pavement followed by a man's silhouette, his head bent against the rising wind. My heart contracted as shadow and form converged and became one.

A beam of moonlight spilled momentarily over the ground, bathing everything in a blinding radiance.

119

Lucien!

I got up quickly, sending my cup spinning in its saucer, and hurried to the desk to put money down. Then without waiting for any change, I rushed out.

I stood briefly looking up the prom, searching for a glimpse of the receding shape. There was no sign of anyone but a shadowed darkness receding round a distant corner.

I started walking sharply, then quickened my pace until I was running. My legs felt heavy. It was like moving in a dream when limbs and all motion seemed weighted with lead. There was no one about, so no one heard when I called his name: 'Lucien! Lucien!' Or did I? I never knew. It might have been just in my mind, because he neither stopped nor came back.

When I reached the corner I looked up the street which was a narrow one leading towards the main road. There was an old inn on the right, its sign creaking fitfully in the breeze, throwing the grotesque contorted shadow of a pirate's head across the cobbles. Why I should have felt panic rising in me I don't know, but I felt suddenly bereft, in a world so lonely and without meaning I could neither move forward nor turn back.

I stood helplessly with one hand touching the rough stone surface of a wall and at that exact moment the lean form of a cat streaked out from a side alley, darting over the road into the shadows on the other side.

The sudden movement spurred me on again, and I quickened my pace. By then the sky had unexpectedly darkened, a drift of cloud dimming the moon. Of course it was stupid to race the way I did; the pavement was notched and uneven with treacherous gaps and jutting bits of stone.

I fell.

I don't remember crying out, but my ankle twisted under me, and as I heaved myself rather painfully to my feet strong hands gripped my arms and I heard a familiar voice saying, 'Belinda, are you hurt? What on earth – ?'

His voice died on the question.

I looked up.

He was staring down at me, eyes burning and tormented in his well-remembered face. And I was suddenly

120

clinging to him with my face buried against his coat. Martin.

'Where the hell've you been?' he demanded, with his grip tightening. 'And who the devil do you think you are to imagine you can play games with me like this?'

Before I could answer his mouth came warm and strong on mine.

'Just walking,' I muttered breathlessly. 'That's all – a walk.'

'At *this* hour? And by yourself? Well, let me tell you this, Miss Belinda Carn – it's the one and last time. You're not fit to be let out. Understand?'

'No. I –'

'And you're not going to Canada either.'

'Who says so?'

'I say so. Instead, you're going to do just what you're told and marry me as quickly as we can get a licence.'

I opened my mouth to speak, but he put a hand over it, continuing, 'I love you, love you, *love* you. I rang the hotel again to tell you so. And when they said you were out – oh, Belinda, did you really imagine I'd let things end that way? With a vague promise to meet months later for a sensible discussion?'

'You seemed to agree,' I said. 'That's what I –'

'Yes?'

'Hated, I suppose,' I confessed. 'I didn't *want* you to be practical and reasonable, Martin. I'm not that sort of person. Don't you understand?'

He shook his head. 'Not entirely. But then, maybe it's better that way.'

'And you're not afraid?'

'What of, for Pete's sake?'

'Ghosts?' I whispered.

He took my face between his hands and kissed me again, long and lingeringly, with a sweet sensuousness that told me all I wanted to know. Then he said, 'To hell with ghosts. When *I've* finished with you, my darling, there'll be no room for any. And that's not a threat, it's a promise.'

And I knew suddenly, with conviction, it was true.

'Finished with me?' I queried teasingly.

121

He gave a little laugh. 'You know what I mean.'

So it has been.

Martin and I were married, and during the fulfilling years that followed it was easy to put the harrowing past behind me. Just occasionally a fragment of a tune, a scent or a lingering shadow streaking the dying glow of twilight, may strike a chord of memory. But in a second it is gone, for I know that Lucien is free and at rest, and whatever inexplicable bond there may have been between us no longer has any power to disturb my life with my husband and children.

Lady in Grey

It all happened so long ago.

I was only a boy of eight and had been sent, following an attack of measles, for recuperation to old Miss Martingdale's home on the Norfolk coast. She had been my mother's governess and was a dear old lady with a deep affection for our family. Her home was on the outskirts of Hangersley, a rambling old place at the end of a curving road leading in a narrowing track directly to the cliffs and sea.

I loved it there. In the summer poppies and yellow daisy flowers grew haphazardly along the track, by the gates of the few houses and into gardens. Butterflies of every kind were profuse. It was a lovely, quiet area, with wide stretches of beach filled with shells and drifts of seaweed below high cliffs crowned by gorse and heather. On windy days golden filaments of sand were everywhere, blown in gusty thin clouds towards the cornfields and rich pasture beyond. There was a kind of golden magic about the place which I have never found elsewhere. I suppose it was partly the magic of youth and, of course, the grey lady.

I called her 'the grey lady' because she always wore grey: long filmy grey dresses that blew gently about her slim figure in the breeze, and a pale floppy hat that had a veil draped over it, tied under the chin. I wondered why she always wore a veil, because I wanted to see her face. I was sure she was beautiful. Polly, Miss Martingdale's little rosy-cheeked servant, said she wasn't quite sure but she thought the lady had suffered an accident or shock some time and had been very nervous ever since.

123

'Doesn't go out much,' she said, 'hardly at all in fact. Sad, isn't it? Must have a funny life with that great bossy-looking husband of hers.'

I agreed with Polly. There was something formidable about Mr Verney — that was their name, Verney. He was an artist, very broad and tall, with bold features and a way of walking, head high, looking neither to right nor left, that suggested he had no wish to notice anyone or be in the slightest bit friendly. He had a studio on a point of a cliff looking immediately across the sea towards a lighthouse. When I asked Polly what he painted there, she said, 'Models, so I've heard. Women. Mind you, I've never *seen*. They go there the other way, by the back lane. But — ' she gave me a knowing look ' — some say funny things go on there.'

'What things, Polly?'

She shook her heard. 'I'm not to be saying. Anyways, I don't know. No one does.'

'Not even Mrs Verney, the grey lady?'

'Ah! Now you're asking. What goes on in her poor brain behind the veil no one can tell. But now, young man,' her manner changed, became bright and efficient, 'don't you be so nosey. Let them two alone, and hop along to the little corner shop for a pound of tatties, will you? Tell Mrs Smith who they're for, and be sharp about it. Mrs Straker'll be mad at me for letting you dawdle.' Mrs Straker, incidentally, was Miss Martingdale's housekeeper, a broad competent woman, quite kindly, but fierce-looking, and sharp-tongued on occasions.

I hurried to do Polly's bidding, and on the way passed Mr Verney coming from the village. It was a warm morning with heat already rising from the June sun. He did not appear to see me but marched past, head held high as usual, looking picturesque, I thought, but rather odd, like a character in a play. He was wearing a wide-brimmed sombrero-type hat, and a scarlet smock over dark blue trousers. When it rained he dressed completely differently, in a mackintosh capecoat and tall hat which gave him the appearance somehow of a barrister or important doctor.

Polly told me one day in a burst of confidence that's what he'd been once — a doctor.

'Supposed to be clever,' she said with a thoughtful, mysterious note in her voice. 'But something happened – something unprerfessional,' she continued. 'A woman, I shouldn't wonder. Mind you, I couldn't be sure. So don't you go saying anything to Miss Martingdale. She don't like gossip.'

'I won't,' I promised, with a sense of gratification at being included in Polly's secret.

From that moment my interest in the Verney couple intensified.

It was true, what Polly said; the lady in grey was seldom to be glimpsed. Very occasionally she accompanied her husband for a time on his evening walk which took him in the same direction at the same hour along the sandy lane leading towards the coast and his studio. He appeared hardly to notice her, and she always turned back when the roadway faded into a mere track going over the dunes to the high cliffs. He gave her only a brief nod, of dismissal almost, and I could sense a dejection in her that saddened me. It was as though she wept behind the fragile veil.

Once, when thin rain blew in a grey cloud from the sea, bending poppies on their slender necks, swishing grass and the yellow daisies, I could just discern her profile against the Verneys' dimmed front window. She stood quite motionless, watching him as he took his habitual path from the house along the lane, and I saw that I had been right; she was indeed beautiful, in an ethereal way that did not so much depend on symmetry of features as on grace and that particular fey quality which defies precise description.

'What are you so interested in, Jeremy?' Miss Martingdale said from her chair by the fire; there was always a fire in the parlour, even on warm days, because the old lady felt the cold, and also she said it was company. Certainly, on such a grey day, it was.

I turned my head and glanced back at her. 'It's the lady, the grey lady. She's standing there,' I replied.

'You mean Mrs Verney?'

'Yes. At the window. She looks a bit – lost,' I added.

'You're very perceptive, boy,' Miss Martingdale told me. 'She's been poorly, you know, for quite a long time.'

'How poorly? Like me? Measles or something?'

'No, no. Nothing like that at all. Lost in spirit. Rundown. But don't let us dwell on sad things. Come here and give the fire a poke. Then tell Polly to come and pull the curtains and light the lamp. Perhaps you'd like a game of snakes-and-ladders, eh?'

I scrambled from my chair. 'All right.'

I did as she'd bid, but I wasn't really interested in the game that evening, still piqued by the air of mystery surrounding the ill matched Verneys.

With my youthful imagination roused, I seldom missed a chance of watching for the grey lady during the times I was not on the beach with my shrimping net, or running errands for the housekeeper, or looking at Miss Martingdale's treasures which she kept in a drawer of the vast carved mahogany chest.

There were times, I think, when the aged governess sensed my preoccupation with the Verneys and tried to channel my thoughts in a happier direction. She had tales to tell of days in her far-off youth before she had been governess to my mother; early years when she was employed as 'nana' to the young daughter of an English family in India. More than once she brought out relics of that period – a crimson cloak intricately embroidered in cream silk, small carved ivory animals and numerous pieces of bizarre exotic jewellery. I was interested at first, then bored. The Verneys' present and unknowable future were so much more exciting than an old lady's stories repeated more than once or twice; and although in a vague way I was fond of her, it was always a relief when I could escape from the rather stuffy Victorian parlour to the outside world, or to my own bedroom which directly overlooked the Verneys' house.

Time passed quickly. Early autumn brought evenings and mornings filmed by pale mists, and the nostalgic earthy smell of fallen leaves and woodfires from gardens and moors. My return home was due in the last week of September. I was quite recovered, and although in a way looking forward to meeting my school friends again, a little regretful to have to leave the old-fashioned

126

atmosphere of Miss Martingdale's, which included Polly, chats with the old gardener, carefree solitary days on the beach, and of course Adolphous Verney the artist, and his sad-looking wife, the lady in grey. 'Adolphous' I thought a strange pompous name, but it somehow suited him, and I guessed he might have chosen it because it sounded important.

I never heard mention of *her* name. When I asked Polly, she didn't know. No one seemed to have any personal knowledge of her at all — of what she did when she was alone in the house with their one servant, an elderly tight-lipped woman who acted as housekeeper. Did she sew? I wondered. Embroider pictures to be framed or used as fire-screens? Or did she just stand at other windows of the house, watching for her husband's return from the studio? There was no clue at all. The disagreeable-looking housekeeper kept severely to herself and was an unpopular figure at the small village shop or with anyone who dared to address her. So the mystery of the veiled lady remained unsolved for me.

I left Norfolk at the appointed time only to return eight years later, having heard that Miss Martingdale had died and had left some small bequests to me from among her treasures. My parents were in America at the time so I made the journey alone — a youth of almost seventeen, due to start university the following year. I did not hear in time to attend the funeral, a cause of some relief.

It was a late spring afternoon when I reached the old house at Hangersley. The pale sun was low in the sky, throwing quivering shadows over the sandy road which was exactly as I remembered it — spattered with clumps of poppies, their drooping heads blown on a frail wind from the sea. I was swept by memories when Polly's rosy face opened the door. She hadn't changed much, except for added weight and a few lines etching the corners of her eyes. The housekeeper was still there, but only, I learned, on a visit. She now lived in a 'Home for Retired Ladies' in Norwich. Polly had taken over Mrs Straker's former duties, and had a younger houseservant to assist her.

The ancient gardener worked outside still. He looked, to my youthful eyes, like a wizened old gnome, but years hadn't dimmed his enthusiasm or capacity for tending plants and active work.

'Keeps me young,' he told me, with a shrewd twinkle in his old eyes. 'Knowin' the ways of livin' things is havin' the wisdom of life at y'r fingertips — even cracked ones like mine.' And he chuckled as he spread one gnarled hand out — veined and brown as a knobbly twig from an old tree.

'I'm sure,' I agreed, wondering if mine ever possibly could look like that, and knowing they wouldn't because the course planned ahead for me was so different — scholastic and away from Nature's ways.

He shook his head then, and his elfin grin faded as a sigh rustled his lungs.

'Who knows what'll happen now, though?' he remarked sadly. 'It'll not be the same now th' old lady's gone. Mebbe they'll sell th' place, whoever's got it. Your parents? Is it they has the house now? I've heard the missus had no real kin of her own.'

'I don't know,' I told him. 'They're in America on some business or other. But I'm sure they'll still want you here — if it *is* them.'

'Oh, no, you can't b'lieve that,' the gruff old voice corrected me. 'I've had my day. Any modern fellow'll want to spruce up an' change things. An' I'd not be wantin' to see that anyways. A time to come an' a time to go — that's the way o' life. Like a tree that sheds it's leaves in winter.' He grinned again. 'A tough old leaf, I am, one o' the last to fall. But fall I will an' mebbe I'll rest a bit then, with a pipe o' baccy of an evenin', at my niece's place Cromer way, thinkin' back over the past 'til it's time to leave.'

He broke off, seeing into a world I didn't know, or want to hear about.

'Cheer up,' I said, 'you'll be with us for a long time yet. By the way — ' to change the suject ' — are they still there, opposite? The Verneys?'

The grizzled eyebrows shot up. 'Them? *He* is. Large as life. But *she* — well — ' He paused as though trying to find adequate words to tell me something unsavoury or so embarrassing he couldn't decide where to begin.

He was saved the trouble, for just at that moment Polly

128

appeared to tell him there was a mug of tea for him in the kitchen. I decided to ask the old man about Mrs Verney when the next opportunity arose, or Polly if she had a moment to spare. I discovered, though, that she had become more fussy about household affairs than when I'd first known her, and always seemed to have some duty or other on her hands — well, it was natural with only a young girl to help. I did find a moment however after the evening meal, when I insisted on helping Polly to clear the table and carry things out to the kitchen.

I thought she looked a little put out — almost as though I was trespassing where I shouldn't be.

'Oh, *her*!' she replied shortly. 'She's gone.'

'Gone? But where? Why?'

Polly sighed. 'It's a long story. I haven't time now. But you'll be hearing, that's for sure.'

I was puzzled, not only by the abrupt answer but by her air of secrecy. In the past, when I was a young boy, she had always been so forthright and straightforward. And when I went up to my room shortly afterwards, bewilderment gave place to confusion because it appeared that she had lied.

I was staring out of the window at the grey house opposite when I noticed a ponderous form emerging from the doorway wearing a theatrical-looking cape affair and a slouched felt hat reminiscent of the Impressionist painters. He was thinner than I remembered, but the stance, the arrogant manner of walking, hadn't changed.

Adolphous Verney.

He strode down the path and out of the gate into the sandy roadway, taking the usual route he had followed those years ago towards the headland. His figure became blurred as what remaining light there was darkened behind a rising belt of cloud. I was about to turn away when my attention was caught by a vague form emerging from the door — so slight and dimmed I thought at first I'd mistaken a shadow for reality. But when the shape moved forward a few yards I recognised it was indeed that of Mrs Verney — veiled and mysterious as ever — walking, or seeming to glide rather, down the path. I watched with concentrated curiosity, wondering if she was about to follow her husband. But halfway to the gate she paused, standing rigidly with her head turned to the right, then moved and made her way back to the house.

A queer feeling of despondency very akin to fear filled me. There was something 'not right' about the ritual, which apparently must have been going on during the whole period of my absence — something more like a scene re-enacted on a film that had been photographed long ago. And yet Verney himself had been real enough, that I could have sworn. But she? Was it that her obsession with him had turned to complete madness in her? Was she insane? Was that why the old gardener had been so reluctant to give any information about her when I asked?

But why? I was no longer a child — though, of course, compared with his vast age, I might, by him, be regarded as such. Yes, I decided, that was probably the answer. The next day, I thought, when Polly hopefully had more time for me, I'd ask her.

And so I did.

She stared at me for a moment in surprise, then shook her head. 'I told you,' she answered, 'yesterday, soon after you'd arrived, she's gone.'

'But I *saw* her,' I said. 'Last night from my bedroom window. I was looking out. Mr Verney himself was going down the road, and she came through the door and watched him. She appeared just the same; at least I *think* so. She was still wearing the veil. She waited a bit and then went back into the house.'

Polly shook her head, this time more vigorously. 'You couldn't have,' she said definitely. 'She's dead.'

'Dead?' The back of my neck pricked with chill.

'Five years ago.'

'But I — I'm sure —' I broke off, wondering if Polly for some reason was lying or if I could have been wrong and mistaken some illusion created by the fading light and shadow for a physical entity.

'Whoever or whatever you saw, wasn't her,' Polly insisted emphatically. 'I went to the funeral myself. Sad business it was too, although they did allow a Christian burial in the end, poor thing.'

'What do you mean?' I queried sharply.

'She committed suicide,' Polly told me bluntly. 'Threw herself over the cliff – over that great rock there, by his studio. Oh, she'd tried once before. Just before I came here it was. Well, though I don't agree with that sort of thing, I s'pose in a way she had cause. Neglected her, he had, something awful so I've heard.' She lowered her voice. 'There were other women, you know. Models. Any pretty face that took his fancy – well, that was it. He'd have what he wanted of them – and not only for painting – and then,' she shrugged, 'that was that. Packed off like any bundle of fancy rubbish. I shouldn't be telling you this, but I reckon now you're quite old and capable enough to furrage things out for yourself. It's said – I heard it from the old dear who keeps the village shop – that his wife was a real beauty when he married her. Young and innocent, and like the others he had to have her. But *not* like the others in one way. She wasn't having any funny business without it being all legal and proper. So he took her to church and brought her back one day, with a ring on her finger and her name on the register – Ann Elizabeth Verney. It's there in the church records – seen it for myself. Of course ...' She paused.

'Yes?'

'It didn't last. In a few weeks, according to rumour, he'd found new interests. The first was some flighty little piece from Norwich. And after that the poor wife meant nothing to him. Oh, he had her fed and clothed all right, and took her walking with him occasionally for appearances' sake. But she fretted and – well, she must've gone a bit funny in the head, because as I said she tried to kill herself years ago, the first time.'

'How?'

Polly's lips suddenly tightened. 'I'm not going into more details, not now. I've had enough morbid talk, on top of poor Miss Martingdale's death. So let's think of cheerier things, shall we?'

I agreed, knowing from the past that when Polly's mouth took on that stubborn set there was no moving her.

But that evening, as the sun was a mere glimmer of fading light above the horizon, I left the house, unseen by Polly or her assistant, and dallied for a few moments at the front of the house, chatting with the old gardener who was just leaving for his small cottage – more of a shack really – near the village. When he'd left and finally disappeared down the lane, I took a stroll towards the headland in the opposite direction and at a convenient place near a jutting tump of dune not far from Verney's studio, proceeded to wait, hoping he would appear presently on his habitual walk. The hour was right, and a thin veil of mist was already rising, sufficiently fitful to obscure my presence unless he was on the watch for me – and there was no reason why he should be – yet clear enough for me to see whether or not his wife was with him. If so, it was possible the drift of wind from the sea could lift her veil for a second or a casual turn of her head might slip the knot, revealing her lovely eyes. Yes, I was certain her eyes would be beautiful, as those profiled features against the window had been when I'd glimpsed her there long ago. And so I waited with growing impatience, eyes rivetted on the sandy track, waiting for the unknown; senses attuned to seize any glimpse of her. And if she turned back, as on previous occasions, determined to follow quickly and somehow make contact.

I felt oddly excited, like a young boy at the start of some mysterious adventure. As the minutes passed the atmosphere deepened. The brooding silence had become complete, except for the rhythmic breaking of the waves below. The soughing wind had died suddenly. Loneliness seemed everywhere – a melancholy greyness echoed in the looming silhouette of the cliff head with the dark pointed roof of the studio poking towards the green-grey sky.

I drew my jacket closer to the neck as the sense of chill deepened. It was unlikely now, I thought, that if Verney *did* appear his frail wife would be with him. On that brief occasion I'd seen her the previous day she'd appeared considerably more delicate than I remembered. But there'd been no mistaking her identity, and Polly had been stupid in fabricating a story that she'd died. But why on earth should she? Unless ... I shivered violently, realising that I'd half believed her, and half not; Polly normally wasn't one to enjoy frightening anyone – especially myself who'd been such a favourite of hers when a boy. Was it possible the morbid atmosphere of Miss Martingdale's death had temporarily unbalanced me, and that my own imagination had played me tricks?

As my mind went searching this way and that, I saw the shadowed figure of Verney approaching like some rigid automaton down the lane. I drew further back into my recess between rock and sand, and as he approached the studio to the right, my heart lurched.

He was not alone.

Behind him, only a few yards away as though part of his misted shadow, another followed.

His wife, the grey lady.

Along the sandy path in front of the quaint building, he took a step or two to the cliff edge, and stood there, looking out to sea as he must have done hundreds – no, more like thousands – of times during the last ten years. I had moments of terrible prolonged suspense, watching, until she drifted close against his back and lifted one pale ethereal hand to his neck. The touch must have been feather-light, but he started and half-turned. She moved forward a little, and with a sudden movement threw back her veil, staring up at him.

From where I stood I saw her face clearly. The light for a brief interim seemed to lift, and her countenance was clear. Perfect on one side, the other a garish mask of tortured twisted features – mouth pulled upwards in a sneering mockery of a smile to a gaping hollow where an eye should have been. Horror, terror and revenge mingled in her grimace of hatred, with ivory bone showing through ravaged flesh.

It was terrible. I shuddered, and was about to close my eyes against the contorted mask when a thin arm swung out from a boney shoulder against the shocked man's arm.

For an instant he swayed, before, with a tottering effort to turn, he fell and went spinning with a wild scream into the gaping darkness below the cliff's rim. Was it shrill laughter that followed or a gull's high cry? I never knew. But after a second I saw the wraith-like grey form disintegrate into a drift of cloud, shrouding all else in obscurity.

I reached Miss Martingdale's house in a state of shock, and said nothing of my experience to Polly.

When next morning she told me that Verney's body had been found on the beach below the cliff, she merely added, 'An accident, I s'pose, but it served him right, if you ask me. Suffered all those years, she did, first from loneliness, then having to look as she did after throwing herself over that same place. Yes, straight down. Wonder she lived at all. But her injuries! Mind you, *I* never saw her face. Some of the old folks did, though. From being a real beauty, she was disfigured something awful. And all through him. So maybe he met his — what do they call it?' She glanced at me for the answer.

'Nemesis,' I answered.

'That's right. What a clever one you are, to be sure.'

Clever, was I? After seeing what I had, I'd have used another word: unfortunate.

Because I have never entirely forgotten the sight on that far off evening, and I know now I never will.

The Blue Flower

Some people believe in ghosts, other try to when a suitable seasonal occasion arises, many are completely sceptical, whilst most 'don't quite know'.

I, being a practical, frequently hard-headed businessman who'd taken off to the States in my youth to make quite a considerable fortune in mining, believed myself to be of the sceptical variety until a year ago this Christmas.

I'd heard an ancient great-aunt had been taken to hospital extremely ill, and was not expected to live very long. Well, having a vein of sentiment somewhere deep down in me bred of my Cornish roots, and knowing she had no other living kin, I decided to leave the States for the old country and visit her, providing she was still alive.

I travelled by jet to Heathrow, spent two nights in London and called on her solicitor to check the correct address of the hospital or home where she'd been taken. Then, the following morning, I journeyed by train to Penzance. As the small cottage hospital was situated some miles away − not far, incidentally, from the large family house she'd occupied all her life − I decided to have a brief look at the ancient building I'd known as a boy, then go on to 'Maddern House' on what was bound to be a rather poignant mission.

Over the telephone I arranged with the matron to call in the afternoon, late-ish, the next day, about five. So everything was scheduled and went completely according to plan, in the beginning.

I caught a four o'clock bus from Penzance, having spent my first day in Cornwall for fifty years looking round what haunts of my youth remained — visiting one or two boyhood friends still living there, and glancing round the shops for any gifts I imagined might particularly appeal to a woman of over ninety. After all, it was Christmas Eve. The weather was cold and grey, holding that feeling about it either of a heavy frost to come or even snow later. As the bus chugged upwards along the curling moorland road the sky perceptibly darkened, taking the looming hills into silhouetted shapes of rocks and furze.

At a cross-roads, from which I knew I'd have to walk, I dismounted and followed a thread of lane which the driver told me led directly to the 'old people's place' I wanted.

I stood hesitating for a moment in the grey light, trying to remember; to recall that other rambling house in its own grounds, Rosewarren, that I'd known so long ago. Then, instinctively, I turned and retraced my footsteps the few yards I'd walked, and made my way from the cross-roads in the opposite direction, along a track leading towards the coast. Bearing slightly to the left I recognised ahead of me an immense boulder known in the past as the Camel Rock because of its curious humped shape. Below, round a bend, I knew Rosewarren should be, a relic of Elizabethan days which through centuries had been altered and added to by small towers and a Georgian portico above steps with terraces on either side. In my day large windows had overlooked the gardens; presumably these remained, although the solicitor had told me the grounds in recent years had become a wilderness, neglected because 'the poor old lady' — his words — 'had been under the mistaken impression that she had no longer the means to employ gardeners'. His manner of speaking had implied she had become confused in the head through age, living alone, and constantly dwelling on a past tragedy: the loss of her lover, killed in the First World War. Yes, it was a sad story, and in the deepening twilight, with the first frail flakes of snow driven against my face on a shiver of rising wind, I chided myself briefly for choosing such a morbid evening for reviewing the past.

Then, as I approached the boulder, a glimmer of light zig-zagged across the rough ground, giving an eerie sense of life and movement to the clawing branches of thorn and

136

heather. I paused a moment, with senses keyed, watching and listening — listening to the thin soughing of the wind that gradually rose and fell in a melody of sound resembling the haunting tones of distant violins. I went on, and as I passed Camel Rock the light spread and widened and I saw it was no illusion. The long windows of Rosewarren below were ablaze with the brilliance of flaring candles and glittering crystal chandeliers, and in a white dress someone was dancing — a girl, with her arms lifted to the ever-changing shadows of the lonely room behind the glass. Yet was she lonely after all?

Awed and mystified I hurried closer to the scene, and just for an instant, as the music rose to a sweet crescendo, it was as though another — a man's — vague form took shape and held her. I rubbed my eyes while the snow thickened and the girl twirled this way and that, throat arched, dark hair flying, feet and skirts swirling as though in an ecstacy of delight. In and out of the shadows she sped, one moment nothing but a movement of flickering air, the next clarified into beauty and life. Yes, she was beautiful. Beautiful with joy and hope and love. I watched, bemused and entranced, as she took a blue flower from her hair, offered and tossed it laughingly to something or someone — her invisible companion perhaps? I do not know. It was only seconds later that the scene started to fade. I forced myself to move and rushed to the bottom of the terrace steps, to catch something more of that magic interim before it faded forever.

But it was too late.

When I stopped to gaze at the long windows all was empty and dark; an old house standing bereft and cold with snow gently pressing against its lonely walls.

Shivering, drawing my coat about my neck, I made my way back to the cross-roads, and from there to Maddern House.

To my regret I was told by the matron that my great-aunt had just died. 'Only about twenty minutes ago,' she said. 'I'm sorry that you've come all this way for nothing. Still — I'm sure you would like to see her?'

I agreed.

And when I glimpsed the delicate ivory-pale face against

the pillow, I knew. Old? Yes. But in an indefinable way eternally young, as young as I'd seen her such a short time ago, dancing for joy behind the long windows of Rosewarren.

A ghost? Had she found her young lover at last? Most would be sceptical, I guess, and think it an illusion. The significant thing was that I saw on the pillow beside her a blue flower.

'I wonder where that came from.' the matron said. 'Very odd.'

I didn't answer.

But I knew, and having seen what I did, never doubted. Would you?

The Damned

The children seemed delightful at first; there were four of them — a girl, Sarah, who was the eldest at nine years old, then Rupert and Lucy, twins two years younger, and a smaller girl, Janie, who was reputed to be different and a 'handful', not exactly retarded, but needing special care and guidance to foster what latent attributes and intelligence she had. She was only four.

It was with Janie that I was to be primarily concerned. I had taken on the job of helping out as assistant governess to the children during the summer months of vacation from university, thinking it a challenge and that the salary would certainly be welcome. The district in the border country between the Forest of Dean and Wales sounded attractive, and I thought hopefully I might find leisure moments for a little sketching.

Little I knew what lay ahead.

The family consisted apart from the children, of a newly appointed vicar and his wife. They had been freshly housed after the old clergyman's death in a modern residence on the outskirts of Hawslade village, nearer to the church than the rambling, rather derelict, old rectory. I was rather taken aback at first glance by the new house's prosaic unimaginative appearance. It was square and box-like with a conventional garden in front, oddly at variance with the surrounding landscape of lush green rising to thickly wooded hills. I'd expected — rather stupidly perhaps — an Elizabethan type of dwelling, with maybe a touch of the Gothic about it. But obviously 'Ferndale' had been built on strictly economic and practical lines — to a budget, most likely, by church authorities wanting to keep expense to a minimum.

Still, the back and the interior were more prepossessing, although from the first moment — until I met the children — I was aware of an air of anxiety, of secret worry, emanating chiefly from the vicar's wife, a plumpish but harassed-looking lady who spoke slightly breathlessly in short jerky sentences, while patting her hair into place nervously and frowning intermittently between gasps.

'I'm *so* glad you've been able to come,' she said. 'The children, you know, are darlings, but — oh, dear! There's so much to do. There's Miss Carnforth, of course, but — well, when you meet her you'll see what I mean. She's enough on her hands. You see it's Janie — and I'm not in the best of health. Oh!' She gasped. 'Don't think I'm ill or anything. But there's my husband to consider, there are duties, we're new here, and — you understand? May I call you Caroline?' she broke off, frowning half apologetically.

'Of course,' I said, thankful to be relieved of my rather lengthy surname 'Anstruthers'.

'Well then, Caroline — now that's over. Oh! The salary. I forgot — did my husband mention it in his letter? I'm afraid — '

'Yes, yes,' I hastened to answer her. 'Please don't worry about anything, Mrs Linton. I shall be glad to fit in with any of your arrangements. Truly.'

It was really rather like trying to soothe some bewildered infant. Luckily, at that moment the vicar himself entered the parlour.

He was a tall, thin, slightly lugubrious-looking man, but with a betraying twinkle at the corner of his eyes, suggesting a sense of humour beneath the dour exterior. His presence brought a more normal atmosphere to the interview, and when the children were called into the conventional sitting room my spirits lifted. Sarah was somewhat withdrawn and solemn-looking with long light brown hair that gave her a misleading, slightly old-fashioned demure expression. Rupert was thin and fair, quite handsome; his twin Lucy darker, almost gypsyish, with sharp bright eyes beneath thick brows and a touch of amusement about her lips that was mildly discomforting – why, I don't know. But Janie, the youngest, was quite beautiful with large violet eyes and curling corn-coloured hair reminiscent of a Botticelli angel. It was very hard to believe she was in any way difficult to handle, and I imagined if she was it might be because of her mother's patently tense and nervous condition, combined with the senior governess's age.

I met Miss Carnforth shortly afterwards. She was a solemn-looking long-faced woman, in her fifties I judged, who had no genuine liking for very young children. She was polite enough to me, but I sensed a certain underlying resentment – or perhaps it was suspicion of my ability to control the youngsters.

'You will have to keep a very careful watch over Janie, Miss Anstruthers,' she told me. 'Of course, she's with her mother much of the time, but when she's not she has a worrying habit of slipping away while I'm otherwise employed with Sarah and the twins. They have an hour of lessons each morning. Rupert will be going to boarding school next year. In the meantime I have to see that studies are not neglected in the holidays.'

'I understand,' I said dutifully.

'The easiest way to keep the children occupied when they are free is to accompany them on walks,' she continued primly. 'A great deal can be learned from nature study, although of course Janie is too young to go far. I must point out to you that the country round here is thickly wooded, and –' She broke off hesitantly.

'Yes, Miss Carnforth?'

'There are strange people lurking about,' she continued almost in a whisper, 'not fit company for any children of a nice famiy like the Reverend and Mrs Linton's. *Gypsies* in those dark woods at the back. I've done my best to keep the children to proper footpaths running on this side of the river. It's really quite primitive country.'

'I'm surprised the house – I should say the vicarage – wasn't built on a piece of land nearer to the village. The old rectory was quite a distance to the other side, and when the authorities built this house I would have thought they'd have chosen a plot more suitably placed in Hawslade itself.'

She sighed. 'However, we have to make the best of it. But Janie, with her propensity for wandering, is a great worry to her mother. I hope you'll be able to cope.'

Beyond answering that I would do my best, there seemed nothing else to say at that point.

For the first week the children were far more amenable than I'd expected, and seemed pleased to have my company on the picturesque walks we took from the house. These were mostly in the afternoons when Janie had a short rest following a morning's activity with me, or was engaged happily with her pet guinea pig and rabbit in the garden, where Daniel, the odd-job man, kept an eye on her.

'The child is quite safe with Daniel,' her father told me. 'They get on together, and my wife and I want you to feel perfectly free for an hour or two each day.'

'Thank you,' I said gratefully. 'But I don't want to neglect my duties. I mean – '

'Tch, tch!' He clicked his tongue. 'We're *very* grateful you could come. My wife has been – somewhat run down lately. I think the removal to this place after living so long elsewhere has been a strain. And Janie – being as she is – so highly individual – well, I'm sure you understand?'

I agreed, although I wondered exactly what it was he was preparing me for.

As I have said, those early days held no obvious hint of trouble; even Mrs Linton's spasms of nervous excitability seemed to abate once she realised I was prepared to stay with them.

It was a beautiful summer, and the countryside had an air of mystery about it that set my imagination alight. From my bedroom window at the back of the house I had a wide view of the garden which stretched on one side towards wooded hills; on the other to lush fields and a winding curve of river crossed by a bridge. Beyond that the trees thickened again into forest land, rising to the horizon in a maze of softly blended deep blue shadows intermingled with sudden splashes of gold and pale green. I would have liked to wander there on my own, but somehow it was difficult to find the time, and I had to content myself to keeping to the meadow lands nearer the house.

There was an old gnarled may tree with leafless twisted

branches at the bottom of the garden, standing near the gate leading into the fields. Only one or two withered-looking leaves clung to it, and I doubted that it ever bloomed.

'Oh, but it does,' Sarah told me. 'It had a flower on it when we came, but Lucy tore it off and put it in a jam jar. She likes picking things. But it just died – quite quickly. It was funny, and do you know?' She paused, staring at me very intently.

'Know what?' I prompted her.

'When I touched it – the tree, I mean – afterwards, it – it seemed to *groan*. Can you imagine it?' And she laughed, a little shrilly, in a way that put me strangely on edge.

This was my first intimation of something slightly odd and offkey, tainting the atmosphere. But I pushed it to the back of my mind, concentrating on the normal pleasures of life with my new charges. 'Charges' of course is the wrong word to use, or at least so I thought during those early days. I was young myself, and I'm sure the children appreciated it. They appeared to have no wish to tease, or test my capabilities to keep gentle discipline; neither had I any desire to enforce my will. In any case, except with Janie, I was not required to. The duty properly fell to Miss Carnforth.

There were times, I admit, when I could easily have joined them in having a little harmless fun behind her back, she was such an unattractive, colourless, drab-looking creature. Naturally I refrained, inwardly making an effort to be ashamed of such childish instincts. But it was difficult – the scents, sounds and joys of summer were somehow so enticing and lush with sweetness that year. Buttercups were gold at the foot of the hills, and long grass was a sea of rhythmic green blown on a warm wind. During my first fortnight the last small leaf had already fallen from the old may tree, but lilies in their succulent foliage floated on the river's surface, and clumps of blossom still foamed about the hedgerows.

'Silly old thing,' Janie shouted one day, kicking the ancient may while I held her hand at the bottom of the garden. 'Booh, *you*!'

My hand tightened slightly on hers. 'That's not very kind,' I said, 'the tree can't help being old. It will have flowers again next spring – perhaps.'

143

Janie tossed her fair curls. 'I don't care. I don't like it. *She* says – ' The small child broke off, frowning.

'Who?' I asked. 'Who says what?'

'Nuffink. I don't know. Nuffink!'

I was curious and wanted to know to whom she referred, but Janie's lovely eyes had clouded and her mouth set mutinously. So I dropped the subject and said instead, 'Shall we make daisy chains, Janie?'

She gave a little skip, and smilingly agreed. 'Oh, yes. Daisy chains to dance in round that funny old tree.'

This hadn't been my idea but I saw no objection to it; so we both picked bundles of the starry white flowers, and presently were seated on a tummock of short dry turf while I split the slender stalks to make chains. I finished a long one for Janie, and she squealed with delight when I placed it over her head. Then with a jump of joy she ran a step ahead of me and the dance started – a harmless expression of childish happiness. But I could have sworn at one point, as we circled round, that the wizened trunk shifted for a second, emitting a rasping growl.

Later I told myself it had just been my imagination. There had been a gentle wind blowing at the time, which had stirred one of the branches. Still, despite all commonsense reasoning, the incident was somehow disturbing, mostly I suppose because of the little girl's complete abandonment which had suggested a sinister, subtle touch of ritualistic fervour. However, the notion quickly passed, and during the next few days the little girl became noticeably more quiet and acquiescent. When I look back now, I realise that the other children also seemed preoccupied at that time – a little too good to be true in behaviour. I even found time to start painting for an hour one afternoon when I did a rough water colour sketch of the river and hills beyond. That was the beginning. The beginning of – other things.

It was as I returned across the field towards the back garden that I noticed a group of youthful figures gathered near the gate. The dying sunlight of late afternoon caught the fair hair of the smallest, lighting it to palest gold. Undoubtedly Janie; I was surprised, because I'd left her with her mother that day. She'd told me a dressmaker was calling to fit the child with a new frock.

I paused for a few moments, puzzled, watching from the shadows of an oak tree. Besides Janie, the twins and Sarah were there, and one other I didn't recognise. They were obviously deep in conversation, heads close, as though deeply involved in some childish plot or adventure. While I waited the stranger turned her head, glancing back in my direction as though she sensed my presence. Although some distance away, her countenance for a brief second was comparatively clear and not at all prepossessing – dark, sallow, and rather old-looking for a youngster. I was mildly taken aback, wondering whatever the vicar's children and such a shabby, wild-looking girl could have in common. A gypsy perhaps, I guessed, or more probably some tinker's daughter trying to ingratiate herself with them for her own interests. I moved forward, although by then she'd turned away, and as though possessed of second sight, and aware of my disapproval, had left the four, and cut off across the buttercup field to the left. At least, I *think* it was to the left; but a thin silvery summer mist was rising, and when I rubbed my eyes to get a clearer look there was no sign of her at all.

'Who was that girl you were talking to just now?' I asked the children when I reached them.

Sarah raised her finely arched eyebrows. 'What girl?' she asked, as though I was a little mad.

'Oh, don't be silly,' I said. 'You know very well. The dark girl in the brown dress. I saw her, Sarah, across the field.'

She shook her head. 'There wasn't one. Honest. I expect it was a shadow – or the light.'

'Yes, it must've been,' Lucy joined in, and gave a little giggle. 'A shadow.'

A warm wave of annoyance pricked the back of my neck. They were playing with me. Lying. And I didn't like it.

'Rupert,' I said, more sharply than I'd intended, 'come on now. Not that it's important really. Except that – well, she didn't look the sort of girl your parents would have wanted you to be friends with.'

The boy stared at me blankly.

'I don't know what you mean, Caroline.' The way he said

my name was confusing somehow. Too grown-up for his age.

'You know very well. *That girl.*'

He shook his head. 'There wasn't any girl,' he affirmed, and then he grinned, 'unless it was Janie here.'

Janie laughed. Her large eyes sought mine.

'Do you think it was me?'

'No, I don't,' I told her, 'and you know it wasn't.'

She shook her head and I knew from the now familiar mutinous set of her lips that I would get nothing out of her.

I was disappointed; it seemed that any feeling I'd had of having won the children's confidence was unfounded. With my own eyes I had seen the bedraggled-looking girl. It was natural perhaps that they'd realise her company would be disapproved of by their parents or the rather grim-faced governess. But I was young. The last thing I would have done would have been to tell tales. I could have met her myself, if they'd been honest and allowed me to. But it appeared I was just another interfering grown-up, out to spoil their fun. Well, if that was their idea of me, I thought determinedly, I'd play the part and keep watch.

And that is just what I did – not obviously but subtly, whenever I caught a glimpse of the older children meandering casually on their own to the far garden gate and the may tree. Once there, they would stand together as though whispering, then the three heads would turn towards the strip of woodland, and I knew they were waiting for someone – the girl. It was an instinctive knowledge, emphasised by the very stillness of their young forms. From my bedroom, as I have already said, I had a good view. But nothing materialised until one afternoon when Mrs Linton had taken charge – as I thought – of Janie for an hour, and Miss Carnforth had made a quick jaunt to the village for a loaf.

The weather was sultry, holding the heavy ominous quality of approaching thunder. Over the distant trees a belt of clouds was massing against the yellow sky. If I'd more time, I thought, I would have attempted a water colour. But in a short while I was due to take Janie for a stroll before tea. Her mother was always wearied by her after half an hour or so. I sighed. I really did feel mildly depressed that day.

146

Still, there was no point in glooming so I decided to have a short wander around myself, without bothering about the children.

It was then, before leaving the window, that I saw them — Sarah and the twins running towards the gate, with Janie in the rear, skipping elf-like through the long grass. At the may tree they waited for her. Sarah knelt down to say something. Janie stood quite still for a moment or two then suddenly jerked into action, pointing eagerly to the wood. The children stared, heads thrust over the gate, while I watched, intent on a shadowed shape moving from the trees. After a quick glance back at the house, the boy slipped through the gate followed by Lucy and Sarah, with Janie rushing ahead and quickly overtaking them.

The brown figure swung leisurely but purposefully across the grass, black hair straggling to her waist, long skirts dragging behind.

I stood perfectly still, where I could see but not be seen half behind the window curtain. When the five met, they turned in a group and moved back to the may tree. There was no way of guessing what they talked about as they stood close, obviously deep in some childish — or *was* it really so innocent as that? — conference. Neither was it possible to have a clear glimpse of the strange girl's face. But an overpowering sense of evil possessed me, for which, later I was mildly ashamed. After all, children did indulge in secret games, and however unsuitable the girl might be considered as a companion, she was nevertheless a character and being so completely different in background and blood to the four young Lintons, might attract them for that very reason.

Wondering if I had the opportunity and time somehow to reach them unobserved before the group broke up, I hurried downstairs and left the house by a side door which opened on to a path leading in the shadows of a laurel hedge towards the far gate. I moved as quickly as caution permitted but not quickly enough. By the time I reached the unkempt stretch of lawn the children were already ambling back, Sarah in front, followed by the twins with Janie lagging behind. There was no sign of the girl.

Sarah glanced at me slightly defiantly, I thought, although

147

Lucy looked innocently pleased to see me, while her brother grinned with a gleam of knowing mischief in his eyes. I suspected they were waiting for and already had an answer to a query from me about the girl, and for that reason I didn't refer to her. Janie came running with a bunch of cowslips in her hand. 'Here you are,' she said, 'for you.'

I knew very well it was extremely unlikely she'd picked them, because there were no cowslips growing anywhere near the house. I'd made a pretty good survey of the flora and fauna of the surrounding district, and hadn't found a single one.

'How lovely,' I said. 'Where did you get them?'

She shrugged, and turned her head to the field. 'Over there.'

'Where exactly?'

'Just there.'

'That doesn't mean anything.'

'Oh, don't be stuffy, Caroline.' Sarah's voice held a contemptuous voice. 'What does it matter?'

I might have lost my temper, but at that moment Miss Carnforth appeared from the house. She had a rather ungainly walk at the best of times, and on this occasion marched forward with long strides in a mannish way, leaving a trail of trodden grass behind her.

The children stood in a line, staring belligerently at her approach.

'Where *have* you been?' she demanded. 'You know very well you were all due for a Natural History lesson. And you, Caroline — ' she turned to me, an unbecoming flush staining her long yellowish countenance ' — you were supposed to have charge of Janie merely for a short time while Mrs Linton rested. Yet you all go wandering off — ' She broke off, noticing the faint supercilious smile on Sarah's face. 'Don't stare like that,' she said coldly. 'Come along, all of you. Lately, I must say, you've been behaving very badly indeed. And I will not have it.'

I couldn't help feeling that the stupid woman was making a great fuss over nothing, and yet — glimpsing the conspiratorial look passed between the children — I almost pitied her. Only Janie seemed completely unaware of any tension.

Looking guileless and angelic, she said, 'Mummy won't mind, not when she has my flowers – Caroline's carrying them 'cos my hand's hot. Look! They were for you, but p'raps we'll give them to Mummy, shall we?'

There was something frightening in witnessing such a capacity to lie plausibly from a young child, and in her talent to beguile and charm. Miss Carnforth softened immediately; the unprepossessing features relaxed, and the angry flush faded. 'What a nice thought, Janie. Of course we'll give them to your tired mama.'

She grasped the little girl's hand, and said to me in more conciliatory tones, 'You can have Janie in a few minutes, Caroline. I didn't wish to sound too cross, but there are certain rules here, you know, which have to be observed, I'm afraid. Keeping an eye on children all the time isn't easy. You'll find out in time.'

I had found it out already, and realised that my temporary post was going to be more of a bind than I'd anticipated. It wasn't the work exactly. Janie, after all, was the only one I was directly concerned with, and for the most part she was comparatively docile with me, and at times an enchanting companion. If she was backward in certain practical matters, she was surprisingly quick in an intuitive unchildlike way, almost as though she possessed an elemental knowledge denied to adult human beings. 'It's going to rain,' she might say when there was no trace of a cloud in the sky. And a little later the first few drops would fall, blown on a sultry wind.

'Come and smell the rain, Caroline,' she urged one morning, and I went with her to the back door, from where the damp grass scent crept with refreshing sweetness from the garden, mingled with that of lime and roses and distant river smells.

'I fink that old tree likes it,' she told me, with her eyes turned towards the withered, gnarled shape near the far gate. 'Sometimes it squeaks. It's thirsty then. Have you heard it squeak, Caroline?'

Something in her tone puzzled me. Something undefinable yet sinister, filled with an unnatural curiosity, possessing a touch of – cruelty, perhaps?

I pulled her back into the passage. 'All trees creak sometimes, Janie,' I remarked. 'It's just the wind blowing through the branches.'

'There isn't any wind today,' the child told me solemnly, 'and I heard it. *Screaming*, Caroline.' She gave a little giggle.

'When?' I asked sharply. 'You've only just had your breakfast.'

She gave me a very straight glance then looked down.

'Shan't say,' she replied. 'It's a secret. She says – '

'Who?' My hand tightened on the small soft one. 'Who says what?'

Janie shook her head. 'Not anyone. Not really. I was playing. It's a game.'

I smothered a sigh, and after a few moments the uncomfortable interlude was over and my young charge appeared just like any normal happy little girl again. But my sense of foreboding gradually seemed to intensify during that hot summer. Yes, the weather became increasingly, unusually hot as the weeks passed – so warm that by early September the grass had turned yellowish and the leaves of the trees were already becoming brittle brown. I fancied a faint aroma of scorching permeated the air, almost as though the distant moorland hills were about to ignite. Miss Carnforth's temper worsened, and the more she scolded the children the more openly they defied her. Mrs Linton took every chance of retiring to her room, and when she came downstairs was forever fanning herself, or demanding attention with sighs and moans of apology for being such a trouble. 'It's my heart,' she wailed frequently. 'Oh, I know I'm a useless sort of creature. I can't help it, though, Caroline dear. Poor Edward' – referring to her husband ' – I should be doing so much *more* for him. But parish work isn't really my – Oh dear! What *am* I saying? Do forgive me.'

On such occasions I did my best to soothe her, telling myself she had probably become neurotic in the first place through bearing such a strange wilful family of children. To have four in six years – including the twins, of course – was nevertheless quite an achievement for a highly-strung woman. Dealing with them wouldn't have been a problem in these early days had they been placid or more predictable – but

150

they weren't. Each in his or her own way was completely individual, even the twins, yet sharing some secret bond with their siblings that was disturbing. And as the nostalgic atmosphere of autumn approached, that sense of alliance − of sinister single purpose − deepened.

I tried to convince myself I was imagining things − making mountains out of molehills − it was just that I didn't understand youngsters as I'd thought I did. But it was no use. The stillness of the days, the early mists creeping from the woods and rivers to the garden, the yellowish oppressive skies and haunting doom-like sense of things long gone − together with the intermittent vision of the bedraggled brown girl hovering just in sight − all combined to make me edgy and apprehensive.

Sometimes I caught a glimpse of a shadowed form standing on the verge of the distant wood, watching, always watching, and I knew it was she. A moment later she would be gone. I'd rub my eyes and tell myself they had deceived me, knowing deep down it wasn't so. The girl had been there.

There were times, too, when Sarah and the twins managed to lure Janie to the gate, and if I chanced to see, I'd wait unmoving by my window until a fifth form joined them, and they'd huddle together in a bunch, gesturing and talking − whispering, I guessed − about Heaven knows what. But I knew it was of nothing good.

Miss Carnforth also had become aware of something going on. Twice I noticed her striding over the brown grass towards the gate as though bent on breaking up the meeting. But when she arrived there was no one there but the Linton children. Once I saw her shake Lucy hard by the shoulders. Then Janie kicked the poor woman. I ran downstairs and out into the garden to intercede. But when I got to the old may tree all was quiet. The children were looking guilelessly and uncomprehendingly at the governess as though she had gone mad.

I asked what was wrong. Miss Carnforth stared at me almost belligerently, obviously not wanting to confess her outrage, which resulted from a kind of shame on her part that she could have been tricked so disgracefully by young children. 'Nothing is wrong,' she said coldly, though her yellowish complexion was an ugly crimson. 'We are late for tea, that is all. You needn't worry, Caroline.'

'Oh. I just wondered if that awful girl was being a nuisance.'

For a moment the poor woman looked nonplussed. 'Girl?' she said questioningly, and from that one word I was convinced she'd seen her but would not admit it.

'There was no girl,' Sarah said, icily brazen.

Janie giggled. She was quite clearly enjoying the confrontation and for the first time I realised that the unpleasant character never appeared on the scene unless the youngest child was there. Was Janie then the link, the thread that bound the others to whatever sinister plot was being hatched? The possibility made the whole thing somehow more menacing.

Perhaps I should have brought the topic up with Miss Carnforth openly and discussed what was to be done, but she gave me no chance. There was nothing sufficiently concrete to bother the vicar with, and to contemplate worrying his scatterbrained wife was unthinkable. So silence prevailed about the matter. I found myself looking forward to the day when the vacation ended and I left the uncomfortable household to resume normal studies at college — even counting with relief each day that passed and marking it off in my small notebook.

I no longer watched for the drab shadowy figure emerging from the wood, or tried to keep Janie under my eye. I'd discovered she had a strange grown-up capacity for looking after herself, or rather keeping out of physical danger. In any case, if she was missing for a brief time I knew she was almost certainly with the other children and did my best to allay Miss Carnforth's fears; but the poor governess was quickly becoming more neurotic even than Mrs Linton. Whether the vicar noticed anything amiss I didn't know. He assumed an air of forced good humour in the presence of the family, to which his wife made a pathetic attempt to respond; but the falsity of these occasions increased rather than assuaged the sense of strain about the house.

Meanwhile the days grew more chilly, filled with the insidious encroaching smells of fallen dead leaves and bonfire smells from the woods. The old may tree was completely bare

152

now, with gnarled twisted branches reaching like deformed blackened arms towards the sky. It was stupid of me, I know — and childish — but I kept my eyes away from it as much as possible. There was something menacing to me in its gaunt starkness — something curiously akin to the dreary bedraggled-looking girl whom, although not always to be seen, I sensed was forever on the fringe of the household, watching and waiting for — what?

I was soon to know.

During my last week at the Linton house it happened.

There had been no recent rain, and the insidious smell of rotted dying things seemed to enclose the house like a shroud.

By afternoon I felt stifled. It was as though the earth itself breathed out stagnant heat, although the air was chill at the same time, brushing the skin with clammy damp. Nothing seemed clear. A thin misty pall clouded the atmosphere, even inside the houe, creeping up the stairs as far as my bedroom and lingering there until I could bear it no longer but went down, meaning to take a stroll to the village. The hour was supposed to be my leisure time, and Janie, I presumed, was with her mother. Where the other children or Miss Carnforth were I neither knew nor cared. All I wanted was a quick escape and sight of normal people in a normal environment — a chat hopefully with the village postmistress, or a cup of tea perhaps in the one small cafe where home-made cakes were still provided in a quaint old world atmosphere.

I hoped, but of course there wasn't a chance.

As soon as I reached the hall, the uncanny sensation swept over me that something was wrong — far, far more wrong than usual. It wasn't only the complete silence. It was as though everything in that square, modern, unlovely brick building held its breath while evil wove its insidious pattern of corruption. I had meant to rush out and away, regardless of any lingering sense of duty. But against my will — against commonsense or feeling for self-preservation — my whole being was impelled to the side door leading to the garden, as a fly sometimes appears magnetised to the spider's web. The tang of burning I'd noticed at intervals during the last few days deepened and intensified, draping the bushes and grass with veils of grey; only it was not mist — it was smoke.

I paused for a moment or two, with my heart quickening and thumping against my ribs.

And then I heard it — a high-pitched scream of terror followed by a gurgling, groaning sound interspersed with the crackle of wood that had the impact of obscene laughter. There was a further scream. I moved then, and started running across the dried grass towards the may tree, blinking my burning eye-lids, trying to see through the black and crimsoned pyre of hungry grey that coiled serpent-like to the lowering sky.

I knew the tree was alight, but I knew also, with mounting terror, that it was not only the old tree that groaned. There was something else there — something too horrible to contemplate. But I had to look. I *had* to, because in that moment of aversion I heard something else — a child's high-pitched giggle.

Just for a few seconds the smoke wavered and cleared, and the grotesque scene was clear. All four children were there, with the odious brown girl a mere shadowy elemental shape behind. Janie, like some devil's imp, was clapping her hands and dancing gleefully round the obnoxious spectacle. I was too shocked by revulsion to cry out or even move. It would have been useless had I made any effort. The smoke was too thick round the stunted skeleton tree, and those few moments, though brief, were sufficient to reveal the dead charred body of Miss Carnforth, impaled and hanging from the stark blackened trunk. Her head, tongue out, was sunk from its broken neck on to its burned corpse. There were no longer any eyes — only scorched holes surrounded by bedraggled still sizzling hair.

What exactly happened after that I do not know. For the first time in my life I fainted.

There was an inquest, of course, and following Sarah's testimony backed up by that of the twins that they had heard screams and had run from the house to find Miss Carnforth alight and Janie crying, a verdict of accidental death was recorded.

'There was nothing anyone could do,' Sarah said in her

quiet, gentle, almost pious way. '*Poor* Miss Carnforth.' And she shed a few heart-rending tears. When questioned I could add nothing further. There was nothing to say that would have been believed. In any case, the vicar and his poor wife had more than sufficient to worry about. For Janie had disappeared – completely. And to my knowledge, despite the intensive and prolonged enquiries and searches made by the police, she has never been seen again.

All that was a long time ago. Thirty years. The tragic story is known now as the 'Linton Mystery'. And mystery it indeed is, one on which I still ponder. How exactly was Miss Carnforth hung on the tree? Who set it alight and by what means? Is there an old petrol tin lying somewhere at the bottom of the river? Were gypsies involved? Or did some tramp leave burning paper around that ignited the tree, and the unfortunate woman in trying to put out the flames become their tragic victim?

No one will ever know, or even guess, an inkling of the truth.

Except I, perhaps, who have no proof.

And Janie? Ah, yes, Janie – wherever she may be. I prefer in dark moments of remembering to believe the wicked demon that possessed her exists no longer, either in this world or the next, and pray the small spark of good in her – the soul – has somewhere found peace.

Perhaps one should be sorry for the damned.

I *have* tried to be – however ineffectually. The truth is, of course, I would rather not recall the matter unless forced to: through a chance phrase on someone's lips, a dry acrid smell of smoke on a yellow autumn day or a high-pitched giggle from childish lips. Small things, but potent.

There is another angle to the story which I discovered years ago when perusing an old history book.

Near the site of the ancient may tree a woman, Anna Cox, condemned to death by the Church, was burned centuries ago as a witch. To the last she denied the charge, but all appeals failed.

So perhaps, in her own gruesome way, she has had her revenge.

It was certainly a mistake for a vicarage to be built on

that particular patch of ground. I heard fairly recently that the family moved soon after the tragedy, and incidentally that the other young Lintons grew up into perfectly normal well-balanced human beings. Shock, apparently had mercifully erased the terrible incident from their minds. I prefer not to speculate as to their part in it.

And the brown girl? Did she ever really exist?

So much hinges on the answer which I have long since ceased pondering over. Whether tangible or not, the shadow of evil is a dark and powerful force, and one I prefer not to dwell upon.

Tit-For-Tat

I suppose many people might think me a bit mean − the way
I'm acting to Alice these days. But really! When you come to
think of it, she's got off lightly after what she did to me those
years ago. There has to be a kind of justice somewhere, that's
what I say to myself when I look back − and Alice certainly
asked for it.

Of course you don't know what I'm talking about. How
could you, when you've no idea − not an inkling − of the
deep friendship there used to be between us.

Even as children we were close, living next door in the same
street, going to the same school and having the same little
secrets, as children do, if you understand what I mean. There
were little differences, of course − in appearance mostly.
Alice was never what you could call a beauty, being the lean,
pale kind, tall and leggy with a yellowish complexion, and
teeth that jutted out. Whereas I was plumpish, pink-cheeked,
with masses of fair hair that was my mother's pride. Every
night, even when I was tiny, she put it in curling rags so I'd
look nice the next day.

As we grew older the difference showed more, naturally.
It was always me the boys liked, but Alice had it in other
ways. She was the clever sort. My, the way she could talk!
Oh, yes, I admit it. What she lacked in looks she made up
for in brains.

The trouble was, of course, that men didn't seem to appreciate it. They wanted the other thing. You know, that certain
bosomy 'something' you're either born with or not. And that
was where I won. I was a bit sorry for Alice in those days,

and got her to try lipstick and swing her hips a bit when she walked. The trouble was that Alice's hips weren't – well, they weren't the swinging kind. In fact, you'd hardly know she had any at all. And the bright slash of red on her mouth didn't have the right effect because of her jutting teeth. So I gave up trying to help her, and concentrated more on my own pleasures.

It was when we were both seventeen that Alice got a job in the local library and I had my first serious affair with Arthur Battram. Arthur worked in a chemist's shop, and was never what you could call a Romeo or heart-throb, but I knew he liked me – I'd only got to cast an eye or shrug a shoulder in his direction, and he'd come trotting after me like a lean shaggy dog 'on the scent', as they say. Well, that's how I first met him, buying Rose Musk over the counter. Later, when we were properly acquainted, I quite though he'd marry me after all the favours I'd allowed; but somehow he never came to the point – which was a bit humiliating, when you come to think about it.

My mother thought so, too. It wasn't that I'd been passionately in love or anything like that. But there weren't many available young men around at that time, and I'd fancied a wedding ring on my finger.

The upshot of it was that Ma and I moved to another district. More 'high class', she said, where 'Mr Right' would obviously appear one day. Meanwhile I took a job at a hairdresser's where I certainly smartened myself up with a perm and more expensive make-up. I put on a little weight, but the men I met those days didn't seem to mind – in fact, they appreciated it.

And so time slipped by, waiting for Mr Right, who was slow to turn up, and meeting Alice occasionally for a coffee together, exchanging gossip, or a drink at The Bull. I generally had pink gin or a cocktail whereas for Alice it was strictly non-alcoholic – fruit juice or tonic water.

I couldn't help thinking she'd become a bit of a prude, and her looks if possible had worsened. Admittedly she was knowledgeable with a whole heap of clever talk at her fingertips or – to put it accurately – on the end of her tongue. Politics, literature and music, the classical kind. No jolly joking or pop. As for television! Well, to put it bluntly, Alice had become just a dreary bore, partly I guess because of all those books, and because she hadn't got what it takes to catch a man – not even without a wedding ring. Whereas I . . . oh, I had my little affairs through the years. But time passed, and we were both still unmarried when I got a surprise one day – quite a shock really! – a letter from Alice telling me she was engaged, and would like Bert to meet her old friend. Could she bring him around some time, any evening, to Acacia Villa? That was the home in the select suburb left to me on my mother's death.

I said yes, of course, with just a teeny weeny tinge of – not jealousy, I was never the jealous sort – envy niggling in my bosom. I was rather proud of my bosom, actually. Bosoms were in vogue at that period – you know, the Raquel Welch era! – and who had thought a plain Jane like Alice would have hooked a husband before me? Oh dear, that remark *does* sound a little common, but you know what I mean.

And so it was all fixed. I made myself up, subtly but daringly, adding pink gloss to my lips, and had my hair permed and tinted to a really ravishing corn gold. I bought a new dress too – blue satin – and one of those alluring corselettes to wear under it that were advertised to contain curves but also enhance sexual allure. Well, after that, I wanted to impress Alice's fiancé, didn't I? For her sake as well as mine. A woman should always strive to look her best in company. Always, I told myself resolutely.

So the evening arrived. I had arranged to have some buffet refreshments in the lounge – cute little cucumber and tomato sandwiches, sausages on sticks, with banana trifles in glasses and many other titillating little etceteras to tempt the palate. And of course a bottle of the best white wine, and sherry as well in case Alice's intended preferred it, with fruit juice for my old friend.

To my astonishment when it came to drinks – oh, what a vulgar expression! – I discovered with quite a shock that Alice's habits had changed. 'Wine, if you please, Doris,' she said with an almost smug tone in her voice. 'The white sort. Bert prefers sherry.'

I glanced at Bert because it seemed to me a little infradig

159

for any woman to speak for a man. He just nodded his head, saying nothing but staring at me all the time. I couldn't help feeling a weeny bit flustered, and maybe flattered, because I knew my bosom under the luscious satin hadn't escaped his attention. Not that Bert Stringer was anything much to look at, and certainly no answer to a maiden's prayer. He was thin, like Alice, with a rather long jaw in a lean face, and wore spectacles. But there was a certain learned, penetrating air about him that told me he was no fool. Then why, I wondered, had he fallen for Alice? She was as plain as ever – more so if anything. Her teeth seemed to protrude further, and her silly way of talking – that put-on ridiculous accent of 'plaise' instead of please; you know the kind of thing – positively rankled and got on my nerves. She was wearing green, too, which only emphasised her sallow skin and drab hair. 'Alice, dear, you poor creature,' I said to myself, really thinking of Bert. 'Being in bed with *her* will certainly be no joy-ride.'

And from that moment I decided to instil in him a vague suggestion of what-might-have been. A bit bitchy of me, maybe, but surely natural under the circumstances? Alice turning out to be such a show-off, parading her intended before my eyes like any sexy glamour girl. Perhaps if she'd been a little less cock-sure I might have acted differently. As it was – well! I played all the tricks I knew, being my sweetest, most charming and kindly self, flattering him in any unobtrusive way I could. And when Alice broke into the conversation with bursts of clever talk about books, I resorted to silence with just the slightest inclination of the head – that's the lady-like way to put it, isn't it? – and always maintained my dignity.

The upshot of that evening was, as you might expect, that Bert soon 'phoned me and enquired if I would like to accompany him to a concert the next day – Bach, I think, at Coronation Hall. I knew I should be deadly bored, not being the classical type, but I accepted, and that was the beginning.

Alice never got Bert to the altar after all – *I* did.

Oh, I was sorry for her in a way, but she really shouldn't

160

have been so uppity and toffee-nosed at our little get together.

I wore pale pink at the wedding, with a small halo hat covered in tiny rosebuds. Alice was invited with other guests to the chapel where Bert was a prominent member, but she didn't attend the ceremony. As we drove away to the reception I caught a glimpse of her, though, standing behind a few well-wishers on the pavement. She looked absolutely green.

Now, I'm not going to say married life was all romance and a bed of roses! But then you don't expect it, do you, with a man like Bert? I mean he was all for learning and giving his opinions on politics and the state of the world and that sort of thing, whereas I didn't care a damn. Excuse me, I don't usually go in for swearing. But there are moments — especially in bed — when a feminine woman like me with a good plump body and fine shape yearns for other things. And I must admit that although Bert did his best at the beginning of our life together, those moments gradually grew fewer and fewer, and in the end declined altogether. However, I put on a good face of contentment and connubial bliss to the world, and soothed any injured pride I felt by remembering I had a wedding ring on my finger. I was Mrs Bert Stringer.

Then, one dreadful evening two years later — dreadful because of the consequences — Alice reappeared at Acacia Villa. Just to see how her old friends were, she explained with a stretched, gleaming, new kind of smile on her plain face. I had to ask her in naturally, and Bert literally jumped from his chair when she entered the lounge.

I couldn't blame him. She looked so different — wearing high heels, and a smart orange-coloured suit, with a sort of tiny pill-box hat pushed forward, half covering her knobbly forehead. She wore gloves, and just a hint of make-up that somehow drained the yellow from her skin. But there was something else quite startling — her teeth. They had changed dramatically and no longer stuck out at all. In fact, two rows of perfectly white dentures gleamed like pearls between her scarlet lips. She'd obviously had the old ugly things out and made this special visit just to show off the new look. In fact, I had a pretty shrewd idea she could even have manipulated the whole operation and occasion for that very reason.

To show off.

Her revenge!

And revenge indeed it was. It came out casually – over-casually – during the first five minutes of our conversation that she'd 'come up on the pools'. Quite a tidy sum that took my breath away, and I could see Bert was impressed too. I began to feel slightly flustered; I think actually the fluttering feeling in my chest was the beginning of my heart trouble – the trouble that eventually had such dramatic and terrible consequences. You see I was not feeling at all my best that day. For one thing I was tired, and hadn't troubled with any mascara or 'rose-blush' – the things that are so essential to middle-aged beauty. My hair needed a new perm too, and my dentures compared with Alice's were a shade dreary and had sunk in a little. Yes, I think Alice's brilliantly gleaming teeth, her swagger, new smartness and clever talk, completely bowled Bert over. Especially the teeth. He never took his eyes off her the whole of that ghastly hour. I did my best to be gracious, of course, but what with my fluttering heart and knowing I looked my very worst that day, the whole meeting was just a dreary failure for me.

Perhaps you can guess what happened.

A month later – only two days after I'd got my own new pearly set of dentures, which were quite striking, I can tell you – Bert left a cold little note for me on the mantelpiece when he went to a new job he'd just acquired at the opposite end of the town. In it he said he was leaving me and joining Alice, and hoped I'd be civilized and give him a divorce.

'I'm sorry for your sake, old girl,' he wrote – Fancy that! Old girl – 'but you can't say ours had been much of a marriage, now, can you? The truth is we've nothing in common – never did have, and never will – whereas Alice and I were meant for each other from the beginning. Cheer up, it's not the end of the world.'

For me it was, though, if you can call death the end – although I manage to conjure up a bit of haunting now and then. I expect that surprises you a bit, my being a ghost. Well, it shouldn't really, not after what I'd gone through. It was my heart did it, of course, and Alice's teeth combined with the pools were responsible for that. Men always fall for a bit of money. Mind you, I don't go in for complete materialisation — too exhausting for an inexperienced newly-born ghost. But I do manage the teeth. And when Alice wakes at night sometimes, suffering from a nightmare, there they are — *mine* — my new dentures that cost me so much, grinning from the bedside table where her own sit so smugly in a glass of water.

She screamed once, giving Bert quite a jolt. He sat up as she explained.

But when he looked, of course, I'd faded them away.

So, you see, you can't really blame me for my bit of psychic tit-for-tat.

I don't envy her, not really. Bert was never much fun in bed, and the way things are, never will be. Poor Alice.

The Stone Unicorn

For five years, since his retirement from the stone mason's and carpentry business that had been his life during the previous sixty decades, old Jethra Luke had been banging about, hammering and chipping at a secret fabrication in his shed. No one in the small town had the faintest notion what it was – no one, that is, but Marty Poole, the halfwit; and what Marty knew he kept to himself, being as stubborn as a mule in his loyalty to Jethra, who was his hero and friend.

Some suggested, with sly winks and knowing glances over pints of ale in The Mariner of an evening, that the old man – getting towards ninety, and of a religious turn of mind – was fashioning a monstrous tombstone for himself; others, that it was some fancy chariot to carry him heavenwards when the last trumpet sounded, or even perhaps a weighty coffin!

Whatever it might be it was certainly no ordinary undertaking. Nothing so sensible as a good boat, a table, chest, or sound old-fashioned wardrobe. The secret creation evolving in Jethra Luke's shed was more solid than wood. Granite or stone – you could tell that, by the sound of it – and a sufficiently wearying business to leave a wild look in the old man's eyes whenever he stepped out for a breath of air, or to fetch his bits of shopping from the fishermen's store.

These short interims were generally taken at twilight, and a queer couple they looked indeed as they padded along the wharf: Jethra a little ahead of Marty, wearing his old jersey and wollen cap with a bobble on top, head thrust forward, thin hair blown in the wind; Marty, tall, bent and gangling, only a step behind, carrying a string bag. Their very walk, ponderous and purposeful, gave their sombre figures a haunted, doom-laden quality against the fading greenish sky.

They spoke to no one on the way. It was as though both were equally driven by the dark mission that filled Jethra's days, relentless and unknowable.

The odd couple lived together on the premises which had belonged to the Luke family for generations, neither having kith nor kin of their own. The routine of their mutual existence was a mystery. When they ate, what they spoke about in rare leisure moments − if at all − was beyond speculation. All that registered to the outside world was the hacking and hammering.

But Marty knew.

Marty, in this one respect, was favoured above all other human beings, and watched wide-eyed, open-mouthed, as the hours, days and weeks went by, seeing Jethra's creation gradually take shape from chisel and hammer − his 'hoonicorn'.

'*Unicorn*,' Jethra corrected him, 'there edn' no haich in "unicorn", 'cept where the horn is.'

'Horn like a hoss, eh, master?'

'Horses haven' no horns,' Jethra said, with a strange dreamy look coming into his eyes. 'Only cows and unicorns − and unicorns are special. Folk doan' b'lieve in them any more, and that's why this one's comin' alive, see, Marty?'

Marty nodded, but there was no comprehension in his vacant eyes, only wonder. Wonder that anything or anyone so learned and above all other men as old Jethra was, should have chosen him as his buddy. It was true that Jethra, from his earliest days, had showed a potential addiction for knowledge, and his preoccupation with the 'hoonicorn' dated from the short term of schooling he'd had as a child when a sensitive youngish woman teacher had encouraged his reading capacity by lending him a book of ancient legends and folk lore which through their illustrations had stirred his imagination profoundly.

'Are unicorn's really true?' he'd enquired one day, fascinated by the picture of the noble-looking horned animal, rearing with hooves raised as though galloping to the stars.

'If you believe in them, and want them to be,' she had answered evasively. 'Noble and beautiful things are born in the mind, Jethra — thinking minds, like yours and mine.'

She had smiled, and although he had not completely understood her, the unicorn had remained embedded in his deepest being as a symbol of the unobtainable secret wonders of the world.

And now, after all these years, he was creating one. Something to defy and put to shame much of the ugliness that seemed to be sweeping through civilization, spoiling life and especially that of his own small town where the old cottages were being pulled down and modern atrocities put up. The people, too, were changing. Most of the old folk had gone, like the herring which had fled when the Gulf Stream had changed course. Summers weren't calm and quiet and beautiful like they once were. Instead, the raucous voices of strangers filled the evenings. Not that he minded furriners, if they were the right kind. But the tourists now who filled the twisting narrow streets at holiday times seemed to have no true feeling or care for the place. They left ice cream cartons and greasy paper bags reeking of chips littering the gutters after days of poking round juke shops where fish lofts and net works used to be. And it wasn't only Treliss — all the world seemed to be going wrong, filled with drugs, bad behaviour and fornication. False gods were worshipped, and ugliness eating the good things of nature away. That was the reason for his unicorn. Something beautiful and rare created from a fairytale of his youth.

Nowadays fairytales weren't believed in by the young. Their interest was in guns and computers — money grubbing in big cities — drugs, vice — shouting and screaming on those squat boxes called 'The Telly'. Oh, he didn't blame them. Not really. It was the fault of their elders, the parents who'd somehow lost their way in life and got values upside down. The magic — the true magic — would soon be lost forever: of learning the ways of nature, of bird and beast and the secret beauty lying hidden in the dreamy pools and coves of the coast, and in the wild lanes curling through lush valleys of the hills. He recalled, as a young boy, wandering

166

from the little school where Miss Wilmott taught, over the hill to his grandparents', Rosewarren way, where his Grandma always had a piece of heavy cake ready for him, and on cold days a bowl of steaming broth, before he returned to his own home half a mile away by the sea. They were his mother's parents, owners of a smallholding where there were a few animals and fowl. Life had been a busy one for them, often hard but somehow fulfilling and rich with affection. What a wondrous thing, Jethra had often thought, if a unicorn could appear there. But though he'd wished and wished, it never had.

Now he realised unicorns had to be created from the fire of physical effort and imagination. And he was doing just that. Building and carving a symbol that would enrich rather than defile his own corner of the world; calling up the dreams and visions of countless pioneers and inhabitants of Treliss who now lay buried in the cemetery sloping down the far slope of Rosewarren Hill beyond the town. He'd contrive somehow to stir them to life again. Oh, it wasn't a thing he could put into words. But through his craft, hands and staunch dedication, he could do it. And Marty, his companion, simple though he might be in mind, had that certain quality of innocence and unsullied devotion which kept at bay any temptation to slacken his efforts.

And so the work continued, and the days passed by, until a certain evening when Jethra laid down his tools, rubbed his hands on his apron and stepped back to take a critical look at the completed sculpture.

No modern thing, no ugly monolith meant to bewilder ordinary decent folks into believing themselves clever beyond normal understanding, but something so proud and wild and free, its spirit – carried from the fire of Jethra Luke's heart – might light the flame once more of far-away forgotten things. A flame so bright that the dreams of the dead themselves would be called to life again.

Ah, yes! he thought, with satisfaction. His unicorn was indeed a splendid thing.

So that night, late, with only a small torch to guide them, Jethra and Marty between them managed to hoist the stone unicorn into a cart kept in the back yard, where Marty –

167

who was tremendously strong-shouldered despite his thin gaunt form – was proudly settled between the shafts, elated and eager to drag the precious sculpture – the revered 'hoonicorn' – to its site on the outskirts of the cemetery.

The evening was a typically Cornish one of fitful moonlight filmed intermittently by a curling sea mist, swirling down cobbled streets and humped grey cottages – a night of magic in which reality could so easily become diffused into illusion. Except for an occasional light behind a curtained window, there was no sign of human life. If any rattle of the cart was heard, no one bothered to pry. Few holidaymakers were about at that time of the year and most of the locals were abed, so for the most part all was dim and shrouded in mystery.

From the sea somewhere a ship's siren hooted, followed by the high shrill crying of a gull. Up the hill, head thrust forward, Marty pulled, with Jethra pushing behind.

When they reached the cemetery a wan beam of moonlight filtered transiently through the drifting mist then died again, absorbing the area of gravestones and memorial slabs into sullen grey.

Marty paused a moment to get his breath.

'Come on, lad, don't give up,' Jethra wheezed. 'Not far now. You know where it's to stand. That patch of common land at the far end. Good view from there. Proud an' fine for all to see – my unicorn.'

'Ar, the hoonicorn!' Marty agreed, and giving a great sigh of satisfaction, lowered his head and started pulling again.

Occasionally, when the moon half slipped from behind a drift of coiling cloud, glints of pale marble and black granite glimmered eerily amidst ancient stones and crosses. Shadows briefly filtered across the scene, giving an eerie sense of movement and phantom life.

But it was not until Jethra's creation had been heaved laboriously from the cart and finally, after tremendous effort, hoisted on to a hummock directly overlooking the burial ground, that the miracle happened.

Proudly, with its front hooves lifted, head raised, single horn pointing allegorically to the heavens, the legendary creature seemed to arch its neck further for a second, while the clouds and mist parted, sending a flood of brilliant blue radiance, giving a dazzle of splendour about its flanks, flared nostrils and curved shining head.

'The *hoonicorn*!' Marty breathed. And it seemed the slabs of tombstones opened; wraiths of forgotten lives – of dreams and aspirations never realised in physical existence, but invoked from sleep by the fire of man's longing and fervour – rose one by one from their earthly beds and with exulting ethereal arms reached towards the hidden stars: Thomases and Williamses, Pengellys, Paynters, Treens, Clarks, and countless more from long-gone generations. The unending throng who'd started life's journey as pioneers in different spheres on land and sea – some to succeed, others to fall and fade before their time. A phantom throng circling joyously in defiance of Time's laws round stones and monuments, while frail whispered music rose on the sighing wind.

There was Tommy Jones, a seaman of the nineteenth century who'd painted in his spare time, and hoped to immortalise with his brush the folk and places he'd seen in foreign climes. He'd been jeered at by the authorities. Then Sarah Phillips, the widow of a fisherman, who'd raised her only son by hard work, hoping to leave him with a good wife and family at his cottage door, only to see him lured by bad company to a wretched end. Then Jonathan Smith, and poor little Lily Bream – oh, so many! So many defiled and disappointed – sleepers in the dark earth, who were risen as immortal dreams now to fulfilment.

Awed, Jethra and Marty watched as those ghosts of life – of phantom fagility, assumed the ethereal substance of spiritual grace. Very rhythmically in a pale grey cloud, lit to rainbow transluscence they drifted towards Jethra who observed no skeletal frames through the mist – only the undying creative surge kindled to life by his own strength and faith, to awakening.

He took an involuntary step forward. In a circle they seethed round him. Once more he heard the faraway voice of his young school-mistress whispering sweetly, as sweetly as the sighing wind, gentle flowing of streams over stones, and brush of air through leaves and trees: 'Yes, unicorns are true, Jethra, so long as you believe in them.'

And he believed.

For a second or two youth returned to him in a wave of joy. His bent spine straightened; he stood proudly erect, eyes fixed on the blazing creation of his dreams – the unicorn. Above him the magnificent creature was lit to splendour by a wild flood of brilliant moonlight bursting through cloud and frail mist. Shadows and shapes billowed round his feet while the whole world seemed to sing. 'Ride, Jethra. Ride,' echoed the voices of the dead. 'Tis yours to ride – to ride the mysteries of the world, Jethra – of space and time and distant stars. Ride, ride!'

He glanced down once; they were all there, the ones he had known – pale ghost faces of lost days come to life again. Ivory bones immortalised and beautified by memory, refurbished with the flesh of dreams. And a song seemed to swell his whole being, a song of triumph and a knowledge greater than earthly things. For that fleeting period Jethra indeed became a king. He took one leap and was astride the fabulous beast. There was a rumbling and a quiver of the earth as with flying tail and hooves the animal galloped straight up into the magical moon-washed sky, carrying Jethra to the far realms of eternity.

Then, gradually, the light deepened from a fleet of clouds blown from the sea, obscuring the shrouded dead. One by one the graves yawned, reclaiming their own.

A thin wind sighed and soughed round the trees and tombstones; whispered voices and music died. And then came the rain.

It was morning when Jethra was found lying stiff and cold by a pile of wet broken stone, including a smashed animal head, his friend Marty staring down on him.

'The hoonicorn,' the youth was muttering. 'It was the hoonicorn. I see'd en ride it – up – up –' And the bemused eyes were lifted to the sky.

'Poor thing,' a woman murmured to the little crowd standing by. 'He doan' know what he's saying, that's for sure.'

'A great shock for en,' another remarked. 'They say it was a real thunderbolt. My, what a storm! Would you b'lieve it?

170

An' to think old Jethra had been workin' so hard for so long just to end up with a hoss's head and a load of stones f'r all the trouble he did take.'

'A funny hoss at that,' someone else remarked pityingly.

''Twas a *hoonicorn*,' Marty protested, 'an' he rode it. Right to Heaven, he did.'

No one took much notice of Marty, of course. Born simple-minded, it was assumed the shock had proved too much for him and shattered what few wits he'd ever had.

The freak storm for a time became the popular topic of conversation at The Mariner, and throughout the small town. One of the first inhabitants to arrive on the scene before Jethra's body was taken away commented several times on the strange look of youth transfiguring the old man's face. 'And so serene,' he added, 'that's the word – like as if he'd seen some shinin' vision before the bolt struck. An' maybe he had – who's to tell?'

'Who indeed?' someone murmured. 'No one can say but old Jethra hisself, an' he's not likely to come back an' tell, I'm thinkin'.'

There was a short silence as the last remark registered uncomfortably. Folks died every day, of course, in one place or another, but Jethra Luke's passing had certainly been strange and extremely dramatic. No one really believed in ghostly visitations, but rumours start in peculiar ways, and in time can grow into a kind of legend – which is certainly what happened at Treliss.

On certain nights, it is said, should thunder strike from the sea, the form of a gold-horned creature can be seen through a flash of lightning, rising to the storm-tossed sky. Bravely astride, a figure clings to its wild free neck, and then – visitors are told – 'Jethra rides again'. The graves open in the old cemetery, and singing can be heard by those with the ears to hear.

A tantalising story, no doubt, and one to titillate the imagination, but no more than that.

Only Marty knows differently, and he is now too old and wrapt in memories to bother about tourists. The sight of his bent, quaint figure plodding up the hill to the cemetery with a bunch of primroses, snowdrops, or merely a touch of greenery in his hand, has become accepted as part and parcel of the town's history and normal life. No one bothers to wonder concerning his thoughts as he sits by the humble stone commemorating Jethra's life and death. And if they asked there would be but one answer.

'The hoonicorn. Jethra's hoonicorn. I seed it. I knows.'

Which makes him, in his own way, a character more unique, and far-seeing perhaps in some ways, than most of normal humanity.

A Quick One

When I entered the tap room of The Mariner most of the crowd there were gathered round the bar discussing ghosts and hauntings. A suitable subject for the season, perhaps, but not one that appealed to me particularly just then. I was tired after the long journey to Cornwall from London. That same evening I had to drive a further five miles to the outlying hamlet where my sister and her family lived. It was cold, and for the first time I wondered if the Yuletide visit was a mistake. Sleet had been falling since I left Bodmin; my engine had jibbed unpredictably en route, and I'd not had a decent meal for eight hours. So my spirits as well as my body were chilled as I drew up at the old inn.

The hostelry stood on the moors overlooking the harbour of St Inta. The thought of a pint by the glow of a good fire in quietness and warmth was cheering. It was natural, therefore, that the morbid subject under discussion depressed rather than elated me.

The group there was a mixed one — fishermen and farm workers, I guessed, a tin miner or two, and several more flamboyant looking individuals who could have been artists or writers. They were talking of hauntings. At any other time I might have been stimulated by the company. As things were I felt mildly irritated, and took my glass to a recess where a cheerful rosy-faced customer was sitting, apart from the rest.

He was elderly, with a white beard, pink cheeks and twinkling eyes under a fringe of grey hair. An amused smile crossed his face when I joined him.

'Always the same, surr,' he said, 'they will get down to rum tales of "ghoulies and ghosties" at Christmas. Though why they should always turn to graves an' dyin', beats me.'

He chuckled, and his head shook for a moment over the mound of his navy jersey. I noticed a cap on his knee. A fisherman probably, I thought.

'You're quite right,' I agreed, 'and I don't feel like that sort of stuff just now.' I paused, then went on to tell him of my uncomfortable journey down.

'Ah, well,' he said, 'tek no notice of them theer tales, surr. Cod's wallop, that's all 'tes. Sit back an' enjoy your mug full, that's what I do say. Good ale this. Best in all Cornwall. Bin comin' for years here, I have — on an' off, as you could say.'

'So you live in these parts?'

'Roun' an' about,' he answered. 'Roun' an' about. Not like them theer trumped up ghosties as seem to bob up just once a year as though they wus bits of a plum puddin' or turkey!'

He laughed, a low rumble of sound that held a comforting ring in it.

I began to feel better.

We were silent for a few minutes, then he remarked reflectively, after rubbing a broad work-lined hand over his grizzled moustache, 'D'ye know, young man, for the life of me I jus' can't imagine why ghosts, if there are any, have to be such sad an' woeful critters.'

'No,' I agreed, 'neither can I.'

'Good, good.'

He winked, pulled on his cap, stood up and said, still smiling broadly, 'Good night to 'ee, surr, an' the compliments of the season; all the best, an' Bob's y'r uncle.'

I nodded.

The next moment he had vanished like a puff of smoke into thin air.

Desire

For their first month after opening as the owners and licensees of The Green Man,' Rosemary and Cliff Drake, newly married enthusiastic escapees from the rat-race of town life, were delighted with their project. The inn on the outskirts of a small town in a picturesque country district was of the Elizabethan era, cunningly modernised while retaining its air and appearance of antiquity. It was large enough, as Rosemary pointed out, to cater for a small number of paying guests if they wished, during the summer. There was besides a delightful garden area which sloped down over a stretch of lawn to a curling river with hills rising gently from the opposite bank to heather-carpeted moorland.

'Oh, but it's lovely – lovely!' Rosemary exclaimed, as she had done on previous occasions. And then the inevitable question, 'But I wonder – why so cheap?'

Cliff laughed.

'Thinking of a ghost, are you? A haunting?'

'Well, of course not. Don't be silly, darling. But –' she paused for a moment knitting her brows '– it *could* have got a name for something, couldn't it? I mean, people are superstitious. And if something horrible had ever happened here in the past –'

'I wouldn't be at all surprised at that,' her husband conceded lightly. 'Horrible things happen in most places at some time or other, and The Green Man is pretty old. But in time they're forgotten.

'Not always,' Rosemary interrupted quickly. 'And you remember when we were looking at the deeds and talking

175

to the estate agent, he had to admit it'd changed hands quite a bit during the last few years. You took that point up with him and cross-questioned him about plumbing and dry rot and all the snags there could possibly be ...'

'Naturally. And there wasn't a thing wrong.'

'Not obviously, no. But he wouldn't refer to anything psychic, would he?'

'Now look here, love.' He took her by the shoulders and stared deep and long into her lovely eyes. 'We made a practical commonsense business deal with a straight-forward bloke, and that was that. We just happened to be darn' lucky. The reason the last couple left so quickly was simply to join their grandson and his kids in Canada. So for Pete's sake don't go getting funny notions about ghoulies and ghosties!'

Rosemary relaxed. 'All right. I suppose it was a bit potty of me to suggest it. Probably it was thinking about that room –'

'What room, for God's sake?'

'You know – the one at the top in that funny little tower, with the dormer window. It's being boarded up seems odd somehow.'

Cliff sighed.

'Here we go again. You heard the reason for that – it's not safe. Any bad gale could take the roof off, and if someone was up there –'

'Then why wasn't it taken down?'

'Expense, probably.'

'Oh, well, if you say so.' She shrugged and grinned suddenly. 'It must be wonderful to have a down-to-earth reasoning nature like yours. I expect you're right. So no ghosts! No hauntings. Just you and me – the new licensees of a perfectly marvellous-to-be hostelry.'

It wasn't actually just Rosemary and Cliff, of course. There was the gardener who had been employed at The Green Man since his young days and was now grizzled-looking and old – a silent, rather truculent character, but dedicated to his work and who certainly managed to keep the grounds in order. Then George, the bartender, retained but only on a part-time basis as Cliff meant to manage the tap room himself. Rosemary, determined to plan ahead for her paying guest venture and also do most of the cooking, took on a daily girl from the village for domestic work, and after the initial opening the arrangement appeared to be working smoothly with the promise of a successful spring season ahead. It was decided that there would be no advertising for guests that first year.

'But if anyone should ask, perhaps,' Rosemary temporised, 'and seemed our sort – you know.'

'Colourful, and a bit vague, and haywire sometimes,' Cliff finished for her.

'Not at all. Everything's going to be very business-like. Meals on time. Prompt opening hours for regulars. Of course –' her voice took on a slightly dreamy note '– it would be rather nice if an artist or two looked in occasionally.'

'Would it? Artists are notoriously poverty-stricken – especially the "colourful", free-beer type.'

'Like you, do you mean?'

Cliff shook his head regretfully. 'I never got that far, as you well know, darling. Just a year at art school, then dear papa's business. God, how I hated it! And there's no need for you to grin, Mrs Drake. There may be more potential genius hidden beneath this blue shirt of mine than you'll ever dream of.'

Rosemary, very much in love, reached out her arms to him, drew down his head and kissed him. 'I don't want a genuis, I just want – us.'

And so it was.

Inhabitants of the village agreed tentatively that the new folk at the pub seemed a nice enough couple.

'A bit on the young side, though,' the postmistress confided to her neighbours. 'Still, mebbe that'll be an advantage. Too wrapped up in each other to go thinking things.'

'Thinking things? You mean . . .?'

'You know very well what I mean, Mrs Bun. *Her*!'

'Well, it could be all tales after all,' the other woman pointed out after a pause. 'What I mean to say is – none of us here in the village've ever seen 'er, and George laughs

177

it off as just bunkum. The truth is, tales get about. That's all. And the last tenants were certainly odd, say what you like. It's obvious, isn't it? Taking off to Canada like that, just as soon as they was properly settled in.'

'But they weren't settled, Mrs Bun. That's just it.'

'Ah, well!' Mrs Bun gathered up her stamped envelope and shopping bag and went to the door. 'We shall know soon enough, I s'pose. But they say this new young woman is a good cook. Makes real tasty snacks. Arthur and I are going to look in one evening and sample things. After all, you must admit, having a well-run attractive local will be a change.'

'Yes, if it comes off, but new brooms sweep clean,' the postmistress quoted forbodingly. 'I prefer to keep my fingers crossed.' And she immediately started busying all ten of them with a pile of untidy envelopes waiting to be sorted.

When the first flow of idle gossip concerning the new landlord and lady of The Green Man had died down, interest naturally subsided. Everything seemed to be going well, the only criticism from locals being that the new decorations in the bar parlour were a bit startling and new-fangled to be right for the place. But as the natives generally gathered in the tap room, and the beer and pasties were good, it 'didn't make no odds'. In fact, as one farmer remarked to another, Saturday night could be more convivial with their wives and womenfolk in a 'separate compartment' as it were – sampling the little pastries and cakes that Missus Drake was ready to serve in the back room and leaving the men to their own brand of bawdier company round the bar.

So on the surface life at The Green Man proceeded on an even keel.

Except for one thing – not really important, as Rosemary confided to Cliff, but odd. Disturbingly so, since the general atmosphere of the inn held that warm, faintly malty smell associated with all hostelries. It first became noticeable after the couple had been in residence for a month: a faint insidious perfume, a fragrance of rose with a musky tinge that drifted at various times along the first landing, permeating halfway down the stairs. During the busy hours naturally it wasn't there, or in the early mornings when healthy smells of cooking and baking issued from the kitchen. But later -- especially after hours, when customers had left – it couldn't be disregarded.

'What is it?' Rosemary queried of her husband. 'You must have noticed that sweet smell, Cliff. It comes and goes, but sometimes it's quite strong. Like now.' She sniffed, and stood quite still, halfway along the landing to their bedroom on the second floor.

Cliff wrinkled his nose. 'Yes, I did catch a whiff of it last night, and thought you might be preparing a new seduction act for your ageing husband.'

She laughed. 'Don't be silly! After just six months that's not very complimentary, Cliff Drake.'

'I was only teasing.'

'I know. All the same, it's odd, isn't it?'

He shrugged. 'Maybe it comes from the garden. That rose tree near the door. There is a draught sometimes.'

'But there's no wind today at all, and it doesn't come from there. I've noticed particularly it's strongest near the foot of that narrow staircase winding up to the tower. Honestly! I haven't said anything before because I knew you'd scoff and say I was imagining things, but it's true. Come on – I'll prove it.'

To satisfy her they went along the landing, passed their own room and took a short turn to the left, from where the unused spiralling steps branched off. At the top, the boarded-up space confronted them, blank and uninteresting, badly in need of paint.

'I'll have a go at that,' Cliff remarked. 'A coat of nice bright green would brighten this dreary corner.'

'Yes – but the scent, Cliff.'

He wrinkled his nose. 'Whew! You're right. Maybe the walls –'

Was it her fancy, or did a soft throaty chuckle stir the air?

'Listen!' she said.

He glanced at her, bewildered.

'Didn't you hear?' She broke off helplessly.

'I heard nothing, and anyway –' he tried to joke '– smells haven't vocal chords. Come on, darling, I've had enough of staring at this gloomy hole.' He paused, adding after a moment, 'And there's no smell either now, except dust. Are you sure you've not been having me on?'

She shook her head. 'Quite sure.' She felt utterly bewildered because what her husband had said was true: the smell had died as quickly as it had risen. No musk, no roses or potpourri or whatever it had been, no low-throated husky chuckle, just silence except for a creaking of floor boards when they moved.

And so it went on.

Sometimes, very occasionally, there were days when it seemed the phenomenon of the unexplained perfume had either evaporated, or – as Cliff liked to think – been a matter mostly of imagination augmented by the lingering odour of fresh paint in the building combined with old wood and furniture, especially of the cedar variety. Cedar itself had a strange sweet tang of its own, as everyone knew.

But Rosemary sensed otherwise, and despite those rare free intervals, the scent continued to return after varying intervals. She was worried. A little of her enthusiasm for The Green Man waned, became clouded by uncertainty, and a habit of sniffing and listening during quieter hours at the inn developed. Cliff was quite aware of his wife's preoccupation, and feeling frustrated said one day, 'I'm going to have that damned tower opened up. The wood's got worm starting anyway. Then, if necessary, I'll get the tower taken away, and be blowed to expense.'

Relieved, but slightly worried at having to cut further into their savings, Rosemary said, 'Are you sure?'

'Yes. There's a bloke I know in the town who'll do it as reasonably as possible. A good chap. I'll get on to him next week.'

But before he could institute his plan, something happened.

The summer dusk had faded into the velvet softness of early night. For some inexplicable reason Rosemary had felt unreasonably tired and gone to their bedroom soon after the last customer had left, leaving Cliff to lock up and see everything was in order for the morning. She had put a loose wrap round her shoulders, and was seated in front of the dressing-table mirror when she fancied she heard a faint rustling sound from the landing, and turning her head saw a thin rim of light zig-zagging in a quivering line from the crack between floor and door. It was only fleeting; she rubbed her eyes to make sure and all was as it should be, with the sound of Cliff's footsteps approaching from the top of the main staircase. A second or two later the knob of the door turned and Cliff entered, bringing with him, to her dismay, an overpowering waft of the sickening perfume.

Her look of alarm and startled exclamation of 'Cliff!' took him by surprise.

'Whatever's the matter? You're frightened!' He was all concern.

But when he came towards her she jumped up. 'Can't you smell it? And there was someone − something − outside, before you came.' She broke off, breathless.

Bewildered, he frowned slightly, stood with his head lifted, drawing a deep breath of air into his lungs, and agreed uncomfortably, 'Just a whiff, perhaps.' But − good grief, darling, we've had it before, far stronger than this. It won't hurt you! Heck!' He ruffled his hair in exasperation. 'There's a perfectly reasonable explanation − must be. And we'll find it, of course we will. Something to do with that old boarded-up cubby hole. We agreed, didn't we? Then try and forget about it until I get hold of Streeter − that's his name, Bob Streeter, the man I told you about. He'll soon put your mind at rest.'

'But the light?' she persisted. 'There was a light outside.'

'A light? Oh, come now!' He sounded mildly impatient. 'Probably my torch. Those stairs are dark, and there's no moon tonight.'

'Don't try and put me off. I'm not an idiot, or − or neurotic. You think so, I can see by your face. There was something there!'

181

Feeling unable to deal with the matter in a rational way, Cliff resorted to teasing.

'Ah, well, maybe I've got a secret mistress – some sly little tart locked up in the bathroom!'

He expected her to respond in her usual laughing, light-hearted way, come to her senses and see the joke. But she didn't.

'Oh, don't! How can you?' She was obviously ruffled.

He grimaced and gave a sigh of exasperation.

'What's the matter with you, Mrs Drake? If you want spanking I'll willingly oblige.' He did indeed look briefly angry, although she knew the threat was nonsense. It was the first time though they'd come near to quarrelling. She softened suddenly, and was about to rush into his arms when a very faint seductive chuckle – the same odious murmur she'd heard before – broke the moment of closeness between them. She stiffened. 'There!'

'What?'

'You heard, didn't you? You must have. A – a sort of laugh.'

He looked discomfited.

'Rosemary, my love,' he said in conciliatory tones, 'no one laughed, because there's no one about but you and me. Darling –' he drew her to him then, and she did not resist ' – in an old building like this there are bound to be occasional peculiar noises and unexplained chinks of light. Now, listen.' He put his hands on her two shoulders and stared very directly and closely into her face. 'If you're not happy here, if the work and the atmosphere are too much for you, we'll get rid of the bloody place, sell it and start all over again, something different, somewhere else. Our love comes first. Remember that, I mean it. You've only got to say the word –'

'No, no,' she interrupted, suddenly vehement. 'I love it here. The Green Man's perfect, and I'm not over-tired – not often.' She smiled. 'Anyway, we took it wondering about a ghost, didn't we? So if there is one, as long as you're here with me, I can cope.' Her natural resilience had returned as if by magic. 'In fact, maybe we could use it for advertising purposes.'

182

He kissed her promptly. 'That's my girl. And now, get that fussy thing off you and into bed. I want you, Rosemary. God, and how!'

He proved it that night, not once but many times, in a manner she had never experienced before. Always their passion had been mutual, but this time there were periods of ravishing lust that left her weak and even a little shocked.

The next morning Cliff appeared slightly subdued, a trifle shamefaced, at breakfast. The night's session was not referred to, and afterwards the day proceeded normally with Rosemary adopting an air of exuberant practicality that deceived everyone but herself. Relaxed and once more at ease, during most of the day Cliff managed to put the whole incident to the back of his mind, and when at odd intervals the memory recurred hazily, it was with a faint sense of surprise and lingering pleasure. Always before Rosemary had evoked a sense of chivalry and sexual respect in him forbidding any show of deeper, primitive passion. He loved her truly – he always would – but it came as a secret gratifying shock to him to realise he was capable of so much more. And she hadn't resisted – or if she had, there'd been no sign of it. What a clever luscious little madam she was beneath her innocently fresh exterior! How warm and soft her fragrant flesh – the feel of her breasts and buttocks – her lips and tongue ... Or had that been in his imagination? Had it *really* been Rosemary?

At this point he pulled himself up abruptly and sternly diverted his thoughts into healthier, more normal channels, vowing inwardly it should never happen again. They were honest, straightforward lovers – almost like teenagers. Yes, that was it. Innocent in an old familiar way. He revered her; always had. God help him if he ever came near to sullying their precious relationship!

That evening he tried to prove the quality of his affection, whispering words of endearment, endeavouring to soothe her so their true relationship could be restored. But Rosemary resisted, and he was hurt. However gently she spoke, despite the pleading little-girl smile on her lips, he was rattled.

'Darling,' she begged, 'I *am* a bit tired tonight, do you mind? It isn't that I don't love you. You know I do, but – '

'Of course,' he replied abruptly, turning his back on her. 'Okay. Last night was too much for you. I understand perfectly.'

She put out a hand, touching his shoulder gently.

'Cliff, last night has nothing to do with it. Please – ' If he had turned to her then all might have been well, but he didn't, and with a sigh she buried her face in the pillow, apart from him.

Oblivion came to her soon after and she slept, leaving Cliff to lie awake, with a strange burning anger in him like a torrid flame refusing to be quelled.

Presently he got up restlessly to take a glass of water, and as he did so a wave of the familiar heady perfume drifted through every crack of the room, cloying the air with its insidious tempting odour. He stood for a moment, glass in hand, fancying he heard something – the rise and fall of a murmuring whisper that could have been the wind's rustling through leaves from outside, or a woman's throaty chuckle. Automatically he put the glass down, went to the door, turned the handle quietly and glanced out. At first he saw nothing. Then, as he waited, staring intuitively up the landing, a dim blueish light penetrated the greyness with a blurred incandescent quality, near the turn leading towards the small staircase. Very gradually, after fading then reappearing, the light resolved into the plump sensuous shape of a woman's form, back view – thighs and buttocks large and radiant beneath a swirling shadow of darkness, presumably her hair. The vision was so momentarily compelling Cliff took an involuntary step forward. Then, following a further chortle of subdued laughter, the form disintegrated, and all was once more dark and still, the air chill and free of perfume, the corridor curiously bereft of life.

He tried to assure himself afterwards that the incident had been some strange illusion due to the misunderstanding with his wife, and too much whisky perhaps, during the evening. Yes – it might have been the latter. And for the first time

184

it occurred to him that he had been drinking more than usual lately.

Why? He wasn't by nature the drinking type of fellow – a fact he'd prided himself on before taking on The Green Man, realising that any successful landlord wanting to keep his health couldn't afford to be. Maybe this recent habit – not addiction exactly, he'd see he never resorted to that – was simply due to nervous tension, a reaction to the changed life style which after all had demanded a good deal of thought and extra work, not to mention financial juggling.

Such commonsense reasoning restored his equilibrium, and for the next few days nothing inexplicable or offkey happened. He was able to joke with Rosemary, and she in turn recovered her normal vitality and good humour, although he fancied there were odd intervals when she was watching him more closely than usual, slightly apprehensively, for any change of mood or sign of his acting out of character. Silly girl! he thought. That wild night had simply been a release of tension from the strain of getting the inn to rights. Now everything was settled and their popularity becoming daily more assured, with 'regulars' and new visitors from further afield, they could afford to relax and get the daily routine on a completely even keel. There were still one or two things to be done, of course, including the opening and demolition if necessary of the small tower room. About this, Cliff set off one morning to see the man he knew in the village. Everything was arranged for an inspection the following day, and on his return Cliff seemed his old buoyant self, and was particularly attentive and considerate to his wife.

'You've got to get out a bit more, love,' he said once. 'I know this place is your "baby" – well, not quite!' His face wrinkled with good humour. 'But you've done a hell of a lot in creating it – baking, painting murals, and all those individual touches that make it unique. But still, you should do a bit of walking around. That was partly the reason for coming here, wasn't it? To the country.'

She smiled. 'I know. And you're probably right. I'll take an hour off now and then – after you've dealt with that

185

wretched cubby hole. I still don't like it. The sooner it's done, the better.'

He agreed, and the following afternoon the plaster and heavy boarding was all removed, leaving a pile of dust, building waste, and rotting wood on the floor. Cliff and his companion set to work clearing it, refusing Rosemary's offer of help; it was during their absence carrying a heavy load downstairs that the sickening odour of perfume mingling with that of dark decay returned. At the same moment she imagined, staring into the interior, that a blurred human shape emerged from the shadows then quickly disintegrated, leaving only a small area of greyish light from the narrow window, thick with filaments of cloying dust and cobwebs.

Hesitantly she stepped inside. Paper dangled in shreds from the walls; one worn rug stood on bare floorboards by a narrow bed. Under the window was a carved bench, and nearby a single chair. From a hook near a small table in a corner an exotically embroidered wrap of some kind hung under a film of cobwebs. There was a scuttling near Rosemary's feet, and she saw with a horrified shudder the grey shape of a rat scampering to a hole near the bed. Air from the newly opened doorway whispered uncannily round skirting board and by worn eiderdown, faintly stirring the threadbare rug as though touched by invisible hands. The whole atmosphere was of life long departed, but somehow potent still and aware of the living. There were remains of dead foliage and flowers of some kind in a cracked jug on the chest. A few dead brown leaves drifted for a second across the rotting wood then crumbled to dust.

Wanting to rush away, yet glued to the spot by some unseen influence and her own insatiable curiosity, Rosemary stood motionless, her heart pumping unevenly against her breast.

Someone once had lived and breathed in that fetid place, she thought. But who?

For an instant the unanswered question seemed to envelop the drab interior with its sinister, prison-like walls, draining life and energy away. Then, mercifully for Rosemary, the two men returned, breaking the unholy spell.

186

If her husband was aware of any uncanny influence, Rosemary didn't wait to find out.

'It's an awful little room,' she exclaimed, gripping his arm. 'How on earth are we going to clean it properly – so rotten and decayed? And smelly. Ugh!' She pushed him into the corridor. 'You'll have to get a new door made. Quickly – soon. Tomorrow. A strong one. It won't take long, will it? Just a door, then – something more permanent.' She broke off, gasping slightly.

'Here, steady on,' Cliff said, staring down at her from bewildered, puzzled eyes. 'You were the one so keen to get it opened up – well, now you can see. The junk'll have to be cleared out first, but it'll only take an hour or two. My pal Streeter here will get it shut off again as soon as possible. With bricks, if you insist. But when it's cleaned and disinfected, though –'

'Yes, yes,' Rosemary broke in before he could finish. 'And then the whole landing could be redecorated again, so that there's nothing left of it to be seen. *Nothing*.'

Cliff stared thoughtfully at her for a moment before pointing out that the idea had been to have the whole tower taken away. 'And that can't be done in a few minutes,' he said, frowning slightly.

'Don't worry about the old tower. Leave it.'

'It's a matter of safety,' he remarked. 'Have you forgotten about the roof?'

She shook her head. 'No, but it's been like that for umpteen years so it's hardly likely to start tumbling at this point, now is it?'

He shrugged, bewilderment turning to anxiety. 'What's the matter with you, Rosie? You're frightened. Now come on, out with it. Tell me.'

'You know,' she replied. 'You've noticed the smell yourself, and I don't believe you haven't seen anything –'

'Such as?'

'Oh – don't ask such stupid questions! The light. That – that – that woman. The succubus. It *must* be a succubus. They call them that, don't they – ghosts. Hungry, sexual ghosts.'

He simulated a laugh, but it didn't work. Neither could he

187

honestly deny what she'd said. He *had* imagined something in rare moments – the luscious shadowy suggestion of fleeting blue light in the corridor, quivering into a sensuous vision of large buttocks and thighs; the slow movement of a head turned over a plump shoulder, with a swirl of black hair. He had dispelled it as an aberration of his senses, or tried to – but had remained rooted to the spot until the shape had faded into the wall near the blocked door.

Sweat had trickled from his forehead and the back of his neck under his collar. At the same moment an overwhelming rush of desire had filled him. Each time the incident had lasted only seconds and afterwards he'd felt ashamed of his own gullibility. Imagination – that's all it was, he'd told himself determinedly, with a feeling of self-disgust. Due to reaction probably, and a certain frustration at Rosemary's recent coolness in bed. Poor girl, though. She was probably just overtired. They could well both be, he reasoned. Despite its charms, the Green Man had entailed rather more hard work, both physical and mental, than he'd anticipated. But they'd get over it eventually, and everything would be fine. His wife was quite right. The sooner that damned cubby-hole was dealt with efficiently and finally, the better.

The business took longer though than he or Streeter had bargained for, due to quite unexpected small mishaps or hindrances. A hammer was missing or a screwdriver lost. Certain materials necessary were in short supply. Streeter inadvertently hurt his thumb. Oh, so many small incidents that delayed progress, and during that time Rosemary's nerves became edgier and Cliff began to look strained and drawn, though he didn't complain. But regulars noticed.

'Our new landlord doesn't seem quite himself these days,' one said to another. And the comment in reply was, 'Maybe he'll take off to foreign parts, same as the last un.'

Even Rosemary forgot her own fears in a sudden realisation one evening that Cliff had lost weight recently. She was all compunction, pulled herself together and said, 'Knock off for tonight, Cliff. You look absolutely exhausted. I can manage the bar with the man.'

He complied without argument, and was on his way along

188

the landing to their room when he saw the luscious back view of the woman's shape slyly emerge from the shadows by the half finished door. A fit of trembling mingled with a shudder as obscene desire overcame him. Yes, he realised the sensation was obscene, and managed to grip the knob of the bedroom door with one hand, the other lifted to his face, covering his closed eyes. At the same moment a drift of the hated sweet perfume followed by a low chuckle drifted on a cloying wave of air, enclosing him in its insidious aura of hungry lust.

'No,' he whispered in husky protest, 'no − no −' His fingers tightened on the knob and the door swung open as he fell, to lie panting, covered with sweat, on the floor. After a lapse of time − how long he had no idea − he managed to get up and drag himself to the bed, where he lay until his breathing eased and the weakness of his muscles had passed.

Gradually faint sounds from below registered: muffled conversation, the tinkle of glasses, all the familiar everyday sounds of a popular bar. Presently he got up, faced himself through the mirror and saw with disgust what a mess he looked: wan, greenish-pale, untidy hair flopping over one eye, tie askew, and eyes wild and staring in his gaunt face.

'God!' he muttered. 'What a sight. Heaven help me to get this damned thing − whatever it is − out of my blood.'

He did his best to tidy himself, and when Rosemary entered the room later, flipped the pages of a book idly, saying he'd had a good read. His manner was flippant, controlled, but she was not deceived.

'You're not well,' she said. 'It's that room, isn't it?'

'Hmm? What? Oh, it's been a bit of a chore on top of everything else. But next week it'll be finished, and that'll be the end of it.'

'I didn't mean that,' she said quietly. 'I've been thinking, Cliff − yes, really thinking. Oh, I know I must have seemed hysterical lately, and − and edgy. Well, I have been. And not without cause.' She paused, swallowed, then continued with deliberate calm, though her heart was racing, 'It isn't right us being here. No — don't speak, let me finish. It's just no use pretending. The Green Man's wrecking our lives. It's wrong, evil somehow. Haunted.'

'But —'

'Yes, I know; we spoke of that sort of thing as a joke at first. It isn't a joke, though. It's — frightening.' She paused before adding, 'And so disappointing. But we have to accept it. And you must admit, Cliff, that after all it hasn't just been *my* nerves.' She gave a wan smile.

He sighed.

'I guess you're right.' He straightened up abruptly. 'Okay! We'll have to accept our losses. Life hasn't been much fun lately, and that's a fact. You've been tense and scared, and I've been in one hell of a sweat at times — drained, tired. And that's no good. I'll get in touch with the agent's tomorrow. The quicker the sale board goes up the better.'

'What will the locals think?'

'They should be used to it by now. Anyway, what's it matter? We're the ones who count.'

So all went ahead as planned. The board went up, the gossip and sly looks started up again in the village. But no immediate sale was forthcoming. Possible purchasers called, appeared enchanted, but were never seen again. Meanwhile, summer passed gradually to early autumn and it became obvious to Rosemary that Cliff's health was rapidly deteriorating. He lost weight, his fresh complexion turned to unhealthy pallor, and he began to suffer nightmares. The illusion or whatever it was of the mistily-blue figure looming in the shadows by the newly blocked-up room persisted at times, but both he and Rosemary endeavoured to ignore it, keeping their eyes averted whenever they hurried along the landing to their own quarters.

They changed their bedroom to the opposite end of the corridor, and for a week or so the problem seemed to be solved. Then one evening, before Cliff turned at the top of the main staircase, he saw from the corner of his eye the sensuous outline of the ghostly seductress taking shape only yards away, moving towards him with dreadful uncanny determination. Her size had increased and there was no turn of the head — no sly inviting glance — but a full frontal view of enormous thighs and breasts below curving hungry lips that approached steadily in a quivering cloud, accompanied by the low odious chuckle.

Plunging forward with the cold sweat pouring from him, Cliff raced to the new bedroom, shutting the door frenziedly behind him, and collapsed on the bed, eyes shut, loathing yet still wanting the obscene image that was sucking his life away.

Presently the door opened quietly. Rosemary stood there, shocked and terrified. 'Cliff. Cliff — what *is* it? What's the matter?'

She stood over him, staring at his glazed eyes. Gradually life and comprehension returned to him. 'We must get away at once,' he managed to say at last. 'Get the bags packed, Rosemary. I'll stay in this damned place no longer.'

Of course, matters were not resolved quite so easily as that, and when, after a good swig of brandy, Cliff could think coherently, he agreed that the following day would be the earliest possible time for their departure. There was the house agent to brief, a notice to go up, all the packing to do, and what staff they had to inform, including the gardener who was forking a patch of earth in a border when he heard the news.

He did not seem surprised.

'I see'd it comin',' he remarked, staring at the couple from eyes shrewd, bright and small as an ancient monkey's in his wizened face. 'It's happened afore. An' 'et's the young 'uns she likes —' He broke off with a cackle of laughter.

'What and who do you mean by "she"?' Rosemary demanded. The old man cocked a thumb towards Cliff. 'Ask him. He'll be knowin' by now.'

So did Rosemary. But she wished to know more. 'Her name, though? Why she — she's there at all. What happened? You must tell us. We've a right.'

'Rights or not won't make no difference. She'm there for keeps, I'm thinkin', an' that's what he meant those many years ago. Oh, yes. I wus only a youngster then. But tales get around.'

'Tales of what?'

'How she did treat 'im. Oh, a real one for the men she was. A buxom beauty in 'er fashion − if you do like 'em fat. Couldn' leave the men alone, though, an' he − 'er husband − a dour jealous kind of fellow. Landlord, he wus.' He paused, with screwed-up eyes, as though trying hard to remember, and enjoying it. 'She hopped it one night, took off with a farmer, new chap to these parts, and went to Australia or some such place, folks did say; that wus the story put out. He went on here for a time, just as though nuthen'd happened. Then 'e went'n hanged isself one night from a tree. Ar! A real tragedy as you could say. Dramatic − that's the word, edn' et? Dramatical?'

With a nod of the head, Cliff agreed.

They thanked the old man and were about to leave him when he began again, 'There's another thing, though. *I* don' b'lieve she ever did go 'way, not really. I reckon he locked 'er up in that theer little room you've bin so worritin' about an' left the sexy madam to starve to death. Mind you, I doan' know. Tis only my own idea.'

With which observation the old fellow turned away to continue with his 'bit o' weedin'.

Rosemary and Cliff stared at each other.

'What a horrible tale,' Rosemary said as they walked back to the house. 'And it's funny how unconcerned he seemed. Do you think − ?'

'Well?'

'Was he trying to frighten us?'

'Laying it on a bit, perhaps. But after what we've been through, I shouldn't think so. He's probably got so used to things and is so much a part of the place now − after all, he must be reaching ninety − that no ghost or succubus has any power to affect him.'

She shivered.

'I wish we could have gone today, Cliff. The thought of another night here gives me the willies. And you look so tired.'

Indeed he looked more than that: completely exhausted, almost drained of life.

He made an effort to sound optimistic.

'In twenty-four hours it will be over, thank God, and we'll have a decent night's rest for a change.'

'I hope so.'

But Rosemary's hopes were to be unfulfilled.

They went to bed early, locking the door firmly, and after half an hour, worn out as he was, Cliff was asleep, leaving his wife awake for another restless two hours, tense and on edge, listening with strained ears to every slight creak and whisper of air blowing through cracks of doors and windows – to the gentle swish of leaves and crackle of branches from the garden outside. Every few minutes she turned her head slightly, peering through a filter of moonlight at her husband's face. He appeared to be at peace, except for the twitch of a small muscle near one eye. Perhaps he was dreaming. She wondered what of. The beastly blue light? The stout covetous form of a loathsome woman's figure? Or was the twitch merely a sign of nerves? Question after question ran through her mind, until at last they began to lose coherence, and she, too, drifted into sleep.

She was woken suddenly by the sharp awareness of something wrong. Her whole body was dripping with icy waves of fear. The air was thick, humid, and reeking of perfume. Sitting up abruptly, she looked automatically towards Cliff – or where he should have been. He was not there.

In a frenzy she rushed from the bed and ran to the door, to find it unlocked and half open.

'Cliff!' she cried, not caring who heard. 'Cliff – where are you? Where – ?'

Her voice died. Just for a few seconds she paused, rigid with terror. The grey light was blurred and uncertain, but sufficiently, ominously clear at the far end of the landing to reveal a large luminous blue shape hovering there, with the form of a man – Cliff's form – spreadeagled before it on his knees, arms outstretched and clawing at the newly barricaded entrance to the tower room, head tilted back and as though gasping for air.

But it was not air he wanted. It was – 'Oh, Cliff,' Rosemary shrieked, 'don't – don't!'

She raced down the passage and reached him just after he fell, to lie in a crumpled heap, tongue protruding between his teeth, his eyes wide and staring, a trickle of foam about his lips.

He was still alive, but incapable of recognising his wife. Rosemary lifted her head, and for the first time saw the gross naked creature clearly – sensuous thick lips curved in derision, immense breasts glowing eerily blue like twin lamps above the lascivious stomach. There was an obscene chuckle of triumph, while the air thickened into a pool of sickening perfume.

'Fiend,' Rosemary whispered. 'You devil! You've killed him.'

But Cliff did not immediately die. He lived long enough to regain consciousness and some wraith-like resemblance to the man Rosemary had married.

'The chest – under the chest – the floor –' he whispered harshly from rattling lungs.

Rosemary put her face near to the travesty of his own, torn by pity and terror. 'What chest, darling? What? Never mind. Don't talk. We'll –'

She broke off with the shocked realisation there was no need any longer to try and spare his strength. What had been left of it following the dreadful encounter was gone.

Cliff was dead.

The inn was closed and after the inquest, which recorded a verdict of 'death from natural causes, due to heart failure arising from some unknown shock', Rosemary insisted that the tower room be re-opened and the floorboards beneath the chest taken up.

The skeleton of a woman was found there in a rotted silk dress, gnawed by rats, surrounded by baubles and cheap jewellery. There was as well a large bottle of perfume and a jar of pot-pourri – the sickly smell intermingling with the stench of decayed flesh.

Investigations proved that she was indeed the licentious wife of the man who'd once owned The Green Man, before hanging himself.

Evil of any kind, however, can sometimes linger in its lustful greed for life.

So exorcism was brought to the inn; but after the dreadful revelations no one cared to live there, and it stands now an empty shell, already no more than a sinister relic of the past.

Only the ancient gardener appeared unperturbed. 'I knowed et,' he said. 'I always knowed et. Tes like a warped bush in bad soil – you never do know as how things is goin' to turn out.'